Heather Graham's Haunted Treasures

HEATHER GRAHAM

13Thirty Books

DEDICATION

To Mya Richard

A sweet little girl who thought my book was pretty.

Happy Halloween

True love is like a ghost, which everyone talks about but few have seen.

Anonymous.

CONTENTS

Dedication

About the Author

VANQUISH THE NIGHT

Prologue

1870, West Texas
There was a curious breeze that night.

Michael Johnston felt it first when the night shadows were just beginning to give way to the pink streaks of dawn. It was the breeze, in fact, that woke him.

Anne's window was open to the night. The breeze entered, seemed to touched him, swirl around him. His eyes opened, and for several long moments, he tensed, listening. He had become accustomed to waking quickly, alert to the first whisper of danger.

But there was no sound, just the breeze.

He slipped the covers from himself and crawled naked from Anne's bed, striding silently to the window. He looked out. The sun hadn't risen yet; the moon was still visible in the sky. Even as he stared at it, it seemed that a dark shadow passed over it. Quickly. So quickly that if he had blinked then, he'd never have seen it... sensed it.

He paused, still and silent by the window, for a long time. Listening. Searching the landscape beyond the ranch house. There was nothing unusual to be seen. A tumbleweed flew a few feet, bounced, flew again. Just outside from where he stood, a shutter broke loose, banged against the house, and went still. Cursing softly beneath his breath, he thrust the window further open, leaned out, and re-latched the shutter.

Then... silence.

The breeze vanished. The tumbleweed hung suspended in midair, then fell. All around him, there was nothing. Just the silence in the stillness of the night.

He wondered how a man who had survived sword-fights, cannon fire, and Indian arrows could feel such a strange unease over something so natural as a breeze.

But it had carried a chill with it...

"Michael?"

Her voice was soft, feminine. He knew it so very well, loved it so very deeply.

He walked back to the bed on his bare feet.

Her eyes were only halfway open. In the shadows, he could not see their color, but he knew it. They were amber. Not really brown, not hazel either. Framed by jet lashes, they were large, wide-set, intelligent, beautiful eyes. Just as Anne was beautiful, with her ivory skin, delicate features, flashing smile, and look of never-ending wisdom.

The heavy skeins of her ebony hair were tousled and wild, an indication of the way things had gone earlier in the evening. She held the pastel-yellow bedsheets to her breasts, and the way her gaze fell upon him, the way her hair curled so enticingly, aroused all the hunger within his body and soul. He smiled as he stroked her cheek.

"It's all right," he said softly.

"What are you doing up?" she whispered. Her eyes widened and focused upon him. "Did you hear anything? There hasn't been an attack anywhere?"

He couldn't guarantee that there hadn't been an attack somewhere, but not near them, he was certain. The citizens of Green Valley had banded tight and close against the possibility of an Indian attack. The alarm would have sounded, they would have heard shouts and screams.

Sometimes, Apaches were silent, stealthy when they came upon their victims. But once they had them...

Well, then they were anything but silent.

The Apaches in this area had been fairly bloodthirsty the first few years following the war. The town always had to keep an eye open to the threat of attack. But recently, a number of the tribes and the citizens of Green Valley had reached an agreement. Walks Tall, an important chief among the Apache, kept his word, and at the moment the white citizens were at peace with him.

Michael wasn't expecting an attack. Still, the members of the militia he headed were always on alert, each man devoting one night a month to guard duty. Most of them, like him, were old war-horses—quick to respond to the slightest hint of conflict. They were a close-knit community, all of them licking battle wounds in one way or another.

"No attack," he said.

Anne caught his hand, holding his palm to her cheek. He thought he felt a shudder rip through her body.

"It's all right. I swear it," he told her softly.

She nodded. A lock of her hair tumbled down over his fingers, soft as silk. It stroked his flesh. Fragrant, it seemed to send the scent of roses sweeping around the room.

It was amazing to him how such a thing, such a little thing, could be so sensual, creating such a swift and urgent desire within him.

Maybe it was just Anne.

Maybe it was love...

They'd both arrived in Green Valley at about the same time. She'd lost her home to Sherman's fires and her husband to a bullet at Sharpsburg. He'd lost his home to a cannonball and his fiancée to a triumphant Yank. Just as he'd lost a little bit of the ability to run, to dance gracefully, and even to mount a horse with his accustomed ease. A saber wound in his knee had never quite healed properly and now he walked with a limp.

But he wasn't bitter. He knew a number of the Yanks at the fort over the hills, and they were all-right fellows. He'd traded with a few downriver during the long years of the war. No, he wasn't bitter.

He just wanted his life to take a new direction.

From the time Anne Pemberton had first stepped off the stage at Green Valley station, he had known that he wanted her. That had been early in 1868. Then there had been a full year when they hadn't had a decent thing to say to each other. Maybe it had been good that they'd spent that year keeping a distance between them. Back then, they'd both still needed time to get over the war.

Then there had been the months when he had hated her for being so damned superior, and she'd hated him for being so right all the time. Then those flying sparks had finally ignited, and there had been one fantastic night when she'd forgotten the past, forgotten all other loves, and fallen prey to the wildness and fury of his seduction. Right in her front parlor. She'd been telling him that he'd no right to chew out her friend Billy over the way he had handled an Apache situation, and he'd been yelling right back that she should be thanking her lucky stars she wasn't staked out on an Apache plain that very moment. The next thing he knew, every longing, every flicker of desire that had been growing over the years had suddenly exploded.

And she'd been in his arms, and he'd been kissing her, and to his amazement, she'd suddenly kissed him back, and he had become tangled in her clothing as he struggled to free her from it. He never did strip her completely. But that hadn't altered either the passion or the tenderness with which he had made love to her.

Funny what war and circumstance could do to people. It hadn't bothered Anne that she had turned her back on propriety and made love with him. But she hadn't been ready to give everything to him either. She didn't like the idea that he was the leader of the militia and dedicated to solving conflicts with the Indians and that was something that he really couldn't change. She'd lost one husband to warfare, and she wasn't willing to risk another.

Sometimes, the townspeople managed all right with the Indians—sometimes, they didn't. But he knew the Mescalero Apache as well as it was possible for any white man to know them. He respected them, appreciated their way of life, and greatly admired their courage and their commitment to their tribes. They were a proud people.

And a warlike one.

Well, things did take time. And though he and Anne rather danced around each other, both expecting the other to give in, there was something strong between them. One day, she was going to be his wife. And in the meantime, he loved her. More and more deeply every day.

He knew that Anne loved him, too. If she just weren't quite so stubborn...

The amber of her eyes was like gold in the room's pale light. She reached out and touched his cheek.

"How odd!" she whispered. "Something... woke me."

"It was the breeze," he told her. He grinned, drew back the

covers, and slid in beside her. Jesu, it was easy to forget that curious breeze now. Her skin was like silk, sensual and sleek against his. And warm, so deliciously warm.

She was shivering, though.

He swept his arms around her, covering the length of her naked body with his own. She was incredibly sensual, her body all curves, her breasts full and firm, the hardened pink nipples taunting against his chest. He kissed her lips softly, feeling the pulse of his arousal become a thunder. "It's all right," he assured her, his lips raised just a breath above hers.

Her eyes shone into his. "I was just dreaming, I think. The strangest dreams, Michael! Something dark had flown across the moon, like a huge black bird of prey. Then there was the most curious yellow light. It beckoned, and I started following it and then..." She shivered again.

"And then?" he persisted.

She shook her head. "I don't know. Then..." Her eyes widened. "I felt the breeze!"

"It's all right, I swear it!" he told her.

"I was so afraid, and I reached for you, and you were gone."

"I'm here now."

She smiled slowly. "I know." Her voice was husky, sweet. "I can feel you."

"The breeze is gone," he assured her.

"It is," she agreed. "Right now it feels like a very hot night."

"Burning."

He smiled, encompassing her in his arms. The power of his body gently forced hers to open, and he allowed his throbbing erection to tease against the soft, sensual flesh of her inner thigh. Then higher... a bit higher. She shifted beneath him, her eyes still on his. A wicked gleam shone within them, teasing and seducing.

"It's getting hotter and hotter," she whispered.

"You just don't know how hot!" he warned. His lips found hers again. Seared them. Then abruptly he rose above her, cupped a breast, lowered his head, laved and tweaked a hardened tip with his tongue. Her fingers dug into his shoulders. He moved lower against her. Lower and lower still. Suddenly, a desperate passion seemed to burst within him. He wanted to make love to her more fiercely than he ever had before. He wanted to make love in a way that somehow...

5

Somehow left a little part of him imprinted on her. As if he could own her...

No, as if he could protect her.

The thought burst in his mind, then faded with the strength of his desire. He touched her, kissed her, caressed her. When she rose against him, determined to love him in return, he pressed her back. Inch by silky, luxurious inch, he caressed her flesh, then flipped her to lie face-down and pressed hot fire at her nape, with the touch of his lips and tongue. He moved down her spine, again bit by bit until he came to the small of her back. His hands circled the curves of her hip, flipped her once again. His caress found the most tender and intimate erotic places. His fingers stroked and parted. His tongue explored.

He was like a tempest with her that night, hot and wild, giving and demanding. In all the times that he had made love to a woman, he had never felt like this. When the end came, it was a sweet explosion, a climax so violent that he held her, shaking with her, lost in blackness, then seeing the startling twinkle of stars against that blackness and finally feeling sweet shudders seize him again and again as they drifted back to an awareness of lying in her bed in her room.

Now dawn was beginning to break in earnest. Beautiful rays of color were filtering into the room. Reds and magentas, pinks and yellows and oranges. The colors of day were coming, sweeping away the shadows of the night.

His arms tightened around her. The strange uneasiness that had swept through him was melting with the shadows. Still, other feelings seemed to take over. The feel of Anne next to him stole into his heart, and for a moment, he felt that desperate urge to protect her again.

Soft, beautiful, entirely sensual, she lay against him, her damp flesh touching his. In any darkness, he could see her, the shape of her, the beautiful curves that were hers, the color of her eyes, of her hair. He didn't want to leave her. He wanted to wake every morning with her naked and replete beside him.

Yes, he wanted to be with her in the darkness, when the night breeze turned cold.

"Marry me," he urged her.

He felt, more than heard, her little sigh.

"Quit the militia," she responded softly. She'd said it before.

Dozens of times.

"Anne, I can't! I'm our most experienced man. I'm also our best hope for peace. You know that."

"All I know is that you ride out all the time. And I never know if you'll ride back," she told him very softly. "And I won't wear widow's weeds again."

"Anne!" he whispered, pulling her close. "How can you say that when life is tenuous at best? Lightning strikes, accidents happen—"

"And I have to deal with them the very best I can," she responded. "I can't add to it the fact that you lead men into a hail of arrows."

"I don't *try* to get killed!" he said angrily.

She touched his cheek tenderly. "No, I won't marry you," she insisted. "Not now."

"When?"

She shook her head. "I don't know."

He pushed back the covers, rising above her. "So if I were killed now, Anne, it wouldn't hurt? It wouldn't cut into your heart just the same?"

"Michael—"

"Anne?"

Her eyes glittered in the darkness. And then it seemed that there was just a hint of tears within them. "Yes! Yes, it would rip me to pieces! Slash my heart, cast me into ungodly desolation! There, is that what you wanted to hear?"

"No, go on."

She stared at him, naked, so very beautiful. So defiant. "All right, I do love you, Michael. Very much."

A trembling seized him. He twisted his jaw to fight it. "Then marry me."

"I can't!"

He let out a long cry of torment. She reached up, long delicate fingers stroking his face. She pulled him down to her. Her tongue teased his lips, entered his mouth, hot, wet, promising.

"I can't marry you. But I can love you!" she whispered.

He groaned again, his frustration palpable on the air. "Anne, this is insane. We're both adults, but you force me to arrive through the back door and exit through the window to avoid any disrespect to your uncle. There's no reason—"

He broke off. Her hands were moving down his body. She knew how to distract a man.

"Anne—"

"I love you!" she whispered.

He sighed. The conversation was over.

Later, he wound his arms around her. She was an incredibly stubborn woman. Maybe she didn't feel the fear that had suddenly stolen upon him tonight.

It lingered.

He sighed. So she wouldn't marry him. Not yet. Maybe he could still hold her, make love to her...

Protect her.

He looked out the window. Light had almost chased away the last of the shadows. Almost.

Then he realized that he wasn't going to get any sleep, not until it was full light. It seemed as if the darkness out there had eyes, and only daylight could close them. Anne was sleeping at last. He felt the smooth rise and fall of her breathing. He held her more tightly.

* * *

Down the hallway, old Jem Turner, Anne's mother's eldest brother, was standing at his bedroom window. He rubbed his grizzled chin, his hazel eyes hard and alert.

There wasn't anything unusual to be seen. But then, Jem knew that the things you couldn't see were often the ones you should most fear.

Well, Anne was all right for now, no matter what the night wind brought in. She and Michael thought they were meeting behind his back, of course, but he knew darned well every time Michael silently entered the house. He didn't judge them. They'd all lived through too much. Actually, he just wished that stubborn niece of his would marry the fellow.

He felt the breeze again. *Soon*, he thought, *soon*.

He'd tried hard to ignore it. Tried to say that legend was legend, and superstition was just plain silly!

But it wasn't, was it?

And how damned odd that he could feel it, just feel it, in a breeze, and know that it was near.

Evil.

Don't leave her, Johnston! Jem thought. *Don't leave her. I'm old and I'm worn, and it's going to be damned hard to make you believe, but he's out there. Watching her. Wanting her.*

Stay. Help me...

* * *

Not far away, David Drago stood on a rise that overlooked the tiny town of Green Valley. He looked down at the cluster of small farms and ranches, and smiled slowly. It was so good, the night was so good. He could feel the pulse of life within him so strongly. He could feel it, almost taste it.

Soon...

He was a tall man, well-built, striking, with dark hair and golden eyes. Eyes that carried a hint of another color, but few people could ever really see that color, or guess at it, until it was too late. As he stood on the rise, a passerby might have thought him very attractive indeed. There was a European sophistication about him that was fascinating. He was a man of the world, accustomed to dealing with any circumstance that might arise. Of course, the world might best him at times, but in the end...

Well, he always bested the world.

Green Valley. How quaint a place when compared with London, Paris, Madrid. And what interesting people. These rough Americans, and the curious red savages.

It was a playground—a playground, indeed.

He'd already found it immensely satisfying.

And down there in one particular farmhouse... she waited.

He smiled, concentrating, and knew that she was with someone. That didn't matter. He could take care of it. He had plenty of time.

He turned and lifted his arms, raising his black cape to the breeze.

Not far away, stone angels and crosses decorated a cluster of gravestones. But where he stood was unhallowed ground. Without Christian adornment. Indigents were buried here. Heathens. The refuse of humanity.

The earth was rich with suffering... just as the night seemed rich with evil.

His smile deepened.

Dawn was breaking. He was weary. But the shadows would come again.

They always did.

Chapter 1

Two weeks later

"ANNE Pemberton!" Cissy McAllistair exclaimed.

"You just can't mean to tell me that you have yet to meet David Drago!"

Anne smiled patiently, biting the thread she'd been using to mend Uncle Jem's good winter jacket. She tied a quit knot before answering Cissy. She really did hate to put a damper on Cissy's excitement. Cissy was young, barely twenty. She'd grown up out here in the wild west of Texas, and although she'd learned plenty about the Apaches, she was innocent of the ways of the world. She'd never had to watch white men killing white men, like they had back East.

"Cissy, I'm sorry, but no, I haven't yet met this paragon of virtue. I've heard people whispering about him, though. They say he's having a big house built on some acreage he bought on the edge of town. Apparently, he intends to stay in Green Valley."

"Oh, I hope so! I hope so!" Cissy said. She was a pretty girl, with cornflower-blue eyes and the kind of white-blonde hair men seemed to go crazy over. Not that Anne felt any jealousy for the girl. Sometimes, she felt very old and worn—in just three years, she'd be thirty! Then again, Uncle Jem was always telling her that it wasn't the years, it was the experience that counted, and she'd certainly chalked up some experience; they all had. But she was comfortable with herself. Michael thought that she was beautiful—at least, he said so fairly often—and for her, that was enough.

In any case, it didn't really matter how perfect this new fellow, David Drago, was. She might be as stubborn as Uncle Jem said she was, but she was in love with Michael. And Michael was pretty close to being perfect himself. He had wonderful deep-gray eyes and sandy hair that he let grow too long. He had a rugged face—a really fine one, with handsome features—and there was something indefinably masculine about those hard features that made him a very sexy man.

She had once been certain that only a truly bad woman could possibly share such intimacies as she shared with Michael and not be married. But the woman she was now was very different from the innocent girl she had once been. Besides, she was going to marry him, one day soon.

Just as soon as she managed to twist him around to her way of thinking.

Of course, that might not happen. Michael was damned stubborn, too. And he was responsible, and honorable, and all those other things.

He was a lot like Joe Pemberton had been. And she had loved Joe very much. Maybe not as deeply as she loved Michael, even though she had been married to Joe. But she and Joe had scarcely wed before a bullet had severed the ties between them.

She *was* going to marry Michael. Soon. Her heart started to beat a little more quickly at the thought. How odd that after all his constant urgings, she was going to say yes. She was going to have to, for the sake of the child she had realized yesterday she was carrying.

But she wasn't going to tell him just yet. Not until she had tried every way she could think of to get him to quit the militia!

"You don't understand because you haven't met him yet," Cissy told her, with wide-eyed eagerness. She wagged a finger at Anne. "But you will. Mrs. Simmons has invited him to her dinner party tonight, and you *are* coming, right?"

Anne shrugged with a slight frown. "I suppose so. But Michael hasn't returned from his trip out to Mescalero country. I won't have an escort."

Cissy smiled. "Then you can join the rest of us whose little hearts are fluttering for David Drago."

"Cissy—" Anne began with a touch of impatience.

Cissy waved a hand in the air. "Oh, Michael is handsome, I'll give you that. And he's tall and rugged, and everyone has always envied you, the way he's so determined to have you—even if you are a widow just a shade past your first youth—"

"Thank you, Cissy," Anne managed to interject.

"Michael is wonderful. Why haven't you married him? Really, Anne, perhaps you should, before you—"

"Dry up completely?" Anne finished for her.

Cissy blushed crimson. "Oh, Anne, you're beautiful, and you know it! But you are getting on!"

"Well, I probably will marry Michael. Sometime soon."

"My father says you don't like him belonging to the militia,"

Cissy said. "But if he were to leave it, what would happen to the rest of us? Think about it, Anne. He isn't making any demands on you. What manner of man would he be if he let you push him around—especially when Green Valley needs him so much!"

Anne smiled. Cissy did have a point. But then, Cissy didn't know what it was like to read in the newspaper that someone you loved very much was lying dead on a distant battlefield.

"Well, it's too bad you're not married to Michael. Then you'd be out of the running for David Drago."

"I'm not going to be *in* the running," Anne assured her.

"But you have yet to meet him!"

"As you say, I will meet him tonight," Anne said with a wry grin. "But I won't join your panting crowd of girls—still in the flower of their first youth! I'll have Uncle Jem take me. Then I'll observe this Drago character from the side!"

Cissy bounded up, very smug. "You'll see!" she promised. "Wear something absolutely fetching! You'll be glad you did!"

Anne sighed as she rose to see Cissy out. She leaned against the door frame as she watched Cissy go, her full calico skirt bouncing behind her. Cissy was so full of life, so sweet, so generous, so warm. She was like a lot of the inhabitants of Green Valley, and it was one of the reasons Anne liked the place so very much. People didn't ask a lot of questions about the past here. A new town, it gave people new chances in life.

"Well, Cissy," she murmured aloud, "I hope your David Drago falls absolutely in love with you. I hope you love him in return and you both live in his big new house happily ever after!"

Cissy turned a comer. Anne's gaze moved up the street. Far beyond it, she could see the rise on which the cemetery was located. There was the graveyard with its wrought-iron sign swinging slightly in the breeze, Green Valley Cemetery it read. To the right of the fenced-in area, there were more graves. Years ago, the folks in Green Valley hadn't been quite so generous and open-minded as they were now. Back then, as in much of Texas, lawlessness had abounded here. Rapists, thieves, murderers, and general riffraff had passed through and called the town home. And when they had died, or killed themselves, they had been buried in the section to the right of the fenced-in area. On unhallowed ground.

Their graves were marked not with handsome angels shipped in

13

from the East, as in the more holy section of the cemetery. But with crosses crudely formed from tree branches tied together and thrust hard into the ground.

It just went to show, Anne thought, how far Green Valley had come along since those early times. Much of the West was still wild and lawless. Gradually, though, Green Valley had begun to appeal to a gentler variety of folk. Nothing terrible had happened here in years now.

Then again, maybe the war had exhausted a lot of the men, and they had just been seeking peace since then. Whatever the reason, a time of quiet had come to Green Valley.

But as Anne stared at the cemetery she had seen every day since she had first come to this town, she felt a strange uneasiness creep along her spine. She gave herself a shake, but the feeling persisted. It was like the other night...

The night when she had awakened and Michael had been gone; she had felt the most awful chill encircle her. She'd remembered her dream about a dark shape obliterating the light of the moon.

But then Michael had come back to her, and held her, and the fear had gone away. Strange, how it was back now...

Good grief! She was too old to be getting shivers in broad daylight. Maybe she was afraid because he wasn't back yet. He should be back. He and the militia should have met up with the Apache chief, talked and vowed their peace promises, and returned this morning.

The later he was, the more convinced Anne grew that something was dreadfully wrong.

All kinds of things might have happened. They might have been invited to a special ceremony. They might have met with some inclement weather.

They might have been scalped and murdered by the Mescaleros!

No, she couldn't think that way. She couldn't live with such fear. Of course, it wouldn't hurt to tell Michael when she did see him just how scared she had been! It might help him understand.

Then again, maybe Cissy was right. Maybe she had no right to ask him to give up the militia. What would happen to the town without his expert protection?

She didn't care, she thought selfishly.

Yes, she did.

Anne hurried back into the house. "Uncle Jem?" she called. When he didn't answer, she walked through the parlor, with its attractive love seat and Victorian drapes, and passed into the back hallway. Uncle Jem was out back by the corral. He was leaning over the white fence, patting her Appaloosa's nose absently.

"Uncle Jem!" she called again. Still, he didn't look her way. There was a troubled frown on his face.

"Uncle Jem?"

He swung around that time, and there was a guilty look on his face. Then his expression seemed as innocent as a babe's. "Annie! What is it?"

She walked out to the corral, studying him. He gave himself a little shake, like a man trying to ward off some unwanted feeling. Just as she had been trying to rid herself of her lingering unease just moments ago.

"What's wrong?" she asked him. Tamarin, her Appaloosa mare, snorted loudly. Anne patted her nose and the horse came close, then snorted again suddenly, backed away, and started running wildly around the corral. "Seems like everyone around here is kind of spooked," Anne murmured.

Jem stiffened, a lock of white hair falling over one rheumy blue eye. "I'm not spooked, young lady. Now what made you say a thing like that?"

Anne shrugged. "Fine. You're not spooked. But I need you to take a bath and get dressed up a bit. I've decided to go to Mrs. Simmons's party tonight."

"What about Michael?"

"He's not back yet."

"You want me to get gussied up just for some fool dinner party?"

"Please?"

He sighed. "Humph."

"Does that mean you'll do it?"

"Why are you suddenly all fired up to go?"

Anne shrugged again. "That newcomer is going to be there. David Drago. Everyone has been talking about him. I'm curious, that's all."

"Curiosity killed the cat!" Jem warned her.

"Uncle Jem, I just want to meet a new neighbor." She sighed.

15

"All right, if you won't go with me—"

"You'll stay home?"

She shook her head. "No. I'll go alone."

"Dag-nabbit, girl!" He glared at her, then sighed. "No, you're not going alone. It wouldn't be right. Someone has to look out for you."

She smiled. "Thanks, Uncle Jem. And don't forget the bath," she added, turning around. She still had a lot to do before getting ready herself. She had to make out some checks today and straighten out her credit accounts or she wouldn't be able to feed her horses and stock much longer. And there were piles of mending.

But curiously—and pleasantly!—her day moved along quite quickly. She was actually ready early and managed to get Soukie, their half-Cherokee stable boy, to make two trips hauling in water for a bath.

She luxuriated in the bath for a long time, sudsing herself with imported soap from back East. It was a pity that Michael wasn't back, she told herself, inhaling the soap's sweet scent. Then she realized that her thoughts were wandering down decadent paths and she firmly diverted them. Still, after she rose from the tub, she lingered long over her wardrobe. The dinner wasn't a formal occasion, but she found herself choosing from among her best dresses. The yellow silk with the amber bodice was her best gown, and although it went well with her dark hair and golden eyes, she should save it for when Michael would be there to see it.

She started to set it back on its hooks, but some power other than her own seemed to take hold of her. Before she knew what she was doing, she was climbing into the yellow dress.

She stared at herself in the floor-length mirror. The gown was beautiful, the bodice a darker shade in embroidered velvet. The low-cut neckline emphasized her full bosom, while the corset gave her a minuscule waist which flared into curvaceous hips. She'd left her hair loose, flowing down her back.

She frowned as she continued to stare at herself, wondering why she had felt compelled to display her feminine charms. Had Cissy's words made her feel old? That she had to prove her attractiveness to this newcomer?

She didn't know. With a sigh, she turned away from the mirror. Even as she did so, fear and unease rippled along her spine.

If only Michael would come home!

"Annie, you ready?" Uncle Jem called. "The horses are all hitched up."

"I'm coming," she assured him, and hurried out to meet him. He whistled at her in appreciation. She smiled and curtsied to him.

"How do I compliment a beautiful young thing like you?" he asked affectionately.

"The same way I rate a dashing older gent like you!" she teased in return. Then she frowned suddenly. The moon was out. A black shadow seemed to sweep across it, then disappear. She shivered fiercely.

"Annie?" Jem asked with a frown.

What was the matter with her?

"All set, Uncle."

He helped her into their shiny black carriage. Old Thorn, the carriage horse, sprang into action at Jem's urging. In a matter of moments, they were traveling along the road to Mrs. Simmons's huge gingerbready mansion on the hill.

"Looks like the entire town turned out," Jem said, nodding at the array of carriages and buckboards drawn up on the grounds.

"Looks like," Anne agreed.

Jem found a place to leave Thorn and their own vehicle, then lifted Anne down from the carriage. He drew her hand through his arm and escorted her up the porch steps to the front door. Lollie Simmons, Civil War widow a decade older than Anne, stood at the doorway, anxious to greet her. "There you are, Anne Pemberton! I'd heard that you wouldn't be coming if Michael Johnston didn't make it back, but I'm so glad you're here. Jem, you old goat, welcome. Anne, I am so aggravated with those boys in the militia! They've just about ruined my seating arrangements, and with so many of the young, handsome, and available gone off, all the girls are just pestering Mr. Drago to death."

Anne kissed Lollie on the cheek. "I'm pretty upset with Michael myself," she assured her. "But the house looks lovely, Lollie. And everything smells divine. I confess, I can't wait for supper."

"Well, you'll have to wait just a few minutes, my dear. You see, Mr. Drago has been dying to meet you."

"Oh?"

"Well, you are such a lovely creature, dear. He's heard about you, of course."

And just what had he heard? Anne wondered. That she was sleeping with a man she refused to marry?

"Ah, there he is now, dear!"

Just as Lollie finished speaking, it seemed as if the crowd parted, breaking away as if by command, just so that she and David Drago could stare at each other.

And she did stare. She felt as if she had become frozen in time and space, suspended there, trapped by his gaze.

He was very tall, perhaps even taller than Michael. He was dark, his hair nearly jet, combed back in a masculine and handsome manner. He was very well-dressed in a dark Eastern suit. His skin was pale, but his face...

It was a striking face, one of an indeterminate age. The planes and angles were sharp, nearly gaunt, but very striking nevertheless, classical in their proportions. For all that he was so pale, he appeared to be strongly built, well-muscled and lean. His mouth was broad, full, sensual.

And his eyes...

They were gold, and very strange. They were similar to her own amber eyes, but more *gold*. She studied them, fascinated. Perhaps some other color vaguely rimmed them. What color? She couldn't tell. But it was there, framing the gold so strangely. They were incredible eyes. Striking. Commanding. Evocative. She couldn't seem to tear her gaze away from his.

He started walking toward her. In seconds, he was standing before her.

"Mr. Drago," Lollie began. "This is—"

"I know," he said, and his voice was deep and rich, sensual and slightly accented, as peculiarly hot and chilling as his eyes. "This is Anne!" He bowed to her. "I am David Drago." He paused. Somewhere in the room, a fiddle was playing. "Shall we dance?"

"No."

She was certain that she formed the word. She hadn't come to dance. Not with any man. She was in love with...

"Come, Anne."

His fingers were on hers. His gold eyes were commanding her.

A searing heat seemed to leap from his fingers to spread throughout her body.

It would not hurt to dance with him.

"I've been waiting for you," he told her.

She fought his hypnotic voice and eyes. "Why?" she demanded.

He arched a deadly dark brow. "They told me you were the most beautiful woman in all of the West. Indeed, in all of the country."

"I do believe they were mistaken."

He shook his head. "I know they were not."

"That is kind, Mr. Drago."

"If I am kind, then perhaps you will dine with me tomorrow night."

"I——I'm afraid I can't."

"Why not?"

"There's another man," she murmured.

"Where is he then?"

"With the militia. He could not be here."

"Then you must let me escort you when he cannot," Drago said politely.

No, never.

"That would be fine," she heard herself say.

He leaned close to her. She thought that she heard him whisper. A very fierce swirl of air, so faint she was not certain she heard it, so intense that the feel of his breath seemed to enter into her very soul.

"There is no other man for you. There can never be. I have waited forever. You are mine. And when you are mine, you will feel my touch and know me—oh, so well, my love!"

She tried to pull away from him; she could not. She must have imagined the words, the passion. But she wasn't imagining the feel of his arms around her, the strength of them. She wanted to break away.

But she couldn't seem to tense her muscles; she couldn't break his hold. His eyes were gleaming down into hers again, and she was meeting them. She wasn't sure that she wanted to break away anymore. There was a staggering warmth in those eyes, a fire, drawing her, compelling her.

He spoke. "Anne..." Just her name. So softly.

She gave herself a mental shake. She had to stop this! Then she realized that over Drago's shoulder, she could see her uncle. Jem was watching her.

And there was pure terror in his eyes! Terror that he couldn't seem to hide!

He rushed forward suddenly and tapped Drago on the shoulder.

"May an old man cut in on a far younger fellow to dance with his niece?" he inquired.

A look of fury swiftly passed over Drago's features. Anne didn't like it. It was frightening.

But then she thought she must have imagined it because Drago was bowing very politely to her uncle. "By all means, sir! Anne, it is not the end. Only the beginning," he promised.

She scarcely saw him again that night. That was good! He was so strange. So frightening. She didn't want to be near him.

Yet she could think of nothing else but Drago.

And when she returned home that night, she was still thinking about him. Uncle Jem was painfully silent and absorbed, but she barely noticed, her own mind was so fully occupied.

A breeze seemed to be stirring again. But inside the house, and particularly inside her bedroom, it was hot, very hot. She opened her window and lay down in her bed. It was still so uncomfortably hot.

She found herself ripping her nightgown off and lying naked on the bed.

She had never, never done such a thing before...

And then she was dreaming. He was there. Telling her to bid him enter. He wanted her. He wanted... things... from her. He wanted to make love with her.

She was dreaming; surely, she was dreaming. But she wanted him, too. She was twisting on her bed, waiting, wanting him. Twisting, parting her thighs, feeling an ache grow between them.

Drago...

He was there, a shadow against the moon.

And all she had to do was bid him enter...

Chapter 2

"God in heaven!" Billy Trent exclaimed, not able to look at
Michael, his eyes still fixed on the scene before them.

Michael Johnston couldn't tear his own eyes away.

And he thought he'd seen everything. Just about everything that
one man could do to another. He'd spent five years with the Rebs,
butchering the Yanks. He'd seen the Yanks butchering them right
back, and he'd seen the landscape in South Carolina—the first state
to secede from the Union—once Sherman and his men had marched
across it.

Then he'd come west, to this part of Texas. And he'd met the
Apaches.

And he'd seen what the Apaches did to the white men, and what
the white men did to the Apaches.

This was a Mescalero camp, he tried to tell his numbed mind.
They were, to many, the most fiery, proud, and violent of all the
Apaches. They were warriors, wild, courageous, and cunning. Few
excelled them in the art of warfare.

But this time, none of their skills had saved them.

Not a soul seemed to have survived within the camp. And in all
his war years, and in all his years on the Texas plains, Michael had
never, never seen anything like this.

Far behind him in their militia ranks, someone was sick. He
heard the low, soft moan, and then the choking sound...

"Colonel, what the hell happened here?" Billy demanded.

"I don't know," he said. There had to be an explanation for
this... this... carnage! Not a single body seemed to have been left in
one piece. And the pieces seemed to be scattered so widely that they
couldn't be gathered to put one body back together.

And yet, for all the horror that met their eyes, there seemed to
be a singular lack of... blood.

But that didn't seem to be something that he could just blurt out
to Billy. He opened his mouth, trying to say something. Nothing
came. "I don't know," he repeated. "I just don't know."

Robert Morison, a freckle-faced redhead who had been with him
in the South Carolina artillery and had traveled with him west to

Texas when it was all over, rode up beside him.

"Colonel, you don't think that the Yanks from the fort did this, do you?"

Michael shook his head. He knew that everyone in their thirty-man militia unit, most of them Texas boys, was staring at him. "I really don't think that the Yanks are responsible. They were pretty well fired up when they came through South Carolina at the end of the war," he said. "They tore up the countryside pretty bad. It was Sherman's 'scorched earth' policy. So I've seen what Yanks do when they're mad. It doesn't even begin to compare with this!"

"Then what?" Robert asked. "Wild dogs?"

"Maybe," Michael said. No, no maybe. Wild dogs couldn't have been so neat.

There would have been blood.

"I think we ought to get out of here," Billy said suddenly. "What if more Apaches come upon us here and think that we did it?"

Their lives wouldn't be worth a wooden nickel, Michael thought. He lifted a hand and called out to all the men. "We'll have to report this to the Yankee fort. We'll ride north-northwest till we reach them."

But even as he lifted his hand to start the movement, he froze. He had the sense of being watched.

He looked up. They were in an arroyo, cliffs on all sides. And he saw that they were surrounded by Apaches.

There was nothing to do but stand his ground.

Then one of the Apache horsemen stepped forward, and Michael recognized him. It was the war chief, Walks Tall. The man he'd come to meet. He began to pray that the Indian hadn't just arrived, that he had known what was here...

"Don't move!" Michael commanded his troops. "For the love of God, hold your ground!"

His men obeyed. The Apaches, excellent horsemen, began to descend the cliffs. Dust and dirt flew in their wake.

Then Walks Tall was riding up before him, his feathered lance lifted in a greeting.

Michael decided not to try his weak Apache with the Indian. Walks Tall had learned English quickly and well because it was the language of the people so determined to encroach upon his land.

"We did not do this," Michael said. "I swear to you, we did not do this."

Walks Tall nodded, and made a gesture to some of his men who dismounted and began to gather the victims' remains. They were a burial detail, Michael thought numbly.

"I've known you since you came to this land, Michael Johnston," Walks Tall told him. "I do not accuse you of this massacre. Women and children, never. Ride back with us. Our camp is not far. We've a fresh buffalo kill. Eat with us before you return home. You must be home before nightfall."

Michael, startled by the Indian's words, glanced at Robert.

Robert shrugged. "You think they really mean to have buffalo for dinner and not us, right?" he inquired beneath his breath.

Michael pondered the question. He had known Walks Tall for a long time, too. They had both tried to negotiate while other white men and Indians had killed one another.

"We're safe," he told Robert.

And they were. Just as the war chief had promised, the white men were welcomed into the camp. Several women saw to their comfort. Walks Tall watched the beginning of the activities, then beckoned Michael to follow him.

There was a certain teepee etiquette, practiced by most of the Plains Indians. Michael knew it well, and entered behind Walks Tall, then sat to the left of his host. He accepted the beautifully carved pipe offered to him. Then he realized that they were not alone in the teepee, that someone was seated in the corner.

An ancient Apache woman, her face lined and leathery, came forward. She nodded to Michael gravely, threw some dust on the fire which caused it to spark, and began to dance around the fire while chanting.

Then she knelt before it and lifted her head, staring at Michael.

"We fight a common enemy, white man."

Perplexed, Michael stared back at the Apache.

"Dancing Woman knows," Walks Tall told him gravely.

Michael shook his head. "Knows what? Does she know who killed those poor people so horribly?"

The Apache woman and the chief exchanged glances. "It is not a *who,*" Walks Tall said.

"Animals, then. Coyotes, wildcats—"

"Evil," Dancing Woman told him.

"A white man's evil," Walks Tall added softly.

This was making less and less sense to Michael. If the Indians blamed a white man, they were being extremely kind to him despite it.

"Walks Tall, I swear that no man I know——"

"No man," Walks Tall agreed.

"Evil," Dancing Woman persisted. "An evil whose death lies at the heart."

Walks Tall sighed deeply and tried to explain. "An evil spirit has come. An evil breeze, an evil wind. It is a white man's evil spirit. Dancing Woman felt it when it came. She cried her warning to the Apaches. Here, among my people, we cried to our gods. We made our land holy and brought our children inside at night. But all of our brothers did not heed our warning. You see what has happened to them."

Michael opened his mouth to speak, to protest. But what could he say? Something horrible had happened. Something horrible beyond words.

And even as the chief spoke to him, he remembered the breeze.

He had awakened in the night, afraid. He had known that it was out there.

He didn't believe in ghosts and goblins. But there were times when he wasn't certain that God truly resided in His heaven.

He knew all about hell—he had seen hell, right on earth. He had seen it in the battlefields, in the medical tents.

But now...

Now a crazed old Indian woman was talking about spirits, and to his amazement, he believed her.

Because he had felt the breeze...

Walks Tall, a man who might have been his enemy, was watching him with pity. He pointed a finger at him. "Dancing Woman says that you must fight the evil."

A cold chill seized him. He didn't want to fight the evil. He didn't want to believe in it.

He lifted his hands. "I don't know what I'm fighting."

The old Indian woman spoke then. "You will see the face of your enemy. He will walk where you walk. He will hunger where you have hungered. He will be more powerful than you could dream."

This was madness.

"If he's so damned powerful," Michael said angrily, "how will I fight him?"

"With the strength of your faith. And your love," the old woman assured him. She was staring at Walks Tall again. The two communicated without words in an eerie silence.

"Dancing Woman says that you must go home. You must ride hard and try to reach your town before nightfall. The fate of your men rests in your hands."

It *was* madness. Truly madness. But Walks Tall was rising and so Michael stood, too.

He was supposed to go. He saw that. So there was no choice.

But just as he was ducking to exit through the flap of the teepee, Walks Tall spoke to him one more time. "Look to your woman, Michael Johnston. Look to your woman."

Fear struck him as it never had before.

Anne!

He had felt the need to protect her that night. Felt it so fiercely. And now he was here...

And she was home. Alone.

Look to your woman...

It was madness.

He didn't care. He shouted the orders to his men, mounted his horse, and started to ride like the wind, leaving the others to scramble onto their mounts and follow behind him.

He'd never make it. The night wind was coming too quickly.

And it was chill...

* * *

Ah... there she was!

Drago could see her through the window as he hovered in the darkness.

As beautiful as he remembered, as lovely as life and as beguiling as death! She was a picture to set an urgent edge to his hunger— naked, sleek as ivory and writhing against the sheets. Her skin was flawless, her face perfection. Her lips as red as blood, her hair an ebony cloud, her throat...

Ah, her throat!

He concentrated, seeking to enter her dreams. If only she knew!

He had dreamed of her for so very, very long. Dreamed, waited, and come this perilous way...

He had to possess her mind.

He had to force her to bid him enter. Yes, come in, my love! Come in...

He was nearly with her. He had sent the wind to seductively stroke her bare skin. Tendrils of swirling air rose and fell, caressing, insinuating, touching her here and then there... more and more intimately.

Concentrate, concentrate!

Yes... yes...

He smiled.

He could nearly feel her. The cool silk of her skin. The velvet brush of that glorious dark hair. Oh, he would take care! He would be so very slow, and very careful, nurturing her all the way. He would not lose her again.

Yes, a stroke here. He closed his eyes, sensing the breeze again. Ah, yes, a long, slow caress with the warmth of the air, along the soft ivory flesh of her inner thigh...

Call me, my love, call me...

Yes!

She was going to invite him in!

He opened his eyes, gold and all-seeing in the darkness.

And then...

Chapter 3

"Anne!"

Michael stood at her bedroom door, watching her in amazement. Bathed in an eerie glow of moonlight, she twisted and undulated, her skin sleek and damp.

"Anne!" he cried again, incredulous—and uncaring whether Jem discovered him at that moment or not.

His sense of fear and unease had increased steadily since he had left the Apache camp. He'd never ridden harder in all of his life. His terror had increased when he had galloped into Anne's backyard and seen the horses careening wildly about the corral, snorting, rearing.

The horses were afraid...

He had leaped from his own bay, Sandy, and rushed to the back door, the one that was always kept open. He hadn't cared if Jem had heard the door open and close, or if he'd heard the pounding of Michael's footsteps on the wooden floors.

All he'd known was that he had to reach her.

And there she lay...

He felt it then. Felt the cool and curious breeze. It made the hair prickle at the nape of his neck, just as if he were a hunting pup. The window! Irrationally, unreasonably, he became certain that the evil was entering through the window. He strode across the room and slammed it shut. Then he hurried back to the bed, falling to his knees beside it, desperate to touch her.

"Anne!" he whispered fervently. She had fallen still now. Her naked flesh was very pale. She opened her eyes slowly, her expression one of confusion and disorientation.

"Michael!" she murmured. Was there disappointment in her voice? he wondered.

Who had she been expecting?

"Yes, it's Michael," he said, somewhat aggravated. He had never expected... this kind of greeting.

And now that the breeze was gone...

He wondered if he had imagined it. Could it have been real?

"Anne—?" he began, but all at once she seemed to realize how she had been sleeping. She was sitting halfway up, still confused. Her fingers fell on her bare abdomen and she gave a sharp gasp of surprise.

She stared at him hard. "Michael, what—"

He stood, his hands in the air. "I didn't do a damn thing," he said harshly. "This is how you were sleeping."

A blush flooded her cheeks. "The night was very hot."

"The night is quite cool."

"Well, it was very hot in my dreams."

"Just what were you dreaming about?" he demanded.

She wrenched up the covers, staring at him hard. "How dare you just waltz in here; like this, accusing me of things! You take off for days, and I wait for you—"

"I didn't accuse you of anything!" he flared angrily. He crossed his arms over his chest, striding away from her. He jerked the draperies the rest of the way across the closed window. Damn, she was disturbing him tonight. He was angry and jealous as he had never been before. Why? What was the matter with him? He was so afraid, and his fear was making him touchy. He wanted to walk right out of the house—and leave her to her dreams.

But he was worried. Worried sick.

He wanted her. There was something so sensual and evocative about the way she'd been when he had found her. And still, even though she'd drawn the sheet to her chin, he knew every exquisite twist and nuance of her body beneath it. He loved her. He always wanted her.

"I think you'd better go," she said coolly.

Yes, he should go. Just walk out of the damned place and let her enjoy her dreams!

Suddenly he remembered the Apache camp. The dismembered bodies spread far and wide. The singular lack of blood.

It was evil. White evil, Dancing Woman had told him. He couldn't leave Anne. Not in the night. Not when he felt such strange fear...

And the coldness of that breeze.

He sat stubbornly in the rocker across from the bed, staring at her. "Go to sleep, Anne," he said, suddenly weary. "I won't come near you. I just want to see that you sleep safely."

Her eyes widened incredulously. "I just asked you to leave."

"And I'm not going."

"Well, what if I were to scream loud enough to bring the entire town crashing in on us?"

He grinned. "They all know that you sleep with me anyway."

She threw her pillow angrily at him. He caught it. The pillow toss was worth it. Her sheets had fallen. He could see her breasts heaving with the exertion of her breathing. Her skin still held that fascinating sheen. Her breasts were beautiful. Full, firm, with hardened dark-pink crests that now tempted his fingers beyond imagination.

"Michael—"

"I'm not leaving, Anne," he told her. Then he added softly, "I'm afraid."

"Of what?" she demanded, startled.

He shook his head. "I don't know. The night. The breeze. I don't know. But I'm not leaving you. So good night. Scream if you want to, but I'm not leaving this room."

She gritted her teeth, turning her back on him with an angry, huffing sound. Michael's fingers wound around the arms of the chair and he felt his own jaw grow rigid. Then he heard her voice.

"If you're staying, perhaps you'd be more comfortable in bed."

He hesitated, then shed his boots and clothes. He strode to the bed, caught hold of her shoulder, and turned her around. She stared into his eyes. He felt the fierce surge of his desire combine with some strange sense of anger.

"Who were you waiting for, Anne?"

"Oh! Oh, you bastard!" she cried, her amber eyes flashing.

He shook his head sternly, holding her when she would have wrenched away. "I just want to make sure that you're making love with the right man."

She swung back an arm, but he caught it before her palm could connect with his face. Then he kissed that palm quickly. "I'm the one who loves you!" he told her heatedly, and he stretched his muscled length on top of her, his lips finding hers. He kissed her with searing passion, kissed her long and fiercely. His hand moved between them, touching her, stroking her. Then he shifted his weight, penetrating her, determined to become one with her. The hunger, the passion, riddled him. He swept his arms around her with a cry and let the rhythm of desire seize them both.

Later in the night, he thought that she slept. But he heard her soft, broken whisper in the darkness. "I love you, Michael. I do love

29

you."

The confusion in the words startled him. There was something more there. She loved him, but...

But what?

He ignored the feeling, wanting only to hold her tight.

He kissed her forehead. "I love you, Anne," he murmured. "With all my heart. I'll never let you go, never let anything hurt you," he vowed, his voice still soft, intense.

She turned in his arms. Her eyes sought his. "Oh, Michael!" she whispered, and she smiled, laying her head in the cradle of his shoulder and resting her hand against his chest. "I just miss you so when you're gone. What happened?"

He hesitated. Then he decided to give her the bare facts. "The people of one of the Mescalero camps were cut down. Everyone was killed—men, women, children."

She gasped, horrified. "My God, how terrible. But who? Yankees? Other Indians? Oh, Michael! The other Apaches don't think that you—"

"No, they seem to know that we're not responsible," he said. He didn't add, *And they don't think that it was a* who, *they think that it was a* what.

Should he tell her everything that the Indians had told him? Would she think that he had finally and completely lost his mind?

I'm afraid of an evil breeze, afraid of a spirit, he could have said. And what then?

"Thank God for that!" Anne murmured. She ran her fingers along his chest. "Of course, I wouldn't have seen you back here if they had blamed you!"

He had to say something to her.

"Anne, the Mescaleros think that there is some kind of evil spirit at work here."

Her brows shot up. "Evil spirit!" she said.

"I just want you to take care, Anne. Please. Take care of yourself, watch where you go and what you do. Please, be very careful!"

She did look at him then as if he was losing his mind, but it was a very tender look. She kissed him. "I always take care, Michael. Where could I be more safe than here in Green Valley? You're the one I worry about. And," she added, trying to lighten the tone, wagging a finger at him, "you had best take care. There's a new man in town, you know."

He frowned. Yes, he had heard something about it. A rich
European. He was building a big house at the edge of town. Funny,
though, he couldn't quite remember when the man had arrived. But
then, he was gone quite a bit.

His stomach turned. He couldn't leave anymore. Not now. He
couldn't leave Anne alone.

"So, is he good-looking?" he asked Anne.

"Very," she told him solemnly.

He slipped his arm behind his neck and leaned his head against
it, studying her eyes as she lifted her chin mischievously high. "So, is
he the man you were expecting tonight?"

"Michael!" she snapped angrily.

But it seemed...

It seemed as if there was an edge of guilt to her voice.

She was suddenly afraid, Anne realized. Because of the strange
things she had felt in Drago's arms, the web of seduction that the
man seemed to weave?

No, Drago was just a man! She shivered. It was Michael's talk
now, about the Indians and all, that was frightening her.

Drago was just a man. Any other thought would be insane!

She smiled at Michael. "Jealous?" she teased, and the note of fear
was gone from her voice.

Michael watched her. Beautiful, sweet Anne. He had best watch
out or he'd lose her because of his jealousy. She was smiling, her soft
body draped over his, her fingers playing with the dark hair on his
chest. "I'm just giving you fair warning. He's offered to act as an
escort for me anytime when you're not around."

"Magnanimous of him," Michael murmured. He couldn't wait to
meet the bastard.

"It means that you need to stay home more often," she told him
primly.

He draped an arm around her, sliding down lower in the bed.
For a moment he was still, remembering the Mescalero bodies. Men,
women, and children, ripped apart like rag dolls.

"Ummm," he murmured, trying to keep the fear from his voice.
"Well, maybe I do intend to stick around for a while," he said. He
kissed her forehead. "Think we ought to get some sleep?" He felt that
he needed it. He wasn't sure why, except that he was going to need to

be awake and refreshed and in full charge of his faculties to...

To fight a breeze! he thought.

He closed his eyes. He pulled her more tightly against him. "I do love you, Anne, with all my heart."

She pressed her lips fervently against his chest. "I love you, too."

He was silent then. *Sleeping?* she wondered.

She eased herself beside him, glad of every place where her flesh could touch his. She felt so secure now. So safe, so cherished, so loved.

And before...

She couldn't remember now, but there had been something or someone out there. Something touching and stroking her. Something incredibly sensuous, beckoning to her.

She'd been dreaming. Awful, decadent dreams that had caused her to...

She didn't want to remember. She wanted to lie safe in Michael's arms.

But a feeling of dark unease swept around her heart. If she was safe...

Then someone else was in danger. She knew it. She didn't know how, or why, but she did know.

And she was afraid.

* * *

Rage filled him. He had been so close, so unbelievably close. She had very nearly whispered the words, thought the thoughts, conceived the ideas that would have given him entry.

It wasn't his only way, of course. But he had to be careful with Anne. He had waited too long for her. He didn't want her perfection marred this time. He didn't want her to die. She mustn't find *that* escape...

Furious, he turned from the house.

Michael Johnston. The soldier. The great Indian hunter turned Indian friend.

He was going to die. Slowly. Drago envisioned having him in his power, then slowly draining him of all his strength, so that he could feast even more slowly on his blood...

Then tear him to ribbons. Michael had no place in the world of the night. Only Anne! Only Anne would rule with Drago.

A shadow, a wraith, he moved erratically in the darkness.

He heard sounds. Drunkards singing their way from the saloon. He hesitated, melding into the shadows. Then he waited.

Several men, singing, stumbling, paused in front of the saloon. Two of them managed to throw themselves over their horses. The third tried twice and failed, then swore at the horse.

Drago's lips curled into a scornful smile. It seemed such a pity that he could not be accepted and appreciated for all that he was. He had heard the townspeople do nothing but complain about the Indians since he had come. Especially the Apaches, and most especially the Mescaleros. So he had dealt quite efficiently with a whole campful of the creatures, and instead of being grateful, they were horrified.

And then there was now...

And now he wondered what good could one stumbling, old broken-down drunk be to the town of Green Valley.

The others had moved off. It wouldn't have mattered. He could have taken them all, just as he had fed his great hunger from the journey with the encampment of savages. But he hadn't come to Green Valley just to feed. He had come for Anne.

Why should they mind the loss of just one drunk?

And when he had fed on that drunk, he would be in control again. The night would still be young.

There were other women here. Young ones. Innocent ones. With incredibly sweet, potent blood. Yes, he wanted Anne... but he had a tremendous hunger, made stronger by the waiting. Perhaps, once she was his, his need would be truly slaked. But while he waited...

It was good to know that there were others.

He smiled again.

So much for the taking!

But first, there was the useless man. Who would notice? And if they did notice, what then?

He almost laughed out loud. And then, as a shadow of darkness and evil, he descended upon the drunk.

* * *

Cissy awoke in the night. She'd been having the strangest dreams.

Sweet breezes touched her flesh. The night seemed to be filled with a low, earthly music. The darkness itself seemed to beckon to her.

In her dream she'd been dancing, she thought, with David Drago. He had turned away from Anne and all the other women, and he had been determined to have her. The handsome, sophisticated Mr. Drago, who was so enchanting with his slight foreign accent...

Then he wanted more from her. First a kiss... then he was touching her. She was powerless to stop it and nothing she had ever been taught had prepared her for such a man. She had never imagined such sensations....

Abruptly, she opened her eyes. She wasn't dreaming anymore. There was a breeze coming in from the open window, and someone was calling to her.

She opened her mouth. She should have screamed. Someone would have come immediately.

But she didn't want to scream. She walked to the window instead. He was there. Smiling at her. Handsome as the devil.

"Cissy..."

The sound of her name felt like a caress. Did he really say it? Or did she think it? She didn't know. All she knew was that she wanted him. She could feel the touch of his eyes on her throat, on her breasts. She could feel the heat emanating from him. And oh, that breeze that touched her!

Yes, let me... !

Did he whisper it? Yes, he was saying things, thinking things. *You're beautiful, Cissy. Stunning. I want you, I want more, I want... please, oh, yes, give to me...*

The breeze grew and rippled. She wanted to feel it, had to feel it, all of it. She reached down for the hem of her nightgown and lifted it over her head and tossed it aside. Naked, with a cascade of blonde hair falling all around her, she reached out her arms to the shadowy figure in the darkness.

Yes, take me. Come in...

It was all he needed.

He was inside.

In seconds she was in his arms. In seconds, he had touched her.

Kissed her flesh. Swept her into his arms. He was filled now, so he could take his time. Tease and taunt and seduce her. Lull her into complete obedience.

Yes...

At last, he reached the sweetest peak of arousal. She inhaled sharply at the pain of his fangs when they first touched her throat.

But that was all. Not a whisper of protest.

He drank. Her blood was achingly sweet, the blood of innocence. Of purity. So damned good.

He would see Cissy again.

And again...

He had come for Anne, and he would have her. But now that he had touched Cissy, tasted her sweetness, he might well be magnanimous. He would not maul or destroy her as he had the drunk.

The taste of her was just too good. He would come back and drink again.

And most probably, he would grant her... life.

His kind of life.

Just because he had never imagined her blood could be so sweet. He had to taste it again. And again.

Until it was gone.

* * *

"Just who is the man and where did he come from?" Michael demanded of Anne.

He'd crawled out the window and come around to the front of the house to knock at the door. He was feeling moody that morning. He hadn't rested during the night at all, and he was irritable.

Anne poured him more coffee. Jem was sitting across the table, looking tired and morose, too. Just what was it with the men in her life lately?

"I'm not sure just when he arrived himself. He has a plump little fellow who works for him and keeps tabs on what the builders are doing up at his house. The servant's name is Servian or something like that. He came in on the stage several weeks ago. I think Drago actually rode in at night."

Michael leaned back in his chair. Anne seemed so amused this morning, so ready to take Drago's side!

"I tell you," he said, eyeing her sternly, "people are amazing. No one even really knows where he came from, and you're all walking around with your tongues hanging out over the man!"

"Why, Michael Johnston!" Anne laughed. "You're jealous!"

"And you're just as pleased as you can be!"

She smiled tenderly at him. "Well, if a bit of jealousy will keep you around..."

Jem stood up so abruptly that his chair fell over. Anne looked at her uncle in surprise. He seemed angry. Really angry.

And frightened.

"You're a fool, Anne! You're my niece, and I love you, but you're a fool! Marry this man, and do it quickly, and quit playing your damned fool games!"

Anne stared at him incredulously, her own anger growing, her discomfort great.

"Uncle Jem—"

"Drago is evil!" Jem insisted.

"But you've barely met the man—"

"I'm warning you, young lady! He's evil. You can feel the evil in the air!" He suddenly bent down beside her. "Annie, I know that you've heard the family stories. This man is part of them. This man—"

"Oh, Uncle Jem!" Anne cried in dismay. "You can't be serious! This is America! This is the New World! It's Texas. We've got Indians, not ancient beasts and superstitions!"

"I'm telling you, Anne—"

Michael stared at them both in disbelief. Jem swung around and stormed out of the house, to the backyard.

Anne looked at Michael. Oh, no. He was going to ask for an explanation and she didn't know where to begin to explain the old stories that had come down through the centuries in her family. They were absurd! She bit her lip lightly, lowering her eyes.

"Anne, what—"

She shook her head, determined to distract him. "I will marry you, Michael," she said softly. "I do love you."

"I love you," he returned, but he was still in an argumentative mood. "When will you marry me?"

She lifted her shoulders in a shrug. "When things are settled.

When—"

She wasn't able to finish. There was a pounding on her front door. Foreboding filled her. Michael leaped to his feet and hurried down the hallway, Anne trailing behind him.

Billy was standing at the front door. He looked worn and aged. He stared from Anne to Michael, cleared his throat, and spoke at last. "We need you, Colonel."

"For what?" Anne cried. "You all just rode back—"

"Oh, we're not riding anywhere, ma'am. Sheriff Dougherty just needs to see Michael now." He cleared his throat again.

"Spit it all out, Billy," Michael commanded.

Billy wet his lips nervously. "Old Smokey Timmons is dead."

Michael sighed, feeling sorry for the town drunk. "What did he do, fall off his horse and break his neck?"

Billy shook his head, looking pained.

"Say it!" Anne cried.

Billy exhaled. "No, he didn't fall off his horse. Someone— something!—got ahold of him. Colonel, it's just like it was with the Indians. There's pieces of Billy strewn all over the place!"

"Oh, my God!" Anne breathed.

"I'm coming," Michael said quickly. He turned and gave Anne a shake. "You stay here!" he told her. "Stay here, do you hear me?"

Wide-eyed, she nodded.

Michael started to leave. But some instinct made him pause and turn back to her. He swept her into his arms and kissed her passionately.

Yes, there was evil out there! What was he going to do? How was he going to fight it?

Easy, keep her away from everyone, keep her inside, locked in!

He whispered softly, "Don't let anyone in. Don't invite anyone in, do you understand? Don't go out, don't let anyone in. Not until I'm back!"

She didn't understand. Life had suddenly changed. It had just been breezes and shadows at first. Now it was terrifying.

And Michael was leaving her again.

"Anne!"

"Yes, yes!" she promised. "I understand."

But it was a lie.

She didn't understand anything anymore. Not at all.

Chapter 4

Smokey Timmons was indeed dead.

With Billy behind him, Michael looked on while Mort Jenkins, the town mortician, gingerly collected the pieces of the man, trying to arrange him in the hastily slapped-together coffin that was to be his final resting place.

They were standing outside Sheriff Dougherty's office, just the sheriff, Michael, Billy, Mort, the sheriff's deputy—and the remnants of poor old Smokey Timmons.

"It's just like the Indians, Colonel," Billy whispered. "Just like!"

Michael felt his throat constrict. Yes, it was just the same. A man, torn to shreds, limb from limb.

And there was that same lack of blood.

Sheriff Dougherty, a good man, a tall man with bushy white hair and a rotund belly, shook his head. "If it don't beat all, if it don't beat all!" he muttered.

This kind of thing just didn't happen in places like Green Valley. Sure, they were tough Westerners. Many of the men had been in the war. And they'd all fought Indians.

But they'd never seen anything like this.

Sheriff Dougherty must have heard Billy's whisper to Michael. He stared at him sharply. "All right there, Colonel Johnston. You think you can shed some light on this subject?"

Michael shook his head and the sheriff narrowed his eyes suspiciously.

"Injuns?" he asked.

"I don't think so," Michael replied.

"You just defendin' those heathen Apaches again, Johnston?" the sheriff pressed.

He shook his head again and decided to answer in kind. "Dougherty, the Apaches never mind leaving a calling card. They've never hidden a raid or a battle—or a killing of any kind. What Billy's talking about is something that just happened to the Indians."

"And?" the sheriff said.

"There was a whole tribe of them, a small encampment. Maybe forty or fifty in all."

"Jesus H. Christ, Michael, you gonna make me drag it all out of you?" Dougherty demanded.

Michael faced him. "They were all dead. Just like Smokey here. Every single one of them—"

He paused, amazed at his sudden realization.

"Every single one of them what?" Dougherty exploded.

"Decapitated. The bodies were torn up too, to different degrees. But every single one of them..."

"Was missing his head," Billy said. He giggled nervously. "Someone's not happy with scalps, eh? The whole head has gotta go these days!"

"Gentlemen, gentlemen!" Mort complained. He was the perfect undertaker, always dressed in a neat black suit. He was as slim as death itself with a gaunt face and skeletal cheekbones. He inclined his head toward them, folding his long fingers in a steeple-like fashion. "Gentlemen, I am accustomed to dealing with the dead, but your levity here is—quite frankly!—making me ill."

Michael ignored Mort, frowning, then looked across the dry, parched street that made up Green Valley's main thoroughfare. "The Indians said that it was an evil spirit. A white spirit."

"An evil, white spirit. You want me to find—*and hang!*—an evil spirit for the death of Smokey Timmons?"

Dougherty was going to laugh at him any minute. Michael couldn't quite say that he blamed him.

"Well, I can't help you. I'm damned sorry," Michael told him, "but that's all the Indians would say, and they must have believed it, because they didn't try to blame us."

"Someone killed Smokey," the sheriff said firmly.

"Or *something!*" his deputy, Tim McAllistair, said softly. "It looks like something an animal would do."

"Wild dogs," Mort suggested.

"Wolves!" Billy said.

"Right," Tim agreed. Like his daughter, Cissy, Tim was blue-eyed and blonde-haired, a man of forty who looked as young as twenty. There was hope in his eyes. Just like there was a ray of hope in every pair of eyes now meeting Michael's.

"Wolves!" he murmured. "And none of us heard them. And there's not a tuft of fur anywhere—"

"Or a drop of blood, for that matter," Mort commented.

"Well, hell!" Dougherty exploded. "Something went on! A man don't get drunk and tear himself up like this! Now, until we do find out what's going on in this town, you're all deputies!"

"Don't we need some kind of formal ceremony for that?" Billy asked.

"Yeah, real formal! You're a deputy 'cause I said so!" Dougherty said firmly. "All of you, keep a good eye out. Jesu, how the hell did this happen in a fine place like Green Valley? Hell, we ain't even had no horse thieves here in years and years!" He spun on Michael. "Don't you go discounting those Apaches, you Injun lover!" he warned him.

Michael lifted his hands, staring at Dougherty. "I'm not discounting anything. And may I give you the same advice?"

Dougherty looked affronted, but then he sighed. "Dammit, Michael, I'm just scared. Scared down to my bones."

Mort cleared his throat. "May I—er, take the deceased? Doc Phelan can examine the—er, remains. Maybe he'll be able to give us some clue."

"Yeah, maybe," Dougherty agreed.

Tim, Billy, and Michael helped Mort hoist the coffin up onto Mort's horse-drawn hearse-wagon. Everyone was silent as Mort clambered up to the seat and flicked the reins over his pitch-black horse's haunches. The wagon rattled down the dusty street.

Dougherty pointed a finger at Michael. "If you can spare me an hour or so, I'd like a firsthand report on your latest excursion into Injun territory. I want to hear all about what you found, and what the Injuns had to say. You come too, Tim. I'll buy you both some lunch."

During the meal Michael stared at the bowl of fine stew set before him, but all he could see was Smokey. He had eaten wormy hardtack upon occasion, between battles, with dead men lined up in hearses behind him. But this was different. He pushed the food away and talked as fast as he could, anxious to get back to Anne. He gave Dougherty a thorough report, but he felt sorry for the sheriff because, like them all, the man was left so damned confused.

Tim sat and listened, but with only half his attention. He seemed withdrawn, an unusual way for Tim to be, Michael thought. But then, they had spent most of the morning with Smokey, noon till now with the sheriff, and it seemed that even the afternoon was waning away and they hadn't accomplished much of anything, "Is that it for now,

40

Sheriff?" Tim finally asked his boss. He hadn't eaten much of his stew either.

Dougherty immediately looked contrite. "Yeah, sure, Tim. You go on home now. You tell Cissy we're all thinking about her."

Tim nodded, rose, offered Michael a faint smile, and hurried out of the inn's dining room. Michael could see him walking out on the porch and then down the steps to the street. There was a slump to his shoulders.

"What's the matter with Cissy?" Michael asked.

Dougherty shrugged. "She just took sick," he said. "Tim's awful worried. Says she was as pale as death this morning and has hardly opened her eyes all day. There's no fever or the like. It's just as if the life had been drained right out of her."

"I think I'll take a walk over myself," Michael said. "Cissy is a special friend of Anne's. That is—if you're done with me too now."

Dougherty waved a hand in the air. "Sure, I'm done with you, Michael. Evil spirits!" he said. He shook his head. "Jesu, Michael, what's going on here?" Not expecting an answer, he went on his way as Michael went his.

Michael hurried after Tim McAllistair. When he reached the McAllistair house, he found Anne there.

He'd told her not to go anywhere...

But what could he say? Cissy was a friend. A good friend. And Anne was obviously fine.

She was sitting by Cissy's bed, spelling Jeannie McAllistair, who looked something like a ghost herself. The strain of her daughter's illness was already showing on Jeannie's face. She had a multitude of children, but she and Tim adored each and every one of their offspring. A cold chill seemed to touch Michael's heart from the moment he walked into the house. He didn't feel any better when Anne's grave gaze touched his. He sat beside her on the bed, trying to think of something to say to make Cissy smile.

But Cissy wasn't going to smile. She was lying there as still as death, as white as a sheet, so very young, so innocent, so lovely. He sat beside Anne, taking her hand, and in silence, they both stood vigil over the girl. In another room, Jeannie was quietly sobbing. Her sons and her husband were trying to comfort her.

"What happened to her?" Michael asked at last.

"No one knows," Anne murmured. "Jeannie says that she was

41

fine last night—but that she didn't get up this morning. She's been more or less like this all day."

"Has Doc Phelan seen her?"

"Yes."

"What did he say?"

Anne's beautiful amber eyes touched his. "He said that we should pray."

Michael nodded. He sat with Anne, taking her hand, and they both watched Cissy.

Time passed. Anne stretched, and Michael looked at her. She probably hadn't had a thing to eat or drink since he had left her that morning. He whispered to her, "I'll stay with her. You go eat something."

Anne seemed startled. "Well, a glass of water," she murmured. She still looked uneasy about leaving Cissy.

"Go!" he commanded her.

She did. Cissy remained still. He looked out the window. What a strange day! The sky was mottled with clouds. Time seemed to slip by so quickly. There were streaks of crimson on the horizon. Far off, in the distance, he could almost see the darkness of night coming. How strange. But then, maybe he had never looked for the night before.

Anne returned. Smiling, she sat beside him again, squeezing his hand. "Any change?" she whispered.

He shook his head. Then he rose and leaned closer to Cissy. "Come back, little one!" he murmured. "Come back." He thought he saw her stir at the sound of his voice. Startled, he sat back down again.

"Michael, look! Her eyes are flickering!" Anne cried.

And suddenly Cissy's eyes were open. Startlingly blue against the pallor of her face, they focused fully on Michael. She smiled slowly. "Michael," she said very softly. Then she gazed at Anne, her smile deepening. "See, he's home!"

Anne leaned over her. "Yes, he's home. And we're both worried sick about you. Your mother is in tears."

Cissy frowned. "Why?"

"You've been sick all day."

"Not sick. Just dreaming."

"I'll get Jeannie," Michael said quickly. He stood and went down the short hallway to the McAllistairs' bedroom. The door was open.

He walked in. He gave Jeannie a hug. "She's talking!"

"Oh! Oh!" Jeannie cried. She leaped up and kissed Michael on the cheek. "Oh, thank you, Michael!"

"I didn't do anything," he protested, but Jeannie was gone, and Tim and his young sons, Anthony and Andrew, were grinning at him.

Michael grinned wryly in return.

"How about a drink?" Tim asked him. "I could use a shot of whiskey myself."

"Pa, it's a little early," Anthony, the younger of the boys, reminded him.

"Nonsense, take a look outside. The afternoon is waning. Hell, it's going to be sunset very soon," Tim said. He stood, clapped Michael on the shoulder, and led him into the small parlor. "Damn strangest thing I've ever seen!" he murmured as he poured the whiskeys. They could hear Cissy chatting away with her mother and Anne in the bedroom. "Last night, she was as right as rain. This morning, when Jeannie started screaming, I rushed in and Cissy was as pale and cold as death, barely breathing. We've been praying all day. And now..." He lifted a glass to Michael. "You walk in and talk to her and she's just fine!"

"I didn't do anything," Michael protested.

Even as he spoke, they heard a rapping at the front door. Tim excused himself and went from the parlor to the small entryway to open the door.

Michael heard a low murmur of voices. The newcomer was a man with a low, deep, well-modulated voice. An intriguing one, with just the touch of an accent. Definitely European, but with an edge...

There was something strange about listening to the murmur of that voice.

The hackles began to rise on Michael's neck, just as if he were an old hunting hound. Something was...

No.

Yes.

Evil.

A touch of it, just a trace of it, something that made Michael increasingly uneasy.

He swallowed down the whiskey. After all this time, he was finally losing his mind. An Indian had talked to him about an evil white spirit, and he was hearing and seeing and feeling this *evil* everywhere!

Tim entered the parlor with the newcomer. Michael assessed him quickly, not needing to be told who he was. David Drago.

The man was dark, with ebony hair. More jet than the color of any crow or blackbird Michael had ever seen. His brows were the same shade. But then the concept of *dark* faded, for his skin was a strange shade. It was rather ashen, with a tinge of blue.

No human had blue skin, Michael quickly assured himself.

But Drago did.

His mouth was full and red. His features were handsome, so fine that they were almost too perfect. And his eyes...

They were gold. Gold, yes, really gold. Different from hazel, different from brown, different from Anne's beautiful soft amber. They were really, truly gold. With just a hint, just an edge of...

Of something else.

He was dressed elegantly in black: handsome black frock coat, trousers, boots, and vest. His white shirt was ruffled. His fingers were long, his nails well-manicured. And also *very* long.

"Ah, I need no introduction to this man," Drago was exclaiming, offering a hand to Michael. Unwillingly, Michael took that hand. "The very, very famous Indian-hunting war hero, Colonel Michael Johnston!"

He had never felt such a jolt of unease. The touch of Drago's fingers was like ice. Michael wanted to wrench his hand away instantly.

Michael was a strong man, but Drago was stronger. His handshake was like a clasp of steel. Michael had the panicked feeling of a man finding himself cast into a pit of rattlers—with no way out.

He gave himself a mental shake, fighting the strange power that seemed to steal away his ability to speak.

"Ah, Mr. Drago, I presume. I'm afraid that I hate killing Indians; I much prefer befriending them, and as for my being a war hero— well, sir, my side lost, and so we are not referred to as heroes but as the vanquished!"

Drago released his hand, his gold eyes gleaming with challenge.

"It is indeed a pleasure to meet you, Colonel Johnston," he said. "I came, of course, because I heard dear Cissy was ailing, but her father tells me she is doing much better."

"And I'm certain that Cissy will want to see you," Tim

McAllistair said.

"Well, if I am welcome..." Drago said.

"Anytime, sir," Tim said. "You are welcome here anytime."

Drago smiled. Slowly. It gave Michael the shivers.

"Thank you, Mr. McAllistair. I will take the warmth of that welcome to heart, sir! If I may..."

Drago bowed to the two of them and started down the hallway to Cissy's room.

A moment later, Anne, smiling with relief over Cissy's improved condition, walked out of the room. Tim excused himself to return to his daughter, leaving Anne and Michael alone. "I see you've met my new beau," Anne teased him, her amber eyes curiously aglow. A ribbon of anger snaked through him. Anne just wasn't the type of woman to pit one man against another.

"I don't like him, Anne," Michael told her honestly. Drago did have some kind of a draw, he told himself, and Anne had obviously felt it.

"Really, Michael," she said coolly. "He's an incredible gentleman. Polite, considerate, concerned—"

"And I'm none of those?" he asked her. He wanted to shake her. She seemed so very tall, elegant, and beautiful with her dark hair and amber eyes—and the rather superior way she was looking at him right now. Since Drago had walked in!

Then her lashes fluttered momentarily, and the Anne he knew was smiling at him. Warm. Sweet. "Mr. Johnston, you are all those things, and much, much more. When—and I do mean *when!*—you're here!"

He sighed. "Anne...!"

"Hush!" she murmured. "They're coming from the bedroom. Now, be nice to him, Michael. He's a newcomer in town. You must make him feel welcome. Please."

He wished he could. And yet, as soon as Drago had walked into the room, Michael had felt the presence of evil.

It was his imagination. It was all the awful things that had happened in the past few days.

But the awful things began to happen from the time Drago had come to town.

And, of course, he was jealous as all hell and he really needed to watch himself. Still...

He lowered his voice to a whisper. "He's a newcomer in town. I'm not making any accusations. It's just that he did arrive right when things started happening."

"Things?"

"Like Smokey!" he whispered.

"Michael!" Anne gasped, her eyes wide. "What a horrible thing to imply! Why, you've no right, no proof!"

A moment's shame filled him. Was he just jealous?

No. Drago was... *evil.*

No matter what, that word returned to haunt him.

Tim, Jeannie, and David Drago were back in the living room. Even Jeannie was accepting a whiskey, suggesting that Anne join her. Anne wasn't fond of whiskey, but she cared deeply about Jeannie, just as she cared about Cissy, and the woman seemed to need the drink, so Anne joined her.

Michael noticed that Drago only pretended to sip his own whiskey.

He didn't drink it.

Jeannie politely asked Drago about the progress on his house.

"Oh, it's coming along very well," he said.

"You must be quite busy," Jeannie said. "We never see you during the day."

"Ah, yes, well, I *am* busy."

"And a man all alone! You'll have to come for dinner," Jeannie chided him.

Drago bowed. "A pleasure."

Besides the fact that the man wasn't drinking his whiskey, Michael noticed that he was watching Anne—like a spider about to pounce.

He disliked the fellow more and more.

And Anne! Anne, damn her! She was smiling just as sweetly as could be. "I guess we should all help in that area," she murmured politely. "You'll have to come to dinner at my place too—" she began.

Something in Drago changed. His eyes glittered like gems. He seemed about to burst with pleasure. With... triumph.

But then, Anne added, "—sometime. In the future. We'll have to set up a real invitation at a later date."

The glitter left his eyes.

46

The man was angry, furious, Michael realized.

Drago set down his untouched drink. "Mr. and Mrs. McAllistair, thank you so much for your hospitality. Anne, Colonel Johnston, good night." He bowed deeply, and started to leave.

To his own amazement, Michael suddenly excused himself. Anne stared at him reproachfully. He ignored her, and chased after Drago.

He was down the front porch steps when Michael closed the door behind him. "Drago!" he called.

Drago turned.

In the light of the risen moon, his skin seemed to carry a true tint of blue. And his eyes were surrounded by that other color. He looked as angry as a starved lion.

"Yes, Colonel Johnston. What is it?"

Michael figured he might as well be blunt. He didn't like Drago. Didn't trust him. And he never would.

"You're showing an interest in Mrs. Anne Pemberton. I just wanted to let you know that it's a mistake. She's going to marry me."

Drago was smiling again. He took a step toward Michael.

"Oh, no, little man!" Drago whispered huskily. "I don't think so." Then he went on to amaze Michael with bluntness of his own. "Anne Pemberton is mine!"

Michael curled his fingers around the porch railing, fighting to control his anger. He reminded himself that he slept with Anne, that he loved her. That she loved him.

"Drago, you're mistaken."

Drago shook his head. "No, I'm not. You see, Colonel, I'll best you. Come what may, I will best you, sir. I have the power. It will happen."

A dizziness swept over Michael. Jesu! That was what Dancing Woman had said, that the evil would be more powerful...

His fingers bit even more tightly around the rail. What the hell was the matter with him? He was staring at a stranger and believing in his threats!

He needed faith. That's what Dancing Woman had told him.

"No," Michael said firmly. "I will not let you best me."

Drago started to laugh. "I *will* best you! But I will enjoy the fight, I assure you! You have afforded me tremendous entertainment already, Colonel! I bid you good night."

He started away again, into the dark street. Michael ran after him, suddenly determined to have it out then and there.

But it wasn't to be. Suddenly he couldn't see Drago. There was nothing but a dark shadow in the street.

And the shadow seemed to fly. To touch the moon.

Swearing softly, Michael walked back into the McAllistair house. He and Anne stayed a little while longer, then they walked back to her house.

He was silent, and she took his hand. He glanced her way to find her smiling at him. "I'm sorry, Michael, I really am. It's just that sometimes you seem so sure of yourself with me. I couldn't help teasing you, just a little. Please don't be angry."

He shook his head, looking at her, marveling at how much he loved her. She was beautiful to look at, but beyond that, there was something even more beautiful in the warmth of her smile. Anne cared for everyone. She even understood when he tried to explain how they had to find peace with the Indians. He had seen her hold and cradle little Apache babes and never once condemn them for their race.

She was his life. She was everything good in it. And at that moment he realized just how deeply Anne was endangered.

"Anne," he said hastily, "I'm not angry. But I don't know how to make you believe me! I don't like Drago. I'm afraid of him. I'm afraid of what he might do to you."

Her eyes widened in surprise. "Michael! You're not afraid of anything."

"I'm afraid of Drago."

"The man is just different, Michael. He's a newcomer. You're not being fair, and it isn't like you!"

He paused suddenly, chilled. Then he took her arm, hurrying her along. "Let's get inside before we talk more, all right?"

She sighed with exaggerated patience. "All right, Michael, but—"

She never finished. Michael was pulling her along until she had to run to keep up. There was a shadow behind them, he was certain of it. A shadow that was following them, ready to swoop down upon them. It was coming closer and closer...

"Michael!" Anne cried out.

He ignored her. They were almost at the house. All that they had to do was reach the porch and get through the door.

The darkness! He could feel it descending...

The door to Anne's house suddenly opened. Jem was standing there, beckoning to them urgently. "Come on, come on!"

Michael jerked Anne up the stairs and into the house. He slammed the door behind him.

The shadow, he was certain, lifted.

"What in the hell is the matter with the two of you?" Anne exclaimed furiously.

"Bats!" Jem said.

"What?" Anne demanded incredulously.

"Oh, yes!" Jem said. "I thought I saw some giant fruit bats, hovering right over you."

Anne turned to stare at Michael. "Bats?"

He nodded. "Well, there was *something* out there."

She leveled a finger at them. "You have both lost your minds!"

Jem shrugged. Anne shook her head. "Listen, you two, you just go on ahead and discuss your bats. I'm going to bed."

That was it. Nothing more. She turned and headed for her room.

Michael had a feeling it meant that he wasn't invited. Not tonight.

He didn't give a damn. He'd stay anyway.

Jem was looking at him. "Michael, I've got to talk to you."

He nodded. Jem seemed to... to know something. After all, he'd been at the door waiting for them as if he'd known there would be... a shadow after them.

He was losing his mind, Michael decided.

"Sure," he told Jem.

Jem walked him back to his own room at the far end of the hallway. He gestured for Michael to sit at the foot of the bed, then dug in one of his desk drawers for an album. There were tintypes and photographs and drawings in it. And letters.

He sat beside Michael, flipping pages. He picked out a letter and handed it to Michael.

"What—" Michael began, staring blankly at the page. It had been written in a foreign language.

"Over, over! It was translated by my English I-don't-know-how-many-greats-grandmother."

Michael flipped the letter over. The words were in English.

"Read," Jem said.

It was an interesting letter, tearstained and very old. It had originally been written in the late sixteen hundreds, he realized. Someone had written about a young girl named Helga. She had been beautiful, sweet, innocent. She had died, Michael realized quickly. By her own hand. She had jumped from a castle tower.

Although tears blurred some of the fine print, he was able to read it.

He says that he will not give up, that he will search for all eternity, that he will find her again. Oh, how do I explain to the others how strong she was? They refuse her a hallowed grave, for she was a suicide. They do not know her strength in fighting eternal damnation. And now, though my precious daughter is at rest, I am afraid, for he has the power to fight time. Perhaps he can even fight death.

Michael looked at Jem. "I don't understand."

"You don't want to understand."

"Dammit, I do!" Michael exclaimed. He stood, then began pacing the room. "Jesu, Jem, you weren't there when they found the Indians. You didn't see old Smokey's body. You—"

"You know that there is a connection with Anne, don't you?" Jem demanded.

Michael sighed in exasperation. He didn't know anything except that he'd been plagued with the strangest damned feelings!

"Jem, what the hell are you talking about?"

"Drago is a vampire," Jem said with certainty.

A what? Michael almost shouted.

"Shush, shush!" Jem said. He rose and closed the door to his room. "Listen to me, Michael Johnston. If you love my niece, listen to me! These... are family papers. I've carried them with me for most of my life. I spent years thinking that it was just a legend, that the letters didn't mean anything. Then the other night, right out of the blue, I felt that breeze, that strange breeze, and I knew. I knew that there really is some kind of strange evil in the world. I knew that Drago is a vampire."

"A vampire," Michael said blankly.

Old Jem shook his head. "I guess you don't know anything about the creatures out here. But they know them real well in the old country of eastern Europe. Some say that the first *nosferatu*, or vampire, was an evil prince named Vlad Dracul, or Vlad the Impaler. He lived years and years ago and—"

"Jem, you're making no damned sense!" Michael cried.

Jem shook his head vehemently. "Michael, you've got to listen to me, you've got to understand. This is the New World, the Wild West. No one else is going to help or understand us, or even believe us! Hell, the damned Indians seem to be the only ones with any sense."

"Jem—"

"I'm getting to it, I'm getting to it. First, let me explain the creature. Vampire. Undead."

"Undead!"

"Listen, Michael—undead, evil spirit, what difference does it make? No one really knows when the first one existed, but a vampire is a creature of evil, of hell, of the night. He must rest by day because sunlight can send him to hell for eternity. He must drink blood to survive. He finds the blood of the young and the innocent the sweetest, but any blood will do for a good meal. This creature had a banquet with the Indians. Then Smokey. Then—"

"My God, my God!" Michael breathed, slumping down, running his fingers through his hair. "I've felt like a lunatic, Jem! But you sound like you want to turn me into a madman!"

"Well, I don't—and you've got to listen and use your senses instead of your mind!" Jem warned him, speaking quickly. "I'll try real hard to make it all clear. My father was Irish, but my mother and her family came from a small place in Romania. Near Transylvania. Right from the area where this Vlad Dracul lived, where he impaled his enemies, where the original legends were all born."

Michael shook his head. "Jem—"

"All right, so you don't understand. You didn't grow up with the legends. But the Transylvanian people knew—"

Michael sank down to the foot of Jem's bed, a headache pounding in his skull. "You're trying to tell me that David Drago is—a *vampire?*"

"The Indians were decapitated, right?" Jem said.

Michael paused. "Yes."

"That keeps them from joining the... ranks of the undead. He wanted to feast, not to create other vampires. The same with Smokey. I'm willing to bet he was headless."

Michael threw up his arms. He couldn't tell Jem that he'd been so damned scared himself. Couldn't tell him that all he'd been able to think when he was anywhere near the man was... evil.

"I can help you, Michael. Just listen to me. You're not going to believe me, but listen to me. He's come for Anne. I think he started on Cissy because Anne is still strong. Dammit, don't you see, boy? Anne is Helga reborn! Maybe God is giving her a second chance for her faith, for seeking death rather than damnation! But Drago wants her now just as he did then."

"Jem, this is madness! Why would this fellow have come for Anne? You have to be crazy!" Michael insisted.

Jem solemnly shook his head. He reached into his bedside drawer again and produced a locket. Like the letter, it was very old. It was beautiful, crafted in very fine gold.

Jem tripped the lock to let it open, There was a picture inside. A tiny, tiny oil painting of a woman.

It could have been Anne. Anne in the full, stylish clothing worn by the wealthier classes of the sixteen hundreds.

"I don't believe this!" Michael whispered.

"Fine. I'm mad as a hatter. Don't believe it. But don't leave her at night, Michael. And don't let her invite him in. Ever. He hasn't been able to touch her yet only because she hasn't invited him in."

Damn, he felt so uneasy! He'd known this morning when he had left her—some instinct had warned him—that she shouldn't let anyone in.

Were they all losing their minds?

Or did old Jem really know the truth, as impossible as it seemed?

There was no mistake, no doubt about it. The portrait in the locket was an exact replica of Anne. His Anne.

"Helga?" he whispered.

Jem nodded.

"Vampire," Michael said, repeating the strange word.

"I know you think I'm crazy. Hell, you must think *you're* crazy! But you've got to think with your heart and your senses now, boy, not with your mind and logic. And most important, you've got to know that he's strong. Very strong. Very powerful. But he can be killed. As strong as he is, he can be killed. Not with bullets, not with a sword. With a stake."

"A stake?"

"A wooden stake. Right through his black heart. Or with sunlight. And, most importantly, with faith."

Dammit! Dammit! That's just what the Indians had said!

Evil spirit...

Vampire.

He couldn't believe it.

But how the hell could he deny it?

He rose on shaky feet. "I'm going—"

"Don't leave. Promise me you won't leave."

Michael smiled. "I'm going to be with Anne," he said softly. "I won't leave her." Then he hesitated. "Jem, doesn't Anne know anything about this family legend?"

Jem sighed deeply. "Stories, yes, she's heard the stories. But none of us ever paid them much mind. Sure, Anne knows that she looks like Helga. She thinks it's an amusing family resemblance. She thinks vampires are really just very seductive men whom innocents fall for a bit too easily. That's the stuff of legend to Anne." He shook his head. "That's why we almost argued this morning. She thinks we're cruel and snobbish, that we're assuming that because he's a foreigner he might be evil."

Jem had a point there. Anne always stood up for the underdog. If she thought that they were being unfair to poor foreign Drago in any way, she'd defend him all the more.

Jem said, "My sister, Anne's mother, never believed in the legend. Neither did Anne's father. Of course, they both died right before the war, so all that's left of the family, that I know of anyway, is me and Anne. She's all I've got, Michael. And as crazy as I've always thought all of this to be, I'm the keeper of the truth at the moment. You've got to help me. Don't leave her. And *believe* me. I think I know enough to help you beat Drago, but I can't take him on alone."

"I won't leave Anne," Michael assured him. He nodded stiffly and he walked down the; hall to Anne's room. He paused, then quietly twisted the knob and entered.

He half-expected to feel a terrible chill in the room, to discover that evil had already entered.

But the window was closed. The room was in darkness.

"Michael!" Anne whispered.

He strode across the room to her. She was lying on her bed, clad in white, her raven hair streaming all around her. Her beautiful, warm smile beckoned him. "I love you!" she said.

He took her into his arms. Passionately, tenderly, he made love to her.

No shadows touched them that night. He woke feeling as if the sunlight would allow him to get a grip on the world again.

But he had barely taken his first sip of coffee when word came to him with a message that plunged his heart and soul back into terror.

That morning Billy knocked at Anne's door once more.

Cissy McAllistair had died during the night. Would they both please come?

Chapter 5

It was incredibly painful to see Cissy in her coffin, Anne thought. The young were not supposed to perish, and certainly not someone as young and vivacious as Cissy.

She looked beautiful. Perhaps that added to the sadness. She looked as if she was sleeping, as if she might take a breath at any second. As if her beautiful, blue eyes would fly open, and her lips would curl into a smile.

Michael stood beside Anne in the McAllistair house. Instinctively, she groped for his hand. She looked to the window, blinking. Just last night, Cissy had opened her eyes, she had smiled, she had laughed. But this morning...

Anne was startled when Michael leaned past her, smoothing back Cissy's long blonde hair. He was looking for something in particular, she realized.

Nervously, she glanced around them. The McAllistairs weren't in the room at the moment. Doc Phelan had sedated Jeannie, who was lying down. Her husband and her sons were with her.

But they weren't alone in the room. Doc Phelan, gray and grizzled, a veteran of the war like so many of the men, was watching Michael with sharp eyes. Billy was there, too, staring at every move Michael made. Even Mort was there.

Then Anne saw what Michael had been looking for. There were little marks on Cissy's neck. Several of them. Mort had covered them with powder, but they were still visible.

Anne closed her eyes. Dear God, no. They were all going to start believing in the impossible. She'd known that Jem had cornered Michael last night and tried to tell him about the family legends. Now Michael was going to be convinced that there was a vampire in town and that Drago was it. If they weren't careful, they'd cause an awful panic. It might lead to a lynch mob—just because Drago was a foreigner.

Now those damned marks.

Maybe there was nothing to worry about. Surely very few Westerners had ever heard about vampires or the undead, or *nosferatus,* as the old family members had called them. It was all so ridiculous. But with Drago in town and all the awful things happening, maybe people would begin to believe that it could be possible. She was going to have to talk to Jem. It was all so ridiculous.

Then again, there was Drago.

He was an exceptionally charming man. He had the power of seduction. Unbelievably, he had even managed to draw her in with his charm. Not when she was away from him, of course. Only when she was near him.

He was just attractive. Handsome. Confident.

Not evil.

Yet she shivered. He did have some... power.

Damn those strange marks on Cissy's neck!

Michael stared at Mort, then at Doc Phelan. Mort shrugged. "I thought maybe spiders," he said.

"Would you care to speak with me outside, Michael?" Doc Phelan said. Michael nodded. He glanced at Anne, and she was startled by the intensity of the concern in his eyes. Then he released her hand. "Yes," he told Phelan. "Anne, I'll be right back. Don't leave here without me. Do you understand? Don't leave without me."

She might have gotten angry at the way he was addressing her, but she held her tongue. He was simply worried. She wasn't going to say anything.

Phelan, ancient as the hills but surprisingly spry, clapped Michael on the shoulder and the two men stepped outside. Anne stared at the marks again, then felt a shudder of sorrow sweep through her. Poor Cissy. Poor, sweet, beautiful young girl!

She suddenly became aware of a very strange sensation. A host of tiny shivers was snaking slowly up her spine, and from them both cold and heat seemed to emanate in waves. Before she turned, she knew who she would see.

"She looks stunning, does she not? So sweetly at peace! So very, very lovely."

Drago stared down at Cissy with a tenderness that touched Anne's heart. He was such a strange man. So very good-looking. So very... sexy.

She bit into her lower lip with annoyance. The way she reacted to him was absurd. She was in love with Michael. Drago had a certain attraction, but she loved Michael. No man on earth could be more sensual, tender, demanding, sexy... all those things. She knew it. And though she found Drago attractive, she didn't find him nearly as attractive as Michael.

He couldn't be an evil spirit, a vampire. Such things did not exist. Certainly not in this world! Only in some ancient little town in eastern Europe.

Still... there was that pull.

"How are her parents?" he asked softly.

"Desolate," Anne answered.

"Ah, well, it is to be expected. I came to pay my respects, but perhaps I should not disturb them now."

Anne didn't reply. Just as Michael had done, Drago shifted Cissy's hair. The marks were again visible. He seemed to study them with a curious pleasure. Anne backed away, discovering that she was really nervous around the man.

He stared at her with some surprise, then smiled.

"She is lovely, even in death. But no woman, alive or dead, is more beautiful than you, Anne."

What a strange thing to say!

"Cissy was a very lovely person," she said, her voice cracking.

"You are trying to pretend that you cannot hear all that I have to say to you. You are beautiful. I confess, I am in love with you."

"I'm in love with Michael!" she whispered fervently.

"But you must remember..." he said very softly, his voice trailing away sensually, then gaining momentum again. "You must remember my touch. I can still feel the silk of your flesh, the tips of my fingers running along the length of that beauty."

She was suddenly afraid. She couldn't take her eyes from his. Michael was right. She should be frightened.

"You've never touched me!" she challenged.

"I adore you. You will realize it. I will have you and teach you true ecstasy."

"No!"

"Perhaps you have been holding your death vigil too long. I think you should come for a walk with me."

"Oh, no—" she began to murmur. Then she stopped. His eyes were on hers. There was something so alluring in them. Something that brought back very strange memories.

As if she had known him before!

But she hadn't, and Michael was just outside, on the back porch. Even if Drago's gaze seemed to compel her to take his hand, she would not do so.

"Anne..."

His voice was soft, sensual. It slipped under her skin. It made her feel as if she wanted to be touched by him, stroked by him. As if she *had* to go with him...

"Drago! Get away from here! You're not welcome here!"

Michael's voice was harsh, his eyes flashing with fury.

Anne stepped back, confused. Suddenly Drago was just a tall, handsome foreigner. And Michael was behaving extremely rudely.

But Drago had said things to her, hadn't he? Things that he shouldn't have said?

She couldn't remember. No, it was Jem—Jem and Michael. They were trying to convince her, convince everyone, that Drago was evil. It was wrong. It was just because he was a foreigner. How could they be so prejudiced?

"Michael!" she whispered furiously.

He ignored her. His eyes flashing, his rugged face set, he brought her behind him, still facing Drago.

And David Drago was smiling. Amused with all of it.

"Get out!" Michael insisted.

"Michael, you can't tell the poor man to get out!" she cried, baffled. "This isn't even your house!"

Drago bowed deeply. "I would much rather leave than create a commotion when the McAllistairs are in such deep mourning. Dear Anne, you'll excuse me. Colonel Johnston, I will meet with you one night soon!"

Drago tipped his hat to them and departed.

Michael turned to face Anne. She set her hands on her hips, staring at him furiously. "That was the rudest display I've ever seen!"

"Rude!" He drew her to him, whispering, "The man killed Cissy, and you think that I was rude!"

"Drago killed her?" Anne exclaimed. "Oh, Michael, you are losing your mind. Cissy got sick! She rallied, but she died. How can you blame that on the man? Just because he's a foreigner. Or maybe it's worse. Maybe you discovered that the poor man has been a Yankee, or a Yank sympathizer—"

"Anne—" he began, then broke off. Too many people in the

room were beginning to stare at them. He caught her hand and looked around the room, setting his eyes on Billy. "Please tell Mr. McAllistair that we'll be back tomorrow to help with the funeral arrangements."

He turned around, as if to leave. Then he paused. The others were talking softly amongst themselves again. He released Anne's hand, and walked over to help Mort, who had signaled that the time had come to close the coffin for the night.

But Michael didn't seem to be satisfied with the closed lid. He tied something around the center coffin handle to hold it shut. Anne couldn't see what it was.

He had her out the door and on the porch before she came to a dead stop, determined to ask him. "All right, what was that all about?"

He hesitated, staring at her. "Drago is a vampire."

"I've had it!" Anne said, waving her hand in the air. Oh, she knew it! He'd been fighting too long. He was seeing demons in the man just because he was different.

A vampire! Michael probably hadn't even known about vampires. Jem must have convinced him. Oh, they'd be seeing ghosts and all sorts of things soon!

"Michael, I love you, but this is ridiculous. What—"

"Three times, Anne," he said, swallowing quickly. "He bit her three times. That's what the marks were. Three is the number. She'll come back to join him now."

"Where did you hear that?" she demanded.

"From Jem. And it's your family legend—you should know, you should see the truth!" he told her.

"You've lost your mind! Jem has heard this legend all his life, and he never believed in this ridiculousness before!"

"Drago was never around before."

"Oh, come on, Michael!" Anne exclaimed.

"You come on, Anne! Look at what's happened."

"Michael," Anne told him coldly, walking around him, "you were unbelievably rude, and now you've lost your mind." She started down the steps, and toward home.

He followed on her footsteps. If she weren't so very worried about his mental state, it would be touching. He'd been in half the major battles of the war. He'd ridden out into Indian country for years now. It was only natural that he would crack eventually. He needed peace!

"Anne, he wants you!"

"Michael, I've told you, I intend to marry you. There is no need for this—"

"Anne!" He caught hold of her, swinging her around to face him. "Anne, I'm worried sick! You must know that you look exactly like Helga—"

"She's an ancestor! I *should* look like her! There's nothing so unusual there."

"Anne, dammit, I'm worried about you—"

"And I'm worried about *you!*"

"Anne, listen to me. When I discovered the Indians' bodies, they were all but bloodless. And they were all decapitated. A vampire can't rise from the dead if it's been decapitated. Then there was Smokey. Bloodless, decapitated. And now—"

"Cissy, whose head is in place!" Anne reminded him painfully.

Michael let out a cry of aggravation. "Because he wants Cissy to join him!"

"I thought he wanted me?" she reminded him.

He threw up his arms and sighed. "Anne, he does. He thinks that you're the woman he loved centuries ago, and that you've come back to life. I can't read his mind. Maybe it was just taking him a little bit too long to get to you. Maybe he wants company in the meantime, and maybe he just really liked Cissy, too, and wanted her to have eternal life. I don't know!"

"Oh, Michael! This is just getting better and better! My uncle has been filling you with the family tales, and you're turning a handsome foreigner into a vampire! Michael, please, get out of my way! I love you, but I want you to go home, and get some sleep! This has all been too much for you."

"No." He shook his head stubbornly. His jaw was set.

She gritted her teeth, feeling a little tremor of desire. She was frustrated, but she loved him like this, when he was so determined.

"I'm going to be with you."

"Suit yourself," she said, walking again. "But I don't want to hear any more about it!"

She walked for a few steps and was surprised to realize that he wasn't following. She turned back. His hands on his hips, he was looking up at the sky.

His gaze touched hers. Suddenly he ran forward, sweeping her off her feet and into his arms. And then he was running like a jaguar with her held to his chest.

She couldn't breathe!

"Michael!" she cried out. It didn't do a thing. He kept on running, all the way to her porch steps.

Once again, Uncle Jem was waiting for them. Michael ran through the door. It slammed shut behind them.

"I've had it!" Anne cried out. "I've had it! Uncle Jem, you quit with the stories. Michael—you quit behaving like a lunatic or I'll not only refuse to marry you, I'll refuse to—" She broke off, remembering Uncle Jem.

"Watch it," Uncle Jem said dolefully to Michael. "She's threatening to not sleep with you anymore."

"Oh!" Anne cried in total exasperation. She walked down the hall to her room and slammed the door shut behind her.

Jem looked at Michael. "Well?"

"There were six marks on her neck."

"Three bite marks," Jem said.

"Maybe," Michael murmured.

"And I'll bet Doc Phelan told you her blood was half gone, too." Michael nodded.

"Don't leave Anne in there alone," Jem warned him.

But Anne wasn't in her room. She was bursting back into the hallway. "Uncle Jem! Why is my room decorated from floor to ceiling in *garlic bulbs?*" she demanded.

He shrugged. "'Cause there's a God-darned vampire out there!"

"I don't believe in vampires!"

"Then humor an old man."

She tossed a garlic bulb at him and stormed back into her room. Michael winced and followed her. She was sitting at the foot of her bed, looking morosely around her. "I do not believe this!" she exclaimed. "This behavior from two grown men."

Michael smiled and reached into his pocket, producing a jewel case. He handed it to her.

She looked at him suspiciously, then flicked up the lid.

It was a delicate, beautiful gold cross. "Oh, Michael!" she moaned.

He sat down beside her. "Humor a young man as well as an old one?" he said softly.

She smiled, handed him the cross, and turned so that he could clip it around her neck. "It's a lovely gift," she said softly. "But Michael..."

"Ummm?"

"I don't think I can sleep with all this garlic."

"How about giving me a chance to make you forget it's here?" he asked her huskily.

She was so angry with him. He was driving her crazy. Both he and Uncle Jem were already halfway there!

But she loved him.

She kissed him gently, meaning it to be just a brief touch, but he pulled her into his arms. His lips molded sensually over hers. His tongue penetrated between her teeth and stroked her mouth deeply.

She did forget the garlic.

Later that night, she awoke. Or perhaps she didn't awake. Perhaps she dreamed.

Drago stood outside her window. Far outside, shivering. He was telling her that it was cold, but that he couldn't come in.

"Come to me!" he whispered to her.

No.

"Come to me, come to me. Please..."

No. She was in love with Michael. But Michael had been so rude. She had to apologize. She just had to apologize.

It was only a dream, but she was suddenly walking. Walking to the window. The garlic was pungent. She needed to crawl over it.

"Anne!"

She awoke with a start. To her amazement, she was standing at the window. Ready to open it and climb out.

But Michael was there, wrapping the sheet around her, wrapping his own warmth around her. "Anne, Anne, Anne!" He cradled her, held her, swept her up and against him.

"It's all right!" she cried. "I was just sleepwalking." She lifted his dear head, cradled his cheeks with her hands. "I was just sleepwalking. Oh, Michael! There are no such things as vampires."

Truly, there weren't such things as vampires, she assured herself with a mental shake. Drago was powerful, handsome, sexy—and far too bold. But there were no such things as vampires!

Michael held her, too weary to fight with her.

He slept finally, his limbs entwined with hers, his arms locked around her, his thigh cast over her hip.

* * *

Jem pointed a finger at him over a cup of morning coffee. Anne was out back, feeding the chickens.

"You've got to kill the creature!" Jem said.

Michael slumped back, staring at Jem. "And just how do I do that? If he is a vampire, he won't die with a bullet."

"But he will die if you decapitate him, or force him into daylight—or drive a stake through his heart. But Jesu, boy, you've got to be careful! Vampires are tremendously strong... Holy water helps," Jem reflected. "But I'm not so sure you can actually kill a vampire with it. Not unless you have a tubfull."

"What a help you are, Jem, what a help!"

"You can't just accost him. I mean, you can't go out and beat up a vampire!" Jem warned him.

"I wasn't planning on trying," Michael assured him. He sighed. Maybe Anne was right. Maybe they *were* crazy. Nonetheless, he was growing more and more frightened. "I've got to find him by day. In his coffin, I imagine. Oh, God! What am I saying?" he demanded with disgust. Then he shrugged. "I'll speak with Father Martin after Cissy's funeral today."

Jem nodded. "Good idea. And you'd better hush up for now. Annie's on her way back in and she doesn't seem to have a lot of patience for either of us at the moment."

Anne came in. Michael went on back to his own house to change into his black suit for the funeral. He returned with his carriage for Anne and Jem, and the three of them attended the service together.

It was the saddest service Michael had ever been to. Jeannie cried as if her heart would break.

Then Cissy was lowered into the ground. Father Martin tried to say all the right words, but a sudden dust storm came up. It started slowly, just as Father Martin began. Then suddenly, it became ferocious. Father Martin, holding on to his hat, looked to Jeannie. "Mrs. McAllistair, we'll start all over tomorrow, don't you worry, we'll see it done right by tomorrow afternoon." By then, people were shrieking, and heedless of the need for a decent funeral for Cissy, they were beginning to run. Father Martin got no further. They would all come back for the service tomorrow.

Everyone there was running for his or her carriage.

As Michael covered Anne and they headed for shelter, he couldn't help but wonder if the cross he had wedged into the coffin the night before had kept its occupant sleeping through the night.

And he couldn't help but wonder if it was still there.

At the McAllistair house, the women made coffee and served food that everyone pushed around on their plates.

While Anne supervised in the McAllistair kitchen since Jeannie was still unable to, Michael took the opportunity to slip outside with Father Martin.

The priest was a young man. For some reason Michael was glad that Green Valley's one man of God happened to be a Catholic.

Father Martin had soft brown hair and brown eyes. He was of medium height and build, but as he crossed his arms over his chest, Michael decided that he was probably stronger than he looked.

Michael tried to talk. He tried again. "Jesu, Father! I can't believe I'm saying this to you, but I think we have a vampire in Green Valley."

Father Martin's brows flew up. "A vampire?"

"I know you can't possibly believe me—"

Father Martin interrupted him quickly. "I'm not sure I know what that is."

Michael patiently explained everything Jem had told him.

"I know it sounds crazy, and it's a long story. It started with the Indians, and they were absolutely convinced that there was an evil spirit afoot, a white evil spirit. Oh, Lord! I—"

"Michael," Father Martin said passionately, "we know that there is the power of good in the world. We believe in God, in the Holy Spirit. So perhaps there are evil spirits as well."

Stunned, Michael stared at him. "Then you believe me?"

"I don't believe or disbelieve you." The young priest suddenly shivered fiercely. "But something is going on here. Jesus in His heaven, my friend, something is going on here. And I'll do anything in my power to help you! I'd be pleased to bless you and your efforts in any fight against evil."

Michael smiled. "I don't exactly know what I'm doing myself, Father Martin, but I've been given some advice, and you might supply me with a few of the things I've been told I'm going to need." He hesitated. "You don't think I'm insane?"

Father Martin paused for a minute. Then he spoke in a rush. "I felt it—something, a while back. One night. I don't know how to explain it. Something came with the breeze, something that had a strange feel of..."

"Evil?" Michael suggested softly.

Father Martin nodded somberly. "And then there was the Indian massacre. Then old Smokey. And now poor Cissy. I don't know the truth. And, of course, the Church isn't taking any official stand, you realize."

Michael nodded. He didn't give a damn if anything was official or not.

"There is something out there," Father Martin said. "Ask what you will. I'll help you."

Michael went to the church with Father Martin, who blessed him and gave him a wooden walking stick with a pointed end—a stake.

He left the church with a small cross around his own neck, a vial of holy water in his shirt pocket, and the stick at his side.

He walked slowly along the empty street until he looked up and realized that it was almost dark. Then he began to run.

* * *

Anne looked worriedly out the window. Almost all the others had gone home now. Jeannie was lying down. The boys were sitting in their sister's empty room. Tim was getting drunk.

Jem and Billy were still there, quietly sipping from glasses of beer.

Anne, growing more anxious, was just about to jump up and run out to look for Michael when he entered the front door. She frowned, worried that he might have hurt himself, because he seemed to be leaning on a walking stick. He gave her a faint smile. She frowned, lifting a brow to him. But before she could say anything, they heard a loud shriek from Jeannie McAllistair's bedroom.

In a panic, Anne flew up. She raced into the room, followed by the others.

65

Jeannie was sitting up in bed, shaking, pointing to the window. "She's out there. My baby is out there. I swear it! I saw her. She was calling to me. She said that she was cold, that she was lonely, that she needed me!"

"Oh, Jeannie!" Anne cried, taking the woman into her arms. "It's all right, Jeannie, it's going to be all right! I'm here with you. Cissy isn't cold! She's with God now. She's going to be fine. But she loves you so much! She'd want you to be well!"

"There's nothing in the window, Ma, nothing at all!" Anthony told her.

Jeannie collapsed in Anne's arms. Anne soothed her until she ceased sobbing.

Michael swung around and walked through the house, past Tim McAllistair who sat in a stupor in his armchair.

He walked outside. There was nothing to be seen in the front of the house. He leaned against his walking-stick stake, then rounded the corner.

And then he stopped still.

It was true, all of it.

Because she was there. Cissy McAllistair, dressed in the beautiful white spring gown her mother had chosen for her funeral, was there. She looked as young and sweet as ever, but she smiled at him in a way that was no longer innocent.

"Michael..."

The sound of her voice was hypnotic. He wanted to go to her.

"Michael, I'm so cold. Come, put your arms around me. Warm me. I beg you, Michael..."

He was moving before he knew it. Somehow Cissy's blue eyes now resembled Drago's gold ones. There was a rim around them. A rim of a different color.

"Cissy?" he said softly. They must have been mistaken. She hadn't really been dead. They had buried her prematurely; he had heard of it happening before. He went closer and closer to her.

That batty old Jem had been right. Drago really must be a vampire. He had given Cissy his deadly kiss...

No, it couldn't be.

Her blonde hair tumbled all around her. Her pretty smile was in place.

"Oh, Michael! I always envied Anne so much. Come to *me* now,

Michael! Come to me. You think you've found ecstasy with Anne. It's nothing—nothing, Michael, like the things I can show you. Like the way I can make you feel. Let me touch you. Let me show you. Let me kiss you."

Something glittered in the moonlight. He realized it was coming from her... mouth. Her lips had drawn back. He saw with mesmerized horror the incredible length and sharpness of her teeth. They dripped clear liquid...

"Michael!"

She called his name in dismay, as if having sensed that she had lost something.

And then he noticed much more. The pieces of graveyard dirt in her hair. The subtle, putrid smell of... death.

"Michael!" she whispered. "I'm so cold. You're supposed to be my friend, Michael. Please come, make me warmer..."

He wanted to. She had caught his eyes, and her power was so strong, he wanted to do just as she asked.

No! Oh, no!

He wrenched his anguished gaze from hers. This wasn't Cissy. Cissy was dead. This was some hellish creation with Cissy's sweet face and youth, yet with the devil's own eyes.

"You come to me, Cissy," he said softly.

She started to move toward him. Smiling. Moving slowly. She was in front of him, ready to sweep her arms around him.

Ready to taste his flesh.

He drew his stake between them. It seemed his silent scream echoed inside him. He took the stake and drove it into her chest with all his strength, seeing in her eyes the shriek of absolute horror she never voiced.

Then she was falling to the ground. He leaned over her. Her eyes were still open. She smiled, and for an instant she was once again the sweet innocent Cissy who had been Anne's best friend. "Thank you, Michael!" she whispered, and her eyes closed.

"Oh, God!" he breathed. He sat back on his heels, covering his face with his hands.

"Michael!"

It was Billy, coming around the corner of the house. Michael looked at his friend and waited for him to express his shock, but apparently Billy had been seeing and understanding a lot more than

Michael had realized.

Billy crossed himself. "She come up from the dead like a devil, right?"

"Something like that," Michael told him.

"You've got to help us all, Michael."

Michael swallowed hard. He nodded. "I'm going to try Billy. But now, you've got to help me, before her parents see her. Let's bring her back to the cemetery."

Together they carried Cissy back to the graveyard and laid her in her coffin. And once again he felt the cold breeze of fear suddenly crash down upon him.

Anne!

She was in the house. It was nighttime. Drago's time.

Somewhere, a wolf howled. Michael stood in the cemetery and looked back toward town. The breeze picked up. It was cold.

He started to run.

Chapter 6

Jeannie was sleeping at last.

Anne returned to the living room. Tim had fallen into a drunken sleep in his chair. The boys were gone. Uncle Jem was on the sofa in the parlor, trying to keep his eyes open.

Anne went into the kitchen and started washing the dishes as best she could. She was worried. Michael had been gone for a long time now, and he had been acting very strangely.

She looked out the kitchen window and thought she saw him hurrying toward the house. She wiped her hands on a dish towel and went out the back door, onto the porch. There was a shadow against the darkness.

"Michael?" she said softly.

But it wasn't Michael. David Drago quite suddenly stepped into view, smiling. "Anne!" he said softly.

All at once she felt uneasy, and was sorry she had come outside. She backed away, watching him. "The funeral was this afternoon, Mr. Drago," she said. "The McAllistairs are all sleeping, if you have come to pay your respects."

To her dismay, he kept walking toward her. She backed away from him. He stopped, reaching a hand out to her.

"I didn't come to see the McAllistairs, Anne. I came for you."

She shook her head, fighting the confusion that threatened to engulf her very soul. There was something about the man that mesmerized her. She had to think carefully to speak. "Mr. Drago, I don't know what impression I gave you, but I'm very much in love with Michael Johnston. I'm going to marry him. I—"

"I intend to change that."

"But I don't want it changed," she said firmly.

Abruptly he was furious. "Well, it *will* be changed this time, Anne! I have waited hundreds of years for you! I have searched nations, continents! And I finally found you here!"

"I don't know what you're talking about!" she cried, starting to back away again. Centuries...

How strange. She'd once had the feeling that she'd known him before. She had dreamed about him, again and again.

She was attracted to him.

She feared him...

They were all losing their minds. Or else it was true, and David Drago was a vampire.

No, that couldn't be! It was legend, superstition. It just couldn't be true!

She should have paid more heed to Uncle Jem, to Michael...

"No!" She mouthed the word. "I have to go in. Michael is coming. Michael will be here at any minute."

He started to laugh. "And you think Michael can keep us apart? My love, you are mistaken!" His golden eyes were latched upon hers, and to her horror, she discovered that she could not move. "I can break your precious Michael's neck with the snap of my fingers," he whispered. "I can send him flying across the state with the whisper of my breath. Anne, you are now mine!"

Deny him! Fight him! she charged herself. But she didn't know how. Why had she been such a fool? She'd sensed his power before. Now she was trapped in it. Its strength was incredible! She couldn't move. His gaze touched her, and she couldn't move.

Fight, fight, she had to fight...

Over and over she whispered, "Michael will come. He will come."

Drago reached for her, finding her wrist, wrenching her toward him. He held her shoulders, staring down into her eyes, murmuring, "I meant it to be so slow! A sure, sweet seduction of the senses. You would have come with me so willingly then. But fast or slow, it doesn't matter. You must still discover all that I can give you."

"I'll never want you! Never."

"But you will. Once I touch you, you will know my power and you will want what I want. Just once, when your blood has trickled from your body into mine, warming it, giving it sustenance, then you will be my creation. Three times, Anne, and you will be mine for eternity!"

He brushed aside her hair. Then fie paused, swearing violently, and Anne dimly realized that Michael's small gold cross lay around her neck.

Dear Lord, please...

He swore again, dragging her with him. "I wanted you! I esteemed you above all women! I searched for you forever! Don't fight me!"

She *was* fighting him, though, struggling with every ounce of strength she possessed, and still, unable to dislodge his secure hold on her. He was taking her with him. Running with him. But then it seemed they were not running anymore; they were not touching the ground at all.

He had lifted her. He had become a shadow in the night. He was holding her, and they were soaring over the town.

She looked down. There was Michael, running back to town from the graveyard.

From the graveyard?

Oh, dear God! Michael was running *away* from the direction in which they were rushing. She began to shiver with dread. Drago was a creature of death and shadows, and he was taking her to the cemetery.

He was taking her toward death.

"Michael!" she cried out.

Drago was laughing. His whisper, hot, throaty, encompassed her. "You'll come to my home, my pet. I'm sure your fool uncle has been wondering where it is. A patch of earth in unhallowed ground has warmed and welcomed me nightly. A small tunnel beneath it leads up to my newly built house on the hill. Richard Servian lives there. You'll come to like the fat little bug, my dear, for he serves me well. Watches over my coffin by day, cares for my comfort at night."

Impossible...

Oh, why hadn't she believed?

She was dreaming. No, they were standing on the unhallowed ground, where the suicides were buried. The atheists who had scorned God. The poor, the unknown, the unloved.

Drago just looked at her, smiling. She heard a noise behind her. She turned to see Richard Servian, the fat little man who had arrived one day on the daily stage coach. Short, plump, he should have been the picture of health, but instead his skin, too, was as pale as death.

"The cross!" Drago roared.

Caught between the two of them, Anne spun around. Servian started toward her. She backed away, striking out. She caught his face, his throat. The man was human! She should have hurt him. But he didn't cry out. And he kept coming for her.

She backed into Drago, and his fingers, cold as steel bars, curled around her arms, holding her in place before Servian. The servant reached out and wrenched the cross from her throat.

The fight was finished from that moment, for Drago held her immobile with absolute power.

First she felt the warmth of his breath against her throat. Then she felt the razor-sharp jab of his teeth. She cried out. His teeth sank deep into her neck. And suddenly, it wasn't painful anymore. A coldness entered her body. And with it, a curious feeling of sweet ecstasy. Yes, she wanted more.

More and more...

* * *

Michael reached the McAllistair house to find it dead quiet. Frantically, he searched for Anne, and stumbled upon Jem Turner, fast asleep.

"Jem!" He shook the man. "Anne... where's Anne? Jem, you have to help me. Where is she?"

"Anne, Anne!" Jem cried, waking. He shook his head. Michael's heart sank. Jem gripped his arm tightly. "My God, she's gone. He's taken her! You'll have to go for him, you can't wait until morning; you have to find him. Three times! All he needs to do is drink three times!" He leaped up. "I'm coming with you. Get Billy to come with us, too. We've got to fight—now!"

Michael knew there wasn't time to dissuade Jem from coming. Billy, as white as a sheet, was still willing to stay at his side.

"Where?" Michael cried. "Where would he have taken her?"

"Where else would the dead find a home?" Jem replied. "The cemetery. He must have taken her to the cemetery, probably to the unhallowed ground. He'll make her sleep with him!"

Michael rushed out of the house with Jem and Billy behind him. Then he realized that although Billy was right behind him, Jem was falling back.

He turned for just a minute. He had forgotten Jem's age. The old man was panting, gasping, his face lobster-red. They should have taken the carriage. They should have—

No, there was no time.

"Go on, go on!" Jem urged him, catching up. He gripped Michael's shirtfront. "Don't forget how powerful he is! Have faith,

Michael." Jem was shaking him. "You've got to win! You've got to win."

Michael nodded and spun around. He and Billy ran the rest of the way to the cemetery.

At first he didn't see Drago or Anne. All he could see was a squat little man standing amidst the makeshift crosses on the unhallowed ground.

The fat man raised his arm. Michael realized he was holding a pistol. "Down!" he shouted to Billy, who fell to the grass and rolled. The pistol exploded. Michael butted the fat man in the gut with his shoulder, and the man went down easily, sending the pistol flying.

When Michael stumbled back to his feet, Drago was standing there. Billy was staring at him in awe and horror. Drago walked straight toward him, but he never moved. Drago swung his arm, and it was as if he were swatting a fly. He slapped Billy against the side of the head, lifting him into the air. Billy crashed down upon a tombstone, unconscious... or dead.

Drago turned his attention to Michael. "All right, little man. It has come down to you and me. It is over. She is mine. And I will tear you limb from limb!"

Michael heard something soft—a word, perhaps—and realized Anne was standing behind Drago.

"Anne!" he cried. Drago stepped aside. She didn't move. She didn't even seem to see him.

There were two tiny puncture marks on her throat.

Michael was overcome with anguish. "No!" he cried in despair.

Drago need touch her only twice more—touch her throat, drink her blood—and she would be lost to Michael forever.

His stake was gone, imbedded in Cissy's heart, buried in the ground beyond. The holy water remained in his shirt pocket. Drago beckoned to him, circling him.

"Come, Michael Johnston, proud Indian hunter, great soldier, warrior, all! Come, fight me!"

Drago was laughing. Anne stood perfectly still, touched by the vampire.

"Anne!" Michael whispered again.

"Don't you see, you fool creature," Drago said to him. "She cannot help you. She is mine, and mine alone. Only I have the power to keep her!"

He moved toward Michael. Impatient, he was now ready for the kill.

Michael reached into his pocket and found the vial of holy water. He splashed it onto Drago's face.

The man let out a chilling scream of pain. He backed away, then fell to his knees.

Good God! Michael thought. Was that it? Had he won?

But Drago was stumbling to his feet. His face was burned where the water had hit him. "You will die slowly!" he promised.

He walked straight to Michael and struck the side of his head.

Michael flew into the air and landed hard, all the breath knocked out of him. He felt broken, bruised, stunned.

Drago was standing over him. A furious Drago.

"First I shall feast upon you, drain the blood from your body. I will leave you barely alive so that you may watch while I take your beloved Anne, here in the moonlight. We will make love upon the earth, beside your rotting, dying flesh, and in the end, I will make her one with me. Then I will grab your near-lifeless form and twist your head from your pathetic body."

Drago smiled and started down upon him.

Michael lashed out, catching Drago in the jaw. Drago just grunted. Michael stumbled to his feet, swinging again.

The vampire struck once more.

Michael sailed, then crashed down upon the earth. Drago dragged him to his feet and struck him again. Michael fought back the best he could, but Drago was gaining strength where he was losing his own.

No matter how many times Michael struck Drago, the vampire seemed to show no sign of discomfort.

"I have the power!" he whispered triumphantly.

And he hit Michael again. Michael felt the sensation of flying once again. Of hitting the ground.

He hurt from head to toe. He couldn't move. He struggled to regain his breath.

What a fool he had been to have left his best weapon embedded in Cissy's heart. But he hadn't wanted to jeopardize her soul, and so he had left it there.

All at once he realized a cross lay mere inches from his grasp. It had been crudely fashioned from branches sharpened at the bottom and thrust hard into the ground, a grave marker to stand guard over some poor soul, made by someone who must have believed in the power of God.

But at some time it had fallen free and intact from the dust.

It could be used as a stake...

The thought had barely entered Michael's head when Drago pounced upon him.

Michael furiously pitted his waning strength against the vampire's puissant force. The dusty old cross lay inches away, just where the fence signified the beginning of the hallowed ground. He could see it so clearly now! Someone had whittled the wood into a very sharp point. And with the rawhide binding around the horizontal, crooked piece of branch, it was both a weapon and a symbol of holiness. If Michael could just get his hands upon it, curl his fingers around it, and plunge it into the creature's heart.

That would be the end, Jem had promised him. Even old Dancing Woman had said death lay in the heart.

Just as life sprang from it.

But he needed more, Michael reminded himself. Father Martin had warned him that he needed faith.

Faith...

God help me, he prayed silently. *God help me.*

But Drago was over him now. And Drago knew that Michael's strength was failing him.

Anne stood just feet away, watching with her sightless stare, caught in the vampire's hypnotic spell.

She could not help Michael now.

And God, it seemed, had deserted him.

He stared at Drago, determined never to give up to his evil. Not until death, not beyond. Faith was the key. Faith in the strength of goodness.

As the vampire smiled down at him, Michael finally realized the true color of his eyes. They were red. Redder when he had drunk his fill of human blood. Gold when he was hungry...

Right now, they gleamed with both colors, hard gold orbs surrounded by red. An awful red.

Blood-red.

Blood-red with the stolen life of his many, many victims.

The vampire opened his mouth. The fangs were fascinating, just like those of a rattler, but far more deadly. They were dripping. Coming closer and closer to his throat. Michael remembered all of Drago's words. He did not intend to make Michael a creature of the night. He meant to rip him limb from limb, and leave him a dismembered carcass as he had done with the Apaches...

"Anne!" Michael shouted suddenly. "Anne, I love you!"

His cry was powerless, but maybe she would hear him before he died. Maybe it would touch her heart. Maybe somewhere, in heaven or hell, she would know how very much he had loved her.

"Anne!"

He heard her sharp gasp as she sharply inhaled. "Michael!" His name, coming softly from her lips, was a cry of anguish. She could see him. She could feel him. She wanted to help him. But she could not fight the vampire's power.

"She's mine now, you fool!" Drago shouted, his fingers biting harder into Michael's shoulders. And then he started to laugh. "By the devil, dear fellow! You've yet to understand the full extent of my powers! But you will, soon. Oh, I promise you. You'll know very, very soon." And he opened his mouth again. The fangs seemed to extend, his whole face to contort. He meant to drink, and drink deeply.

Michael renewed his struggle, pitting the bulk of his strength against the arms and chest of the vampire, keeping those fangs just inches from his neck. Drago swore, and Michael thought he could count it a minor triumph to have held him off for so long, during a vicious fight...

Michael blinked suddenly. Perhaps he was losing his mind, hallucinating. Men in the desert often talked of seeing things that weren't there...

But it was happening. Anne was moving.

He could hear her soft voice. Or maybe it was a voice from her heart, because Drago didn't seem to hear it. It was Michael's name she was saying again and again. "Michael, oh, Michael. God help us, God help us... oh, Michael!"

Miraculously, she *was* moving. He could see her eyes. She was fighting the creature's supernatural power. Ah, that amber fire within her eyes. In it, he could see the fantastic strength of will with which she was fighting.

And he could see her tears, evidence of her love.

She had sunk down to her knees. She was thrusting the stake forward.

Closer. Closer.

He stretched out his fingers. He could almost touch it. Almost! He groped and strained...

Try! He willed her. *Oh, Anne! Please try!*

And Anne pushed the cross forward once again. His fingers closed around it.

And he found new strength.

For a moment, he faltered. What would happen to Anne? The vampire had touched her, put his mark upon her. If he did manage to slay the vampire, then...

"Do it! For the love of God, do it!" Anne pleaded. "Save us both!"

He had to. Whether she perished or remained on the earth to love him, he had to do it. To free her, one way or the other.

"I love you, Anne!" he cried out.

Drago was laughing, laughing, deep within his throat.

The teeth were almost ready to sink into Michael's flesh, to draw his blood. To steal away his life.

Michael gritted his teeth. With a burst of raw energy, he drew up the crosslike stake and managed to wedge it between them even as he struggled with Drago.

And just as the cold teeth touched his flesh, he thrust the pointed stake straight into Drago's heart.

He pushed it hard, again and again.

The vampire glared at him, his red-gold eyes widening. Michael looked on amazed. The vampire was surprised. Stunned.

Drago fell back, his long pale fingers curling around the stake that protruded from his heart. He looked at Michael again. His hands fell away from the stake.

Miraculous things began to happen. Years and years of decay began to take place before Michael's very eyes. Drago became a wrinkled old man. Then his skin turned to leather, which began to turn to dust and ash, crumbling around him.

In horror, Michael backed away. Then he heard Anne cry out.

Anne! They had won, they had bested the creature. They had fought it and bested it with love and faith and someone's pathetic cross from a dusty grave... Anne!

She was still on her knees, just inches away, as beautiful as ever, tears staining her cheeks, her eyes wide and luminous.

"Oh, Michael!" She threw herself into his arms. He held her tightly. He felt her warmth, her trembling. She was alive and well, and fire in his arms. He touched her frantically. Even the tiny pinpricks on her throat had healed.

She reached for him, and he was there. Ready to hold her, finding new strength, sweeping her into his encompassing grasp. She was trying not to look at Drago.

She stroked his cheek. "Oh, Michael. We made it! You saved me from him."

He smiled crookedly. "No, my love. *You* saved *me* from him." He was trembling again in remembrance. "God saved us both from him, Annie. He gave us... life."

Just inches away, a new, cleansing night breeze, warm and balmy, was lifting away the ashes of the vampire's corpse.

Neither of them looked at the remnants.

There was too much to be discovered in each other's eyes. Anne's smile deepened. "I'll marry you," she whispered.

"I haven't asked lately!"

"You will."

"And you'll understand about the militia?"

She nodded. "I'll understand that I'm blessed. You have a rare strength, Michael Johnston. A very rare strength. I pray that our children will have it too."

"Our children?"

"Yes. We'll be starting with just one, of course. Very soon."

"Anne..." he murmured.

Her arms tightened around him. "You mustn't worry! I knew long before Drago came. I just couldn't tell you because I wanted to convince you to quit the militia. And now..."

"Now?"

"Now I know that would be wrong. The town needs you. Cissy said so. We all need you."

He lowered his head for a moment. Cissy. They would all mourn her for a long time. She would keep them all from ever forgetting.

And maybe that was good. They would cherish life so much more because of her!

Anne cupped his face. She kissed him long and deeply before

releasing him and stepping away.

"Billy," he murmured. He left her for a moment, going to his friend, fear lodging again in his throat. But even as he knelt beside him, Billy stirred.

He stared at Michael. "Did we lick him, Colonel?"

"We licked him, Billy. Come on, let me help you up."

Billy wavered for a minute, then stared at Anne, wide-eyed. "You all right, Annie?" he asked.

She smiled and nodded. Billy let out a Rebel cry that pierced the night. He hugged her. Then he turned to Michael. "I'll hurry on ahead. I'll let Jem know you're all right and that—"

"Right. Tell Jem that we had enough faith. Get the sheriff to send someone out here to pick him up," he said pointing to Richard Servian, who was still lying unconscious on the ground. "And take care, Billy! We don't want the McAllistairs to ever worry about Cissy. She is at peace now."

"I know," Billy said softly. He shook his head. "I don't think that I believe it, Colonel. I was here, but I still don't think I believe it."

He headed back to town. When he was gone, Michael realized that he was trembling. He spun around. "A baby?"

Anne nodded, smiling.

"And you're going to marry me?"

She kept nodding.

"Well, you're going to do so right now. I'm going for Father Martin the minute we get back, and I don't care how long he's been sleeping. Jem and Billy can be our witnesses. We'll have to be quiet out of respect for the McAllistairs, but I'm not giving you any chance to change your mind!"

"Michael!" Anne protested.

"And I don't want you to step away from me. Ever."

Her arms curled around his neck. They might be standing on unhallowed ground, but Michael was certain that God was smiling down upon them.

Maybe the legend was true. Maybe Anne *had* lost to Drago once before. Maybe this was their turn for happiness.

All he knew for sure was that she was kissing him, and that it was good. Sweet, tender, loving.

Oh, she could stir his senses so easily!

They needed to get home. Her home, he decided. That would be where they would live. She'd already imbued the place with her special warmth.

And tonight...

Tonight he wanted to return quickly. To hold her in a darkness that no longer harbored evil shadows. To make love to her with a breeze caressing them that was soft and warm and good.

"Let's go home," he said softly.

"And just leave... him?" she murmured.

Michael pressed her head against his shoulder and stepped around what was left of the vampire. There was the stake that now protruded from a swatch of black cloth. There were pieces of bone and ash on the ground.

Michael held Anne very tightly. "Perhaps I never truly understood the extent of your powers," he told the remnants of the creature. "You told me about them over and over again. But there was one power you underestimated. One you never understood." He paused, then smiled.

"The power of love, old boy. The power of love. It's the strongest in all the universe!"

Then, holding Anne to him, he walked away from the shadows.

And into the light of life and love.

LOVERS AND DEMONS

Petersburg, Virginia 1864
Under Siege

By night, by this night, at any rate, the shells and mortar that so often hurtled toward the city, whistling their horrid cry in the air, were still.

There were no battle cries, no explosions, no screams.

The well-equipped Union Army soldiers slept, fiddled, or played mournful harmonica melodies within their camps. In the Southern trenches, the men lay back, seeking whatever rest they could find while their empty stomachs growled in terrible protest of the starvation that had seized hold of the besieged city.

In both camps, the men read letters from their loved ones, read them over and over again, folded them carefully, tenderly, and replaced them in pockets or wallets.

And in both camps, they wrote letters as well. Letters that tried to make light of the situation.

Yet letters in which all men, in blue and in gray, wondered if they would survive the next day's fighting, or perish in the blood-soaked fields and trenches.

Plaintive tunes rose on the air. So many the same from both sides.

So many weary... so damned sad.

Within the city, the people waited, defiant and devoted to their cause. People passionately loyal to Lee, their leader, to the belief that they must be right, that they must, in the end, win their freedom.

Yet they waited in great anguish. First through the days, then the weeks, then the months. Stalwart, they hung on. Determined, they suffered.

The pigeons had disappeared from the streets a long time ago.

Men, women, and children were all too eager for meals to question just what the meat in the pot might be—when they were so lucky to see anything that resembled meat.

The moon rose high. It was a full moon tonight.

Lenore Latham, hearing a distant, mournful song on the air, paused on her mission of mercy. She thought for a moment how much she longed to escape the war. But she couldn't run away. Her youngest brother, Teddy, just fourteen, was in the trenches surrounding the city. Her grandfather, nearly eighty, was in the trenches as well.

Her husband, Bruce, was not in the trenches. He was buried in a mass grave in Spotsylvania County where he had died well over a year ago. Sometimes, she couldn't even remember his face.

Too many faces filled her thoughts now. The drawn, terribly thin faces of little children. The desperate and also terribly thin faces of mothers. The pinched, puckered, wailing faces of infants...

The tortured faces of the wounded, screaming for help, screaming for something to ease the pain... No, she could never run away.

She was now attempting to move swiftly through the graveyard under the cover of the night shadows, going from kneeling angel to gentle Christ, and onward again to a large mausoleum, one that housed the deceased of a very prominent family, on her way into the blockaded city to help where she could.

She wasn't afraid of the dead. And she wasn't afraid of the cemetery. She had traveled through it often enough. But tonight, something frightened her. She held very still, and looked above her. She shivered suddenly, biting into her lower lip.

She wasn't afraid of the cemetery, but she was terrified each time she made one of her forays out of the city, seeking help from those beyond the lines of Yankees that surrounded Petersburg. But she was a native child of the place; she knew the Virginia landscape, the rivers, the forests, the plains, like few others. She even knew the cemetery she walked through now, knew many of the stones she touched, knew the old church that looked so eerily still and dark in the moonlight, knew exactly where and how she must return, time and again, to the city.

She shivered again. It seemed like such a very strange night. That full moon was rising so high in the sky, and there was a low ground fog. Soft, gray, swirling, it now misted around the old white stones of the graveyard, and around the roots of the trees, traveling upward until it seemed that the slender branches were arms with long fingers, white-bleached bone, reaching out to touch, to capture the unwary.

She gave herself a stern shake. The folks in the cemetery were beyond her help.

Others in Petersburg were not. They were desperate for the drugs and medications she was smuggling into the city. Even traveling by darkness as she did now, moving as swiftly and as furtively as possible, she carried her hoard of provisions within the fullness of her skirts—dozens of little vials tied to the wire rims of her petticoats. It had taken hours to secret them this carefully, but once she reached the city, the doctor and his desperate assistants would quickly rip them free.

She didn't have much farther to go now.

She just had to make her way through this town of the dead, and then...

Through the Yankee lines.

She felt a shivering seize hold of her again, and it suddenly seemed that a cloud passed over the full moon. The night was pitched into an almost total darkness, with only a few remnants of light remaining to cast a glow upon the tombstones in the cemetery, some old, some new, some toppling, some broken, some lovingly, carefully tended.

It didn't seem to matter so much now if the stones were new or old, tended or neglected. The ground fog was rising all about to cover them in mist.

From somewhere—far away? Or not so far away?—a wolf howled. The sound was long, and somehow lonely. It seemed to fade away on a shiver...

Lenore moistened her lips, fighting for new courage. She slipped around one of the stones and headed for the fence before the road.

Suddenly, she realized that she was not in the cemetery alone.

A shadow raced just before her, using the cloud's cover of the moon.

A shadow, someone else, *something* else...

She hung back, flinging herself behind a stone, breathing hard. Someone else could be on an errand just like her own.

The shadow had seemed so strange, not quite the shape of a man, not...

It was the moon, the night, playing tricks on her. Perhaps it was the siege, or the whole damned war. She remained braced against a headstone for a moment, biting her lip, realizing the grave was a new one.

There were a number of Confederate graves here. Men killed in distant places, but their bodies found and sent home. The stone she leaned against hadn't been here the last time she came through. It belonged to a Sergeant Peter Barnes, born 1841, deceased 1862, aged twenty-one years, seven months, three days. Her fingers moved over the etched numbers in a sudden strange motion. He had been killed when Bruce had been killed, same day, same battle.

His loved ones had been lucky. He had been returned to them in a box, even if it took a year to have a proper burial.

She had received nothing but paper, and the promise that Bruce was or would be buried with his countrymen somewhere, in some communal grave.

She pulled her fingers away from the stone and told herself sternly that her nocturnal activities were rattling her mind. She had to make it the rest of the way through the cemetery. If some other mercy runner was sharing the sanctuary of the graves with her, then God bless him, and Godspeed. She had to move again herself. She had reached the edge of the enemy lines. She would be running into Yankee pickets very soon, and she would have to keep her eyes open and wary, and pray as well, so that she could avoid them and capture. The area ahead of her might well be closely guarded.

She looked around her stone, and even as she did so, the cloud that had covered the moon shifted. She caught her breath. Beyond the stone wall, she could see tall figures with rifles converging. Pickets, meeting after walking their rounds. She counted them. One, two, three... four, five.

She fell back against her stone again, breathing hard. If they started to move again, she would never get around them. She had to go now, and go fast.

She stood, ready to fly.

Yet even as she did so, a harsh voice cried out in the moonlit night.

"Halt! Who goes there? Halt, or I'll shoot!"

She froze, afraid to turn around.

They *would* shoot her, they would have to shoot her. They wouldn't know who she was, they'd only know that she was the enemy.

Yet even as she started to turn, she heard an ear-shattering shriek. She fell to the ground as she spun around in a panic, desperate to see what had happened.

The Yankee who had cried out the warning had fallen. He lay upon the ground. And even as she stared at him, she heard another cry, a choked off scream...

She nearly cried out herself, she was so terrified. There was another shriek, yet it was farther away, and then another, farther still.

She stared at the fallen Yankee, then realized that his comrades were all fallen around him. She leaped to her feet in terror.

She looked around and saw nothing but the silent stones within the graveyard, and the swirl of the mist around them.

"Dear God!" she prayed aloud in a whisper. She gave up all thought of secrecy for the moment, plowing at high speed through the rest of the cemetery, tripping over stones, feeling them tug at her skirts, running so blindly that she couldn't even avoid the tree branches that leaned down to rip at her hair, threatening to pull her back.

She reached the wall and leaped over it. The Yankees lay before her, all five of them, the first alone, then two sprawled atop each other, two more about six feet away. She stared at them in uncomprehending terror, then, despite herself, she felt her feet being drawn to the first, the man who had called out in his husky voice to warn her to halt...

He was upon his back, his eyes open. Unseeing, staring, the greatest horror imaginable seemingly reflected in their terrified blue depths...

"Oh!" Her hand flew to her throat, and she choked back a scream, then swallowed hard, determined that she would not become ill.

He was a Yankee, the enemy, he might well have captured her, he might have shot at her...

But he was a human being first. And so many Yanks had been her friends before the war.

She started backing away from the corpse with its still staring eyes, fighting an overwhelming sense of panic.

The shadow!

Had she really seen a shadow, running through the graveyard, lithe, furtive, moving in the night? Had it been real, saving her from certain capture? And yet...

Yet done this. This awful horror.

And did it lurk nearby? Had that shadow seized upon these victims, and would it now seek others?

She had never been more terrified in her life. War was horrible——she had seen it. She had stood by Dr. Claiborne and the others, and she had witnessed the things that war could do, and she hadn't thought that anything could be more terrible.

But this...

This was. This hinted of something dark, of something alive in the mist, of something evil...

The night was not evil! she tried to tell herself. It was war, and war was the evil, the killer, the maimer that destroyed the country now, piece by piece.

But she wasn't convinced. She couldn't think straight, and she couldn't reason. She turned from the sightlessly staring Yank, and started to run. Blindly. Down the path, into the trees.

She heard the sound of her own breathing. She saw the stones from the graveyard to her left, surrounded by the mist. They seemed to be moving. She thought that she could hear a cry on the wind again, the cry of a wolf, ragged, mournful, alone, the cry itself reaching upward to the bone-white moon.

Then she heard movement behind her.

Heard the rush of air, the crashing of the trees and brush behind her.

She heard it! So close! A sudden thunder against the ground, or was it her heart? The night was alive with a vicious wind...

No, it was her breathing, so ragged, so desperate!

Because of that shadow...

"Halt!"

She heard the word, felt warmth, energy behind her. She

screeched in wild panic as something fell upon her shoulder.

"No!" she cried, running still, desperate. But the earth was pounding so hard around her now...

And then she shrieked again because something fell, as heavy as the night, as powerful. Fell atop her, catapulting her to the earth, where she rolled in the dirt and the leaves and the tufts of grass. Blinded, she closed her eyes against the dry, flying earth. Her arms were caught; she was thrown back.

She screeched, fighting wildly. Her arms were caught, endless weight was atop her, and she screamed again.

The shadow...

"No!" she cried, and her eyes flew open.

And she gasped as she stared into the hard crystal gaze of her attacker...

Chapter 1

His eyes were blue, a deep, dark, rich blue, enhanced by the detestable blue of the uniform he wore. They were eyes she recognized, for to her amazement, the Yankee officer straddled over her was not a stranger.

Nathaniel McKenna. Colonel McKenna, so it seemed now.

She'd met him at a dance in Richmond at least five years ago, before she and Bruce had been married. It was strange seeing him now, very strange, because she had noticed him the moment that he had walked in. She had been on Brace's arm, speaking with an artillery captain and his wife, when she had looked up and seen him.

Impossible to miss. He was a tall man, well over six feet, with thick waves of auburn hair; those very striking blue eyes, broad shoulders; a handsome, powerful build; and an equally handsome, ruggedly chiseled face. That very first time she had seen him, she had tightened her hold on Brace's arm, perhaps with some instinctive or defensive gesture. She had loved Bruce, and he had been an equally striking man, tall, slim, blond, so quick to smile, so very, very quick to make her laugh. They had been engaged a year, their wedding was forthcoming, she was eagerly anticipating it, and they would be setting up housekeeping on land her grandfather had given her that adjoined land his father had given him. She was very happy then; things seemed wonderful.

But it was, in fact, that very night when she had first realized there was really going to be a war. And Nathaniel McKenna had actually had something to do with that realization.

She had danced with him once. And it had been a fascinating, exhilarating experience. The feel of his hands on her, the very energy of his movement...

And his eyes. The touch of them invaded her soul, seemed to read her mind. A minor flirtation with such a man, a classmate of her betrothed's, had not seemed such a terrible thing...

But when the conversation had turned to her wedding, when she had swept her lashes over her cheeks and promised him an invitation, he had suggested that she hurry her arrangements—before the war waylaid the ceremony. And, as far as that situation went, she might not want him to attend.

"Perhaps the South will secede from the Union, Major," she had told him, for he had been a major back then, before years of war had caused swift promotions among the ranks, "but I do believe that the North will quickly realize that our gallant young men do mean to stand up for their rights and independence just as our Virginia forebears—such as Mr. Washington and Mr. Jefferson and Mr. Madison—did. Do I take this to mean, sir, that you will not be on our side?"

He looked down at her with his handsome features tense and his cobalt eyes unnervingly steady. "You've underestimated the determination of the North, I believe, and men such as Mr. Lincoln. There will be war."

"You didn't answer my question, sir."

He shrugged, looking across the room to Bruce. "What about your fiancé, Miss Tyler? What do you think he will choose to do?"

"Side with the South, of course."

"And if he did not?" he demanded, a dark brow arched. Then he smiled, and his tone was mocking. "Ah, Bruce Latham would not be your fiancé if there were even the least bit of doubt in your mind!"

"You're being excessively rude for a Unionist standing in the middle of a Richmond ballroom," she assured him.

He shook his head. "Alas, no, Miss Lenore Tyler, for the Old Dominion will perhaps leave the Union with her brethren to the south, but she will do so painfully, and only when there is no turning back."

"This is no matter for jest—"

"Ah, that we did jest! For, Miss Tyler, I fear that it will come to war."

"Over in a matter of weeks—"

He stopped the dance, and bowed to her. "So I pray, Miss Tyler, but I do have my doubts."

"Perhaps you should return me to my fiancé—"

"Perhaps, indeed, I should. Perhaps it is even a very fine thing that we should, by circumstance, be enemies. Or perhaps it is even a pity that it is not the other way around, that Bruce Latham is not staunchly behind our government, and I am not the hero of your cause. For, then, I must admit, I'd be most tempted never to return you to your fiancé, but rather to hold you ever tighter. There was

something in your eyes the moment I entered the room, something—
"

"Something of enormous conceit from within your heart!" she charged, but she was breathless, and he was not. He swirled her very easily in the dance, not letting her go at all.

"I did not say what it was within your eyes at all, Miss Tyler. I am quite spellbound, I admit."

"You're no gentleman—"

"Oh, but I am in a way. An honest one." Those blue eyes settled upon her with their dark candor. "There is no chance that I might sweep you away. Certainly, since I count Bruce among my friends, I would not do so, even if you weren't staring at me with beautiful outrage and stunning if very indignant fury."

"Your manners—"

"My manners!" he interrupted softly, and a mild chuckle left his lips. "Indeed, they leave a lot to be desired. What is it with you lovely ladies of the Old Dominion? I can feel you tremble beneath my touch, there's such startling warmth and passion within you! But you'd deny it to the very day you died, since it wouldn't be quite proper."

"I demand that you return me to my fiancé! And if you say no more, I will refrain from mentioning your remarks—"

"You will refrain, Miss Tyler, because you do not care to see his blood spilled—though, certainly, you wouldn't mind the sight of mine at all."

"You're so incredibly sure that you would best him—"

"I am incredibly sure that such a fight would be foolish, for he is my friend, and against such a stalwart son of Dixie, I am surely no threat."

"I find you to be a horrid man—"

"And you are also, Miss Tyler, a beautiful daughter of Dixie. I am sorry to count you among my enemies here tonight. You need say no more. I will return you to Bruce immediately."

And so he did, still sweeping her across the floor, for all outward appearance, as much a dashing cavalier as any man there.

She had hated him then.

She had tried to hate him.

But she had remembered him. Remembered his face. Remembered those moments when he had held her. Remembered the heat, the feeling of energy... Of passion.

That had been so long ago. She'd married. She'd been a good wife. She'd held fast to her Cause.

She'd become a widow.

And she'd seen that he had been right, that his cynicism had been well placed. The North had gone to war, and the war had gone on and on.

And been horrible...

Now, he truly was her enemy. And he was straddled over her, fierce, tense, determined. There was no mercy in his features, rather, there was raw anger mirrored within them.

"My God!" he breathed. *"Lenore!"*

She swallowed hard, clenching her teeth. Him. Of all the hundreds of thousands of Yankees who were fighting against them...

Yet, at the same time, she had another thought. A ridiculous one, she tried to tell herself. But there. Oh, God, there, nevertheless.

At least he was a Yankee. A *man*. Not a shadow...

"Major—ah, *Colonel* McKenna!" she spat back. "I do realize that war has proved quite trying, but do you still believe that you need such violent effort to capture one small woman?"

He didn't smile, didn't bend, didn't flick an eye.

"What are you doing out here?" he demanded.

"Trying to get home."

"Smuggling—"

"No!" she lied swiftly, then was stunned by his further accusation.

"Murdering Union soldiers?"

She inhaled on a gasp, feeling the blood drain from her face. Those men... those Union soldiers, so savagely killed, they were among *his* men.

And he seemed to think that she could do such a thing.

She shook her head wildly. "You can't believe—my God, how? I carry no weapons, you can see that!"

Maybe he did see it. He rose, unwinding his long, powerful length from her body. He reached down a hand to her, but pride kept her from accepting it. She pretended not to see it and struggled carefully to her feet, trying to make sure that none of her medicine vials clanked together.

His hand clamped upon her wrist. She felt his eyes again, and looked into them.

"Why were you running, so terrified?" he demanded.

Her mouth went dry. "Because," she lied, "I know quite well that the area is teeming with Yankees—"

"You knew that when you came out smuggling," he told her impatiently. "Why were you running so swiftly now?"

She shook her head again. "We're at war—" she began again desperately.

"You saw something," he said harshly. "You know who the murderer is!"

She shook her head again. "I can't tell you anything—"

"You'd carry your Rebel loyalties this far!" he exploded furiously.

"No! Yes—what difference does it make if men die by cannon balls on the field, or a sword or knife off! Dead is dead! They perish, they—"

He exploded in a startling oath, pulling her along. She saw quickly that he had moved so very swiftly upon her because his horse was on the trail just behind them and he was now leading her toward the animal.

"What—" She gasped, only to discover herself thrown up atop his handsome, well-fed Union bay. And looking down at him, she stared into those endlessly blue and relentless eyes.

"Let me show you the difference, Mrs. Latham!" he charged her.

A second later, he was up behind her. She felt the wall of his chest at her back, the power of his arms around her. She felt his breathing, the pounding of his heart. She started to tremble, and despite him, despite herself, despite her awful fear of him as a Yankee...

She suddenly felt safe. Safe and yet...

He nudged his bay hard. He whirled the animal around. He was racing furiously back toward the wall of the cemetery.

Back to the place where the men had been killed...

He pulled in on the bay. She could see that others were there now; his troops had come out in number. At least three companies had come, searching the foliage, bringing blankets to wrap their dead.

But the one sentry still lay, his sightless eyes staring at the golden glow of the moon sitting so high above the night.

"Dead is dead!" he said harshly behind her.

She inhaled on a ragged sob, and as if he was suddenly sorry, he spun his bay again.

"Colonel!"

One of his men rushed forward, gravely noting the captive before him with a nod of acknowledgment. Then he was speaking rapidly again. "A slaughter, sir! Each one of them dead, bleeding... Oh, the blood, sir!"

He broke off, staring at Lenore, his eyes widening again.

"Sir, this—lady—is the one you caught in the foliage?"

"Indeed, Lieutenant. The lady is actually an old—I dare not say friend!—but she is an old acquaintance. She is not our murderer. She is merely smuggling, I believe."

"Sir—"

"See to these men, Lieutenant," Nathaniel McKenna said very softly, a deep pain in his voice. "I will see to our captive here."

The lieutenant saluted.

Once again, Nathaniel turned his bay around. He nudged the animal, and they were moving swiftly through the night with a small guard at their heels.

They came to a Yankee cavalry encampment. He leaped to the ground behind her, then reached for her before she could attempt to elude him.

She touched the ground in his arms. She tried to break away but he had an iron grasp upon her arm.

He tossed his horse's reins to one of his men and, leaving the animal behind, he hurried her toward one of the larger tents among the field of canvas. She found herself thrust into what appeared to be his headquarters tent, large and oddly enough, homey.

He had obviously been settled in for the siege for some time. His bunk was covered with a quilt that could only have come from home. There were picture frames on the camp desk in the center of the tent. There were trunks of clothes and books. There were the remnants of a meal upon a polished wooden stand.

A meal...

Ah, yes. The Yanks were still eating these days.

He thrust her forward into the room, then came around her, picking up a glass decanter of brandy and pouring two glasses. He offered one to her, and she backed away.

"Take it. I doubt you've seen or tasted anything so sweet in some time."

93

"I don't care to now—"

"Ah, afraid to fraternize with the enemy! But you're not fraternizing, you know. You are a prisoner, Mrs. Latham. A prisoner of war."

She swallowed hard. There had always been the chance that she might be caught. She had thought about it often enough. Other women had been involved in the war effort. The Yanks had once threatened to kill Mrs. Rose Greenhow if she didn't divulge the names of some of her accomplices. But somehow, Mrs. Greenhow had escaped, only to die later when she drowned in her attempt to return to her beloved Confederacy with British gold sewn into her skirts...

What could he do to her?

Keep her here, so near to him. That, in a way, was a kind of hell all in itself...

She shivered. He came closer, pressing the brandy glass into her fingers.

"Who is murdering my men, Mrs. Latham?" he demanded.

"I don't know."

"You had to see it!"

"I didn't!"

He was closer still. So close she could see that his cheeks were just beginning to darken with an evening stubble, so close that she could feel the warmth of his breath, feel his heat.

Feel her own heartbeat...

"Are you an accomplice?" he demanded softly.

"No!"

"Then what were you doing in the cemetery?"

"Bringing flowers—"

"Bull!" he roared so suddenly and so harshly that she paled, stepping back. But his hands were on her. She threw the brandy into his face, struggling, but his hands were ever more fiercely upon her.

"Let me—"

"What were you doing in the cemetery?"

She spun within his hold and tried to run. There was no escaping him, but things swiftly became worse. Her struggles brought them both crashing down upon his bunk with the fine handmade quilt.

He was over her, touching her, hard upon her. His eyes were blue steel, piercing into hers. His hands...

"What were you doing?" he demanded.

"Nothing—"

She gasped, nearly shrieking aloud. His hands were so intimately upon her, fingers inching up the length of her leg. "Bast—" she began, but her voice faded.

For he had found one of the vials tied to her petticoat. He held it before her eyes.

"Smuggler!" he said softly. "Are you protected? Does some soldier or civilian ride with you, savagely murdering men to protect you?"

"No!" she cried out.

"But you were smuggling—"

"Medicines!" she cried out. "Medicines! Nothing more, I swear it!"

He was silent, his leg half atop her, his arms leaned over her, imprisoning her. "Please!" she whispered suddenly. "I swear to you, I am carrying no weapons. I have medicines on me, and they are so desperately needed! Please..."

Her voice trailed away.

He stared at her. Then his hand came to her cheek. He touched it softly, so softly.

His face came closer to hers. So close...

She could almost feel his lips. She *wanted* to feel them. She wanted to forget the war, to forget the terror, to forget that he was the greatest enemy...

"Colonel!" came a sudden cry from outside.

"There's more of them, sir! More of them!"

More of what? she wondered, feeling his eyes, feeling his tension...

"Dead men!" came the cry. Then a choked sob. "More dead men!"

Chapter 2

Nathaniel stared into emerald-green depths of the woman's eyes beneath him, frozen for a moment.

Lenore...

Bruce Latham had been a friend of his, a good one. They had both known they would go different ways, but many friends were split, families were split, brothers were split. It was a damned sad state. Just because a man was your enemy, didn't mean that he wasn't your friend anymore.

But Lenore...

Perhaps, in that one aspect in his life, the war had been good. From the moment he had seen Lenore, he had been fascinated. He'd been compelled to touch her. She was an exquisite woman, small, slim, petite, with a headful of glorious sun-blond hair that had a wild and elusive way of curling about her beautifully defined features no matter what. She had startling gem-green eyes that seemed to give away her every emotion. She had been born to live life to its fullest, so it seemed to him from those very first glances. To love deeply, passionately. Fiercely. Life would not walk by her; rather, she would take it by the throat and force from it what she would have...

Perhaps. She had been younger then. They had all been younger then.

The war had cost them all...

Yet that night of the dance, when he had touched her, he had felt staggering emotions. It had been nearly impossible to return her to Latham's side. He had been shaken, wanting her more in those few minutes than he had ever wanted a woman in his life. Feeling something between them, some great energy like lightning, something that seemed to scream that they should have been together, lovers then and there...

But, of course, she had been Latham's fiancée. And as the nation careened toward war, and men lined up on the proper sides, he had heard that they had married.

He had sent them a gift. A green crystal candy dish. He had done the shopping himself, having discovered that the emerald color of the crystal was so very like her eyes.

Later he had heard that Bruce Latham had been killed on the battlefield. He had sent his condolences, but whether his letter had gotten through—or whether she had bothered to open it—he did not know.

He had known, of course, that she lived in Petersburg. He had thought of it every horrible day since the siege had begun.

But he had never expected to come upon her in the dead of night, right outside the cemetery, smuggling, while...

While so nearby, his men were being slaughtered one by one by some murderer with ungodly strength and speed.

What did she have to do with it? What did she know about it?

If only he could believe the light in her eyes! They were upon him now, wide with horror.

She had seen the men left dead by this murderer...

And now there were more...

More of them, dead. Not in battle, just dead, slain and bleeding in the midst of their dreams of peace.

He stared at her, gritting his teeth tightly together. He leaped to his feet then and hurried outside, for one moment actually forgetting that after all this time, he really held Lenore Latham within his grasp.

Several of his men were waiting for him outside. Lieutenant Andy Green had come forward and stood right before his tent. Andy's young face was torn with anguish and fear, but a fear he would fight in order to find out who was so brutally destroying their companies.

Just beyond Andy was a sorrel mare. Nathaniel gazed from Andy to the mare, and walked over to the horse. Two of his men lay draped across the haunches of the animal. They looked as if they had been savaged by beasts. Young Tim O'Connell, twenty years away from County Cork, his red hair matted with blood, his merry green eyes never to see again. *Oh, God!* Nathaniel thought. He wanted to whisper a prayer, but those were the only words that came to him. Oh, God. Maybe it was prayer enough, because God Himself had to know that something wasn't right here.

The other man was Curtis Trent. A crusty old sergeant. One of the best men to be had anywhere, any time.

"Eight tonight," he said bitterly.

He felt a presence behind him. Lenore. She was staring at the bodies with horror, shivering.

97

What could she know? he wondered. She couldn't possibly have anything to do with this. The war was doing horrible things to men; desperate times called for desperate measures.

The situation in Kansas and Missouri had been beyond horrible for years, men killing men in coldblooded murder, but they weren't behaving like that here in the East. No matter what, they weren't committing cold-blooded murders. There were codes of honor and behavior here, and they had all been raised with them. Flags of truce were recognized, battle lines were recognized...

Someone was murdering his men. Desperate times...

He spun around and looked at Lenore again. She had already seen the men killed earlier. But she was looking at Timothy O'Connell with tears burning her eyes.

Yes, there were horrible things in the war... but sometimes, people remained human, empathy survived. Lenore was as horrified at the sight of Timothy as any of them might be.

And he was heartily glad, and heartily sorry, both at the same time. Maybe he had wanted to believe the worst of her. Maybe he had needed a reason... not to want her so badly now. In the middle of duty, in the middle of this.

Lenore's eyes, shimmering with their emerald beauty, remained locked upon Timothy. She was dressed in black—a mourning gown, or a shade in which to slip through the night?—and her hair was escaping the neat knot that had been twisted at her nape when she had begun her foray. Now it spilled about her in shades of gold like sunrays against the darkness. Her beautiful features were thin and drawn, and she was definitely slim—everyone residing within the city of Petersburg was slim these days.

Ruffled, thin, exhausted, disheveled, worn—she was still the most elegant, beautiful woman he had ever seen.

He tore his eyes from her for a moment, remembering his rank, remembering the war and the situation that had so completely filled his mind and his life—until she had walked back into it.

He remembered his men—staring at him for help, looking to him for salvation.

"Gentlemen, we're in for some rough times ahead. Many of you have been with me for a long time now, and we've survived rough times before, bitter, hard times when the enemy walked all over us. We dug in then, and we're going to have to dig in now. We're going to have to forget about normal night and guard duty schedules. We'll divide the companies under my command evenly. Lieutenant Green, you'll see to the divisions. Four hours sleep, then up, and the next group down, and no one to be alone at all. See to it that all the men remain in their companies, and no matter what our losses, see that there are not fewer than twenty men to a company."

"Aye, sir!" Lieutenant Green agreed, saluting sharply. Then, looking past Nathaniel, he seemed upset. "Colonel, what about the lady you've, er—encountered?"

Indeed, what about the lady? He was a colonel in the Army of the United States of America. Did he denounce her as a smuggler, perhaps as a spy? See to it that she was turned over to the proper authorities, taken to Washington, perhaps?

At least, he thought fleetingly, she'd be safe, she'd be far away from this horror...

Yet he wondered if she was actually in any danger herself. She hadn't been a hundred yards away tonight when so many of his men had been slaughtered.

Maybe it didn't matter. Maybe he just wasn't ready to give her up quite yet, and maybe, despite the damned war, he was ready to risk his own life to see her back to her own kind of safety.

"Mrs. Latham will have the use of my quarters this evening," he said smoothly. "God knows, I shall not be sleeping. In the morning, I shall see to her."

He spun around and looked at Lenore. She was returning his stare, her chin high. She was trying very hard not to look at the horse that carried the bodies of the dead men.

Yet beneath her calm composure...

Her lip was trembling. Her lower lip. Just slightly. He wanted to take her in his arms, swear that it would be all right.

Except that she wouldn't want his comfort.

And the words would not be true...

He bowed swiftly to her, with all the courtly manner he could remember from a thousand years ago—before the war. "Mrs. Latham, as you can well see, this has been a distressing evening. You'll excuse me if I'm occupied. The young fellow there,"—he paused, pointing to one of his aides—"is Sergeant Jenner. He will be just beyond the tent flap throughout the evening, ready to bring you anything within his power, should you find yourself in need."

He turned and quickly left her with Lieutenant Green on his heels. He had to order one company of the men on to make contact with his superiors, to report the strange and horrible murders. He had to pray that someone would send back an answer.

He wanted to look back.

He wouldn't allow himself to do so. Not until morning's light.

They had lost men before. But never by daylight. As soon as the sun was shining...

He would see to her fate himself.

* * *

Lenore watched him go, her heart, her mind, her emotions all in a tempest. She'd been caught. He had stripped contraband right from her petticoats.

At least she hadn't been taken with weapons or documents! she thought swiftly. Perhaps when he realized that she had carried nothing but medications, he would let her go.

Perhaps.

Perhaps he would turn her over to the Union government, which would send her to a Northern prison, try her for God knew exactly what, hang her by the neck until dead...

No. She clenched her teeth together hard. Nathaniel would never do such a thing; surely, he would not...

He had left her because of what had happened.

She didn't realize that she was standing there, shivering, until the sergeant entrusted with her care stepped forward. "If you'd like to make yourself comfortable within the colonel's tent, ma'am... Perhaps I could bring you some hot coffee?"

She found herself nodding numbly, and she swirled quickly to reenter Nathaniel's tent. She walked straight to the bed and sat at the foot of it, still shivering. She realized that Sergeant Jenner had been commanded to see to her comfort. He had also been commanded— silently, of course—to see to it that she didn't exit the tent until Nathaniel returned.

Did she intend to leave? she wondered wildly. Escape, run, try to reach home?

With that murderer out there?

Ah, but a murderer who sought to slay Yankees, not Southern

women.

How could she know that? she wondered in anguish. And, after all that she had seen tonight, did she have the heart, the strength, to run again?

She was still sitting there in near darkness when Sergeant Jenner returned. He brought her hot coffee, and much more. He carried a cup of something steaming—chicken stew, so the aroma promised—and a basket of biscuits. He set the tray on Nathaniel's desk and turned up the glow in the gas lamp there, offering her ample light, and, it seemed, more warmth. Badly needed warmth.

"You didn't say as how you might be hungry, ma'am. But if you've been—" He cut off, not saying that she had been in the siege city itself. "If you've been around in these parts, you probably are mighty hungry."

She moistened her lips. She was starving. She shouldn't be able to eat a thing, not after what she had seen, but she had lived hungry so very long now.

She stood and walked toward the desk. She should refuse the food, show some pride.

Pride?

This man was a Yankee, her enemy, her jailer.

But there was something about his face that was so appealing, something that seemed to speak of his own weariness, and his longing for it all to be over.

She smiled hesitantly at him. "Thank you for your thoughtfulness. I am very hungry indeed."

He tipped his cap to her. "Then I shall leave you to enjoy your meal," he said politely, and he departed. A moment later, when she had devoured the hot stew, she realized that he had left quickly to allow her to consume the food with all reckless speed—and in something far less than a ladylike manner.

It was good; it was delicious. And the coffee that he had brought her was strong and sweetened with a touch of sugar. She managed to drink it slowly, savoring every small sip. A certain amount of guilt assailed her that she should be enjoying such a meal when others she loved still went so pitiably hungry. Yet even as her thoughts sent her flying into an emotional war, she heard a sudden commotion outside the tent, and she leaped to her feet, her heart slamming hard against her chest. She shouldn't have cared so much, she should have thought in a philosophical manner that any dead Yank was one less man to shoot against her own kind.

But as she rushed to the entrance, lifting the canvas, those were not her thoughts. She was praying.

Please, God, no more dead men. Please God, let there be no more!

As she looked out into the night, dimly lit by the small campfires of the men, she saw, across the field where Nathaniel's brigade was encamped, a number of prisoners being brought forward by a guard of Yankee soldiers.

She jumped when she heard Sergeant Jenner suddenly at her side.

"It's all right, ma'am. They weren't just taken; they've been transferred over so that they can be brought north tomorrow morning by wagon from here. No one's going to be hurt, ma'am. And no one else..."

"Has been killed?" she inquired softly.

He nodded.

She bit her lip, looking at those men clad in gray. She would recognize some of them, perhaps. The Army of Northern Virginia was protecting Petersburg during the siege, but any able-bodied man left in the city had been sent out to fight. A few who weren't so able-bodied had been sent out, too.

Her heart seemed to leap as she saw them. No, they weren't being hurt, they would probably eat, and maybe they would even survive prison camp to tell their grandchildren about the war. But watching them, she felt a terrible guilt again. She should run, she should hide, she should get as far away from this place as she could...

She closed her eyes for a moment, feeling a sensation of dizziness. She couldn't escape; she had barely moved before and Jenner had been right on her, watching her every movement.

Even as she thought this, Jenner's voice startled her back to reality.

"The colonel will be back soon, ma'am. Perhaps you'd like to get a little sleep, or rest, or perhaps I could bring you more coffee...?"

She shook her head wildly; she could still see the tattered prisoners being walked by the campfires.

She started to turn, then felt her heart freeze. She spun back, staring at the prisoners again, seeking desperately, searching...

Bruce. She had seen Bruce.

But they were already disappearing into a tent.

She couldn't have seen Bruce. He was dead. He'd been killed over a year ago...

But she could have sworn...

"Ma'am?" Sergeant Jenner said. "Are you all right?"

She nodded, but she wasn't all right at all. She was dizzy.

Bruce... it had looked like Bruce, but not like Bruce. No, it had looked almost exactly like Bruce, but something had been wrong, something about the eyes, about the face...

Something about the way she was feeling right now...

"Ma'am?" Jenner said gently again.

She shook her head blindly, turning swiftly back into the tent. She walked to the desk, her fingers gripping the chair behind it.

Bruce could be alive; she should feel elated...

No! She had to be seeing things. He had been fighting beside Jay Laughlin, and Jay had come to see her himself. He had apologized so earnestly about the body, but lest she spend her days in endless, fruitless prayer, he assured her that Bruce had died. He'd been struck three times—in the head, the heart, and the gut. There was no way that he could have lived.

But she had seen him!

No, not him, someone who looked like him!

She covered her face with her hands. She started to shake again, determined that she had to know the truth.

"What?" she heard suddenly, harshly. "What is it?"

Her hands flew from her face, her lashes rose, and her eyes went wide.

She hadn't heard him, hadn't heard him come at all. But Nathaniel was back, staring at her with his sharp blue eyes, his demanding gaze.

He looked very tired, very worn and weary. Yet he stood there, just inside the tent, staring at her so intently, hands on his hips, his stare relentless.

She felt a shivering sweep over her again. She couldn't forget that he was a colonel in the Union Army, one very distressed at the awful loss of life around him.

One who had accused her of being a part of it...

One who had known her husband very, very well. One who had gone to West Point with him, one who had been in the military with

103

him a long time, long ago, when it had all been one military, and the enemy hadn't been composed of friends and brothers.

One who would recognize Bruce instantly if he were to see him.

She shook her head, moistening her lips.

"What is it?" he demanded again roughly. In a minute, she thought, he would stride across the room, take hold of her shoulders, shake her. Shake her and shake her until...

"You-you have Confederate prisoners," she told him, discovering that she had very little voice.

He nodded. "Yes."

"You've-you've seen them all?" she demanded in a hoarse whisper.

He cocked his head at an angle, mystified.

"Yes," he said, then it seemed that a slow dawning came to him, and he did cross the room, his hands falling upon her shoulders, his blue eyes very intense. "I see," he murmured, and she tried to pull away from him, but he held her tight, staring at her.

"You thought you saw Bruce," he said simply.

"Yes... no..."

"Listen to me, Lenore," he told her, his voice tense with emotion, "it-it isn't Bruce."

"But he's so much like Bruce—"

"He isn't Bruce!" Nathaniel assured her. "He was captured a few nights ago, and when I first saw him, I thought I had taken a ghost for a captive. But I came closer to him, and I knew instantly that he wasn't Bruce. You would understand if you came closer to him. He isn't Bruce, he is nothing like Bruce was, nothing at all! He's eluded us a few times, but we always manage to get him back, and each time we do, I think of Bruce, but... Lenore, it isn't he!"

She lowered her head quickly, believing him. As startled as she had been, as taken by the resemblance, she herself hadn't been able to believe it had been Bruce. Something inside her had simply felt so...

So cold.

Her hands were shaking, her lips were still trembling. She had to forget the man she had seen, had to forget all the Confederates who were prisoners here.

They, at least, would eat.

And her petticoats were still loaded down with the vials of

medicine that Nathaniel had still let her keep after he discovered she had them.

She lifted her chin. "What are you intending to do with me?" she asked him coolly.

He was silent for what seemed to be forever. She should have wrenched away from him, hard, but she didn't; she just stood there, stiff, trembling.

And wondering why she wished so desperately that she could forget the war and lean against his chest, and feel his arms come around her and hold her very tight. She was achingly aware of the man, of the strength of his arms, of his scent...

She gritted her teeth and stared at him hard, determined to betray nothing of her emotions. Surely, it would all be over soon. He had never made any pretense of his heart, his mind, his loyalties, even if he had left with her the medicines she carried.

"What do you intend to do with me?" she demanded.

"Take you home," he said.

Her heart slammed within the wall of her chest, then took flight. "Take me home?"

"Well, I can't actually see you to your door, but I'm bringing you as far as the river, at least."

"But—"

"The woods are full of Yankees and Rebels. And worse."

"You're not going to—arrest me?" she whispered.

"If you'd had a single bullet on you..." he said, his voice trailing away with the unspoken threat. "But you didn't," he said very softly.

"Why?" she asked him.

"Maybe for old times' sake!" he said softly. Then his hands fell from her, and he turned away, striding across the tent to pause behind his desk, his shoulders very broad and strong, his back very straight. Then he swung on her again suddenly. "And then again, maybe just because it's *you*. Maybe I just don't know why I'm doing what anymore. But I've got leave for twenty-four hours. Enough to get you back." His voice had seemed to grow angrier and angrier as he spoke. He stopped suddenly, his fingers wound into fists at his side. "Get some sleep!" he commanded abruptly, harshly. "We leave at first light!" he ordered.

Then he spun again, with military crispness, and exited the tent.

And, shaking, she sank down to the foot of his bunk. Sleep.

Dear God.

On such a night, she would never, never sleep.

Chapter 3

It seemed a very strange circumstance to be leaving a Yankee camp with Yankee protection instead of a Yankee guard.

Strange circumstance, indeed, but then the whole night had been very strange.

By the first pale streaks of dawn, she found herself faced with something else very strange—a well-fed horse. Nathaniel had acquired her a fine mount, a Union cavalry gelding, and it was far healthier-looking than most of the people she had left behind in Petersburg.

She was leaving the Union camp with her petticoats still laden with countless vials of essential medications. Not enough, never enough, but the morphine she was carrying would ease some of the agony for the men who were shot down in the trenches, caught by mortar fire, or victims of the steel of countless bayonets.

She was still leaving with the very precious morphine for pain, the ether for surgery, and the laudanum, and so much more!

And she was leaving with Nathaniel by her side.

How very, very strange it all was.

As she sat there on horseback, waiting for Nathaniel to mount his own fine cavalry horse, Lenore could still see the last faint glows of the Union campfires. Someone played softly and sadly upon a harmonica, a song she recognized about a boy returning home and his father coming to pick him up at the telegraph station. He was told to go to the depot, but the old man shook his head and said, "You do not understand, he is coming back to us dead."

She stared down at her hands. The song, so soft upon the crisp air of dawn, was haunting. It was a Union song, for the boy had joined "the boys in blue," but at this point in the war, maybe it didn't matter so terribly anymore.

When she glanced over at Nathaniel, now mounted, she saw that the night had certainly left its mark upon him. His handsome face was deeply creased with lines of exhaustion and care. He was not just losing his men to cannon balls and shot.

They were being murdered...

But not by daylight, so it seemed. And so he was willing to

escort her safely back to Rebel lines.

"Ready?" he asked her.

She nodded, then waved a hand to the men, the enemies, who had been so very kind to her, and it suddenly seemed unbearable that it could come to a point where one of these men might have to shoot her brother—or be shot by him in turn.

If they were to make the battlefield again, that was. Someone, *something* sympathetic to the Rebel cause was decimating them before they could reach the field...

She gritted her teeth. Damn. She should be glad; what difference did it make how the enemy died, as long as the enemy went away?

But there was a difference! She was at a loss to explain exactly why—dying from a gunshot was certainly one of the most horrible ways to go—but there was just something about this...

The Union harmonica player had been joined by a fiddler now, and they were singing a startlingly rousing chorus of "Rally 'Round the Flag, Boys."

Another day was breaking.

She glanced over at Nathaniel to discover that he was studying her intently. He still had that weary look about him—she supposed it would take a long, long time for that look to go away—but he rode with his back and broad shoulders very straight, and she thought that he would go to any length of exhaustion, as long as he felt he was doing all that he could for his men.

Or, perhaps, all that he could under the *circumstances*.

And she was one of the circumstances of war, at the moment.

"Let's go, Mrs. Latham," he commanded, his deep blue gaze an enigma as he studied her. He nudged his bay. She didn't make the smallest movement, but her well-fed Union cavalry horse fell right into step with his. In a matter of minutes, they were passing out of the camp. Men stepped back, saluting Nathaniel, nodding to her. Their faces were drawn.

They were men with a bond that was tighter than that of men sharing a common cause in a war.

They were fighting a different battle now as well, and they all seemed to know it.

They passed by Lieutenant Green and a company of mounted men. Sergeant Jenner was with him. Lenore found herself lifting a hand to wave to him. She bit her lip, realizing she had been befriending the enemy. Jenner didn't seem to notice her sudden hesitance. He raised a hand and offered her an encouraging smile. "God go with you, ma'am!" he called out suddenly.

"God go with you, too!" she cried fervently. She meant the words.

Nathaniel was looking back at her. She still couldn't read his eyes, but there seemed to be a ray of warmth within them. He reined in, waiting for her to draw to his side.

"Stay with me," he warned her. "We're leaving the camp behind now, and—"

"The woods may be full of Rebels?" she asked quietly.

"If it were only Rebels, Lenore, I'd be tempted to throw you headfirst into the lot of them!" The words were spoken low, but with a startling intensity. She looked at him again, swallowing hard, but still could read nothing from the steady appraisal of his eyes. She remembered that once there had been a moment, back when they had first met when she had read clearly the longing in his eyes when he looked at her.

Once upon a time, she had actually had some flesh on her bones. Her face hadn't been drawn and haggard. Her hair hadn't been worn in absolute abandon with strands escaping all over the place. Once...

Once was so, so long ago!

They rode in silence for several long moments. Then she was startled again when he spoke softly, his previous anger seeming to have faded. "I was very sorry to hear about Bruce, Lenore. I wrote to you. Did you ever receive my letter?"

"Yes," she said quietly. "I did." It had been the perfect note of condolence, entirely proper. She had dropped it immediately, finding herself in tears again when she had just managed to stop the flow.

She fought a new rise of them right now, blinking quickly and furiously as she stared at him. "Were you in the battle when he was killed?"

Nathaniel stared over at her. "Yes."

"Then... did you know... did you see...?"

"Lenore, there were tens of thousands of men there! No, I didn't see Bruce. There were men everywhere, downed men, dead men, injured men. You can't begin to imagine—"

"You forget where I live," she reminded him with quiet dignity.

"Every day, I watch while they bring the men in. The downed men, the injured men, the dead men."

"I haven't forgotten where you live," he said, a note of bitterness in his voice. "I've never forgotten where you live." He reined in for a moment, pausing, a frown tugging upon his brow. Lenore did likewise, silent as he listened. She couldn't hear anything amiss. They were traveling land she knew very well, holding close to the trail that wound through the trees in the dense forest area rather than taking any chances on the broader, open road, or even using any of the shortcuts across what had once been fields rich with grain, tobacco, and cotton.

They had come quite a way from the Union camp. Lenore could see one large red farmhouse on a slope in the distance. She could see the trampled fields, a little outcrop of rocks dumped at the far corner of one of them. She could see or hear nothing else.

"What is it?" she asked him at last.

He shook his head. "Maybe nothing." He nudged his bay, and they started moving again.

She shivered suddenly, feeling as if someone had drawn an icy nail down the length of her back.

"That man..." she murmured, following behind Nathaniel again. "That man last night—"

He reined in again, twisting in his saddle, a mustard-gauntleted hand riding upon the ridge of it, his blue eyes grave now as he looked at her. "That man is not Bruce," he told her again. "There is a strong resemblance. But if you were to come near him..." He paused, shrugging. "You would know," he said simply. "Lenore, I told you, I'm sorry, very, very sorry about Bruce. But don't grasp at straws. I know that you loved him—"

"I did love him!" she cried huskily. "Very much."

"But he's dead. He isn't my prisoner," he assured her. He turned back, nudging the bay, starting once again down the trail through the dense thicket of trees.

But he had barely gone another twenty feet before he reined in again. Lenore's bay nearly blundered right into his, but she pulled the horse in swiftly, maintaining her seat while the animal swung around.

"Shhh!" Nathaniel warned her.

"I wasn't trying—" she began with exasperation.

"Shhh!" he warned her again, and this time, she thought she

heard a distant rustling sound.

Then there was no need to wonder if they were hearing things. There was the sudden, near-deafening boom of a cannon, followed by a cacophony of sound—yells, shrieks, cries, bugles—not too far distant down the trail from them.

Men were going to war.

Nathaniel swore suddenly and loudly, offering no apology when he stared at her with new consternation. "Stay behind me and follow me fast!" he commanded her.

Her horse started to rear up. Nathaniel swiftly swung his own mount around, grabbing her reins at the horse's bit. "I can ride—" she started to protest.

"But we need to move fast!" he snapped back. "Else I'll be returning you and your precious cargo pierced with bullet holes from both armies!"

He was suddenly moving them along so quickly that a rush of wind brought tears to her eyes. Branches slapped her shoulders and face, and she ducked low, gripping the pommel of her saddle, unable to do anything but accept the plummet of the wild ride. Through it all, she could hear the horrible sounds of the fighting going on around them. Was it a skirmish, or a full-scale battle? That much she couldn't tell, only that the cries seemed to be everywhere, cries of challenge, Rebel cries, shouts, commands, orders. Then there were shrieks of pain, there was the horrible sound made by horses when they, too, screamed...

They broke through the foliage, coming to a small stream surrounded by oak trees and shielded by a low stone fence. Nathaniel leaped down from his horse, smacking its rump to send it into the safety of the trees. Then he reached for her, drawing her down. His arm still around her, he forced her downward until they came to the shield of the stone wall, and there he hunched down himself, pressing her shoulders until she sat, her back to the low wall. She closed her eyes, trying not to hear the battle.

She felt Nathaniel slump down beside her, his back to the wall as well.

A second later, she felt his fingers entwining with hers, and her eyes flew open to meet his. His piercing blue gaze was steady now. She looked down at their hands, laced together, his large and covered in the mustard-colored cavalry gloves, hers suddenly seeming so very small. Rough hands which had once felt like silk, she thought ruefully. But her hands were such a very trifling matter now. She wondered if she would ever again care what they looked like.

And she wondered if she shouldn't pull from his touch, but she didn't. She just felt like leaning her head upon his shoulder and crying.

"It will be all right; you've simply got to stay down. So far, this thing is a skirmish, and I don't think either side is really going to get anywhere."

"I'm not afraid—of this," she told him, and she meant the words. Apparently, he believed her. He was still touching her, still holding her fingers laced with his own. He stared ahead at the stream. "Such a waste," he said angrily. "Such a damned waste."

"The—the murders...?" she inquired hesitantly.

"The war. Every damned day now is a waste. Of my men, of the Southern men. Petersburg will have to fall—"

"It won't fall!"

"It will fall!" he said angrily. "And you damned well know it!"

"Then Lee will move on to Richmond—"

"If he loses Petersburg, he won't be able to hold Richmond. The army will have to abandon them both."

"Then Jefferson Davis will just move his capital elsewhere and…"

"And he'll be captured, and his cabinet will be captured. It's over, it's all over—except the dying."

He was right, she knew it in her heart, but like so many others, she denied it. Lee was invincible; he could not fall. The South could not lose; they had fought too hard, too long.

And Virginia had been the place devastated by it all. Virginia had seen so many of the battles; Virginia had given too many men. She started to draw her fingers away. He held them tightly. There was passion in his eyes again when they met hers. "You know that I'm telling you the truth. You've seen the men come in. You're fighting with old men and little boys, and, God help them all, they are a brave and valiant crew. But it's over. Every damned death is a waste." He broke off bitterly, looking back to the stream. "And some even hideously more so than others!"

The murders. He had to mean the murders.

Now she did start to pull her fingers away. He held fast, and she tugged upon them. "I don't know what you're trying to accuse me of again—"

"I don't remember accusing you of anything!"

"The hell you didn't!"

His brow shot up, and a sudden curl touched his lip. "The *hell* you say?"

She tossed her head, her hair suddenly falling completely free of its pins and cascading down around her shoulders. "Your language, sir, has been atrocious!"

"Ah, but I'm not a sweet, demure Southern belle," he teased. "But then again, I'm not so sure that I remember you as ever being *demure* to begin with..."

"Go to hell, Colonel!" she said with dignity. "Hell. H-E-L-L."

"We may all be going to hell!" he assured her, laughing softly.

But then they heard the retort of a cannon. Not too far from them, a tree split. Branches seemed to explode and come hurtling through the air.

His arms were suddenly around her, bringing her down, his body shielding hers. Despite herself, she started trembling. They held still for a long, long time.

Finally, Nathaniel eased up, but he held her against him, against his chest, his arm still protectively around her. She bit her lip, then said softly, "Nathaniel, I never murdered anyone." She felt a choking sensation in her throat. "I can't believe that you could—believe such a thing of me!"

His hold tightened. "The war twists things," he told her. "But I don't suppose I ever thought you could have murdered anyone. I thought that you might know, though, who was doing it, and, yes, I did think that someone might be running with you, to protect you."

She shook her head vehemently, twisting around to stare into his eyes. "I don't know who it is, Nathaniel. I swear it. I would never..."

"A good enemy is a dead enemy," he said softly.

"I would never condone murder," she whispered.

He nodded, setting his chin upon her head, his arms around her waist, the cold stone to his back. He was silent for a very long time. The sounds of the battle seemed to be fading away. She closed her eyes. She hadn't slept at all. It was absurd. She was in the arms of the enemy, in the midst of battle. She felt safe here, and warm. And for the first time in so very, very long... secure.

She heard his whisper suddenly. "I love you, Lenore. I fell in love with you the moment I saw you. Nothing has ever changed that."

A molten lava seemed to sweep through her. She wanted to twist in his arms, crawl closer, be warmer. She wanted to feel his lips, wet and hot, closing over her own. She wanted to be held, loved, cherished. And by this man.

She swallowed hard, stiffening, yet not pulling away. Her voice was harsh when she spoke. "Don't love me, Nathaniel. Nothing has changed, nothing has changed at all. You're my enemy."

"You're mine. It doesn't change how I feel."

"You're not allowed to feel, because you're my enemy!" she told him urgently.

"Would God that that were true!" he said vehemently.

She started to pull from him.

"Sit still!" he commanded, and now she felt the warmth of his whisper at her ear, stroking her cheek. "Sit still. Whether you loathe me or love me, my sweet belle, I'll not let you kill yourself! Relax. You're not going anywhere."

"Then you must stop saying these outrageous things," she told him very properly.

He laughed softly. "Not so outrageous as you want to think, Mrs. Latham," he assured her. When she tried to move, he held her fast. She let out an aggravated sigh, but she didn't try very hard to move again. She closed her eyes. She listened to his heartbeat.

She eased back against him, encompassed by his warmth and strength. Amazingly, she began to feel as if the world itself was fading behind her. She was so tired, and so comfortable here in his arms.

The battle continued in the distance. Lenore felt it all slip away. Incredibly, she slept.

* * *

She awoke later to the gentle sound of his whisper. "Lenore. It's over; it's nearly night."

"Oh!" She started, and drew swiftly from his hold, leaping to her feet, nearly falling again. But he was there to steady her.

"Listen, you've got to stay here for a moment, and I'll be right back. I've got to see if anyone is still out collecting the de—the wounded. I'll be right back. Lenore, no matter what your feelings for me, don't leave! I'm bringing you home; I just want to see that you get there safely."

His steady gaze was her last warning. He started to walk away. She felt a sudden chill breeze, saw that twilight was indeed coming quickly. "Wait!" she cried to him, rushing to him.

"Lenore, I'll be right back!" he assured her. "Stay here!"

He turned from her abruptly. He whistled, and in the twilight, she saw his horse trot forward. He leaped up on the animal, then looked down at her. "Stay below the rocks!" he warned her fiercely. "No one can see you there. You'll be safe until I return."

He was right, of course. She had been kept safe from an entire battle there. Nathaniel, no matter what his uniform, had his own code of honor. If there was danger out there, he would meet it first.

She swallowed hard. "Hurry," she told him, stepping back.

He nodded, turned, and, way too swiftly, disappeared into the growing shadows. She turned and gazed at the water. Her stomach was growling again, but the water looked very inviting to her parched throat. She hurried to it, sank to her knees, dipped her hands in, and began to drink, shivering as the cold touched her lips and flesh. Still, it was good. She strenuously washed her face and throat, then shivered again, rose, and came back to the rocks. Darkness seemed to be falling with incredible swiftness.

How many nights had she come through this terrain and not cared in the least if the sky was pitch-black?

Why this sudden new fear?

"Lenore...!"

Her name! Whispered on the air. She felt as if the cold of the night was descending upon her, enwrapping her. It entered into her, rose to her throat, started to choke her.

She spun around. She had imagined it; please God, she had merely imagined it...

There was nothing there. No one.

But it came again.

"Lenore... Lenore..." It was a hissing sound, it wasn't real, it was all too real. It was a rasp, it was terrible, it was drawn from lungs that could not be accustomed to breath.

"Lenore, I would never hurt... you. Lenore, Lenore, Lenore, Lenore, come to me, touch me, Lenore..."

Nothing! There was nothing there, just the sound, echoing in her mind, reaching out, nearly touching her.

She screamed and spun, running blindly, desperately into bushes. She heard a thrashing behind her, and she ran harder, shrieking.

"Lenore!"

It was her name, called again. Not on the wind, but in a husky, male voice. A voice that commanded, that compelled. A voice that was...

Human?

The earth pounded behind her. Horse's hooves. Then, suddenly, he was upon her, leaping down, catching her shoulders. They fell to the earth and rolled together, and when he held her still, straddling over her, she met Nathaniel's worried blue gaze with her own eyes insanely wild. "Nathaniel, we've got to move; it's here, it's here!"

"What's here?" he roared.

"Get off me! We've got to go! It's here!"

"What's here?" he demanded fiercely again.

"I don't know, I don't know, I don't know! But please, God, oh, Nathaniel, I beg of you..."

He was still frustrated, but the terror in her tone had reached something within him and he was quickly up, sweeping her from the ground, depositing her upon his own horse. She didn't know where her mount had gone, and she didn't care. He swung up beside her, and she was glad to ride with him, she was desperate to touch him, desperate to feel his touch.

"Ride, Nathaniel, ride! Please!" she cried to him.

He obliged her, sending his horse hurtling forward in the shadows.

The moon was just rising, she saw as they exited through the trees.

A moon still huge and full...

It caused her to shiver, and yet, even as she felt the cold engulfing her, she saw the Lawry house in the beam of light. Stripped and abandoned, it was of no interest to anyone. The smugglers used it sometimes to hide weapons by night that were picked up the following day. There might be ammunition there, guns, swords.

There were sturdy bolts upon the doors...

"There, Nathaniel, there!" She pointed out the house beneath the golden glow. "There, please, take me there!"

"If you are that afraid—"

"Oh, God, Nathaniel—" She began to cry.

"I will take you anywhere you want to go," he promised softly. "To hell and back, lady, if need be!"

She leaned against him, closing her eyes. And she realized suddenly that she was not just afraid.

She was more terrified than she had ever been in all her life.

For *him*, as well as for herself...

Chapter 4

The old farmhouse had seen better days before the war. Then the white paint had most certainly been bright instead of dingy gray; the railings on the broad porch would not have been so sadly weather-beaten. But no matter what the place looked like tonight, Lenore didn't care. It seemed a haven from the *thing* out in the darkness and the shadows.

Lenore ran in the moment they dismounted after reaching the place, turning to implore Nathaniel to join her swiftly. He followed closely behind her, barely taking time to tether his bay to one of the broken porch railings.

Inside, she paused in the hallway, then hurried to the left where the parlor stood. The house itself appeared haunted—the draperies ripped from their cords, the once beautiful brocade loveseats and chairs now coated with a fine layer of dust. No one had tenderly covered the furniture before leaving, as a family would before a trip. This place had been abandoned. Lenore had heard that the owner had been killed at Manassas, and his wife, a Northern girl with no local kin, had simply left everything behind, brokenhearted, and with nothing to return for.

Lenore had been in the house at least three times before. It had already been looted of any decent tableware or silver. It was abandoned, pillaged, yet it still seemed to be a miraculous place of sanctuary.

She stood in front of the fireplace, stretching her hands out as if a blaze burned within it. She felt Nathaniel behind her, watching her.

"I can't start a fire, you know," he told her softly. "Every sentry on both sides would be reporting the smoke."

"I know," she told him, turning around at last. He was staring at her, just as she had felt he was, his hands on his hips, his head slightly cocked at an angle. Despite the fact that there was no heat, she felt a shade warmer. He created a dashing figure with his encompassing blue Union cloak cast over his shoulders, his dark uniform jacket beneath, his hat brim pulled low over his forehead, and at a rakish angle with the tilt of his head.

He must have thought that she had lost her mind, behaving with

118

such a desperate degree of panic. But even now, she fought to control the shivering that awful voice had caused in her.

She thought of the dead men suddenly, and she felt as if she wouldn't be able to endure it if such a thing were to happen to Nathaniel.

Especially if it were to happen because of her.

"You should go back, now!" she whispered fiercely.

"I won't leave you here—"

"I've been in this house before."

"—in the darkness," he continued, as if she hadn't spoken. Then he was suddenly crossing the room, sweeping away the distance between them. He caught her hands, stared down at them, felt the ice within them.

"What happened?" he demanded, looking from her chilled fingers to her eyes.

She felt the blood drain from her face. "It called me!" she whispered.

"What?"

She jerked her fingers free. "When you left, *it* called me. By name."

He shook his head, frowning. "Lenore, this *it* you're talking about has to be a man—"

"What man can kill so many so swiftly?" she charged him.

"Did you see anything?"

"No," she admitted.

"Then you felt the breeze. It was a long, horrible day with the battle raging all around you. You—"

"I heard my damned name whispered!" she cried out furiously, backing away from him. "And if you don't want to believe me, then don't! Go home, go back to your Yankee camp! This is really more our territory than yours at the moment. I'm safe, just go—"

She broke off because he *was* going. He had turned his back and was starting for the door.

And she didn't want him out there. She didn't want to be left alone, but more than that, she didn't want Nathaniel out in the darkness of the night.

"Nathaniel!"

She cried out his name and went flying after him, throwing her arms around him, forcing him to turn around. "You can't go out there. You can't go out there tonight!"

She didn't know herself just how terrified her words sounded, or how large her eyes glowed, how pale her cheeks seemed. Looking down at her, Nathaniel felt his heart begin to thunder. How incredible to like every little nuance about a woman. He was in love with the delicacy of her face, the green fire in her eyes, the little point in her chin, the one tiny dimple in her left cheek.

He set his hands upon her shoulders. "I was just going out for my saddlebags, Lenore. I've some real food in them, some not too terribly old bread, even a square of cheese. No wine, I'm afraid, but I do have a canteen of fresh, clean water."

Her fingers, entwined in his coat, began to fall. "You're not leaving?"

"No. I would never leave you in the night."

She lowered her head, and he set her to the side, stepping past her. He was going back outside. She listened to the door open, then she swirled around and followed him swiftly, watching the darkness, the foliage, the shadows, while he unsaddled his horse and gave it a freer rein to sample the overgrown grasses at the place, then looked back to her.

She had remained on the porch. She didn't see anything in the shadows...

And a breeze had picked up again. She closed her eyes, but there were no whispers within it.

"Let's go in," he told her. He had his saddlebags and his cavalry sword, and what looked like a Spencer repeating rifle. She knew the gun—her grandfather had taken one off a dead Yank and had sworn that afterward it had saved his life more than once.

It was a good weapon...

But was any weapon enough?

She shivered, turned, and hurried into the house. He came in behind her, but didn't follow her into the parlor. She heard him on the stairs, hesitated a moment, then came back and followed him up. "Nathaniel?" she called softly. Up here, not even the full golden moon gave her much light.

She heard the striking of a match, and he returned her call. "In here, Lenore." She hesitated, biting her lip, then hurried down the hallway to the end room. A soft amber glow from the candle he had lighted gave the room an air of comfort, the candle glow shining warm against the shadows. He was there, seated on the windowsill, looking out. She saw why he had come. From his vantage point, beneath the glimmer of the moon, he could see a great deal of the land surrounding him.

"Come closer!" he told her in a low voice.

She did so, moving on her toes, softly, though there was no one to hear. They were certainly alone in the abandoned house.

She stood by him, and he set a hand upon her shoulder and pointed eastward. "Yankee encampments," he said quietly, and she saw the multitude of small star like blazes that were the men's cooking fires. "And there," he murmured, and when he pointed again, she could see the outskirts of the city of Petersburg, and likewise many small fires that blazed into the darkness. No sounds of gunfire or chaos filled the night. The troops were settled in their tents and trenches.

He handed her his rifle suddenly. "Take this. I'm going to make certain the downstairs is secure."

She accepted the rifle he thrust into her hands. He swept his heavy cloak from his shoulders and set it around hers, then he strode from the room, leaving her in the light, walking out into the shadows.

"Nathaniel!" she cried softly, but he didn't hear her, and he didn't return. In a few moments, though, she heard the sound of the front door being bolted. Minutes later, she heard locks snapping on the windows, and she closed her eyes—praying it would be enough.

Yet, oddly, she felt secure for the moment. Maybe it was because Nathaniel was with her. Maybe it was because she didn't hear or feel...

The whisper.

No, it was gone. And for now, they were safe.

He was back in just a few minutes then, tugging his gloves from his fingers, tossing them upon a nightstand. "Well, no one is going to sneak up on us." He shrugged. "If an entire company shows up and shoots the door down, we're in trouble. But we're not going to be surprised by anyone."

Watching him, Lenore nodded. He tossed his canteen to her, and she caught it, then took a long grateful drink.

"Picnic, madam?" he inquired, then elaborately ripped the cover from the bed, flipping it over to create a blanket on the bare planked floorboards. A soft scent of roses filled the room as he did so, and Lenore realized that the house's last Yankee lady had set flower petals into her sheets, beautifully embroidered sheets that now gleamed whitely on the bed.

Nathaniel tossed his saddlebags down, sat Indian-legged upon the spread on the floor, and began to dig into the leather satchels. He produced bread wrapped in a towel and a hunk of cheese, one knife, and two apples. Lenore stared at him, and he quickly offered her an apple. "You must be starved," he told her.

She shook her head. "I ate last night," she told him. "But *you* must be starved."

"Well, I admit that I am," he said, picking up one of the apples. "But I can't imagine eating unless you accompany me every bite."

Despite her fear, she found herself smiling. The fear began to fade. He was with her.

And she bit into her apple, and Nathaniel did the same. And in a matter of moments, they were speedily setting into all the food, Lenore breaking the bread, Nathaniel cutting the block of cheese.

The food was very quickly gone. Lenore savored a long last sip of water, then handed back his canteen. After a moment, he stood and strode to the window.

He stood there, broad shoulders squared, arms crossed over his chest, looking out into the night.

She longed to walk to him, longed to touch him.

She shouldn't. She mustn't. He had told her that he loved her. Foolish. But she believed him. She had felt the same draw from the very first, felt as if something bound them ever since he had come into her life again. She remembered his words that long-ago night, and she admired his wisdom now, just as she admired the deep emotions he felt for his men, his determination to lead them, to fight for them, to die for them.

He shouldn't love her; they had nothing but pain ahead of them. He couldn't come with her.

She could never leave with him.

But suddenly, it didn't matter. All that mattered was that she did get to touch him once. Feel his arms around her. Feel his warmth, his passion, all that he had to give. The opportunity might never come again, and dreams might sustain her for the rest of her life.

She couldn't let the night, with its shadows, with its golden glowing moon, slip by her...

She stood and walked softly behind him, hesitating. But he had heard her quiet movement, and spun around. When she would have backed away then, he reached out.

She was drawn into his arms, held there tightly. For a moment, she saw the blue-gem fire of his eyes, then she felt the pressure of his lips upon hers, felt the trembling within them both as he held her. Fiercely, his mouth formed over hers, his kiss one that both demanded and savored, a touch that spoke of a poignant hunger, so very long denied. Her fingers curled into his nape. She reveled in the thick, rich feel of his hair, in the touch of her fingers upon his neck. She hadn't known the extent of her own loneliness until this moment, nor had she ever realized just how deeply Nathaniel had touched her.

She had loved her husband.

Yet being held by this man had been a secretly burning desire since he had first walked into that room so very long ago. She had never, never seen it, recognized it, admitted it.

Until now. Now, floodgates seemed to open...

His mouth parted hers with a dizzying liquid heat. She felt the stroke of his tongue, hot, deep within her, sensually, excitingly suggestive. The warmth seemed to fill the length of her.

His hand cupped her cheek as his lips continued to sear her own. She felt the gentle stroke of his fingers upon her throat, the strength of his arm around her. Felt the sweetly burning liquid fire of his tongue, probing, seductive, sweeping away what remained of reason and thought.

Then, suddenly, the kiss was broken, and his eyes, cobalt in the candlelight, were hard upon hers. He stared at her, no words escaping his lips for long moments. Then he spoke harshly to her. "It's a dangerous game you're playing, Lenore."

"Game?" she said softly. Then she thought that he meant the smuggling, but he continued swiftly.

"No half steps, Mrs. Latham. If you're seeking nothing more than comfort from the night, you had best do it from a distance. If I touch you again, there will be no turning back."

She blinked, realizing his warning. Her lashes fell. Yet once again, things of the past made so little sense now. Ah, yes, once upon a time, she had been the proper lady. She had never thought to share more than a kiss before marriage; she would have died rather than take a Yankee for a lover.

Once upon a time...

Her lashes raised. She met his eyes. "I'm afraid of the night, yes. Yet I'm more afraid that we'll part ways here tonight, and I'll never know what it would be to... have you."

He inhaled sharply. His hands were suddenly upon her shoulders, spinning her around. His fingers, trembling but seeming certainly well-practiced and sure, worked upon the length of tiny buttons that ran down the back of her black gown. He pressed the fabric from her shoulders. His lips touched down upon her bare flesh, and from that simple touch, fire seemed to radiate throughout her. He spun her again, and this time his fingers swiftly sought the tie to her chemise, tugged the satin ribbon, and bared her breasts. The sweep of his hands upon her, palms rubbing her nipples, fingers caressing the fullness around them, brought a soft moan to her lips. She closed her eyes, but his hand stroked up her throat to her cheek again, fingers threading into her hair, arid she was compelled to meet his gaze once again.

"I do love you!" he told her very, very softly.

But she couldn't repeat the words, no matter what lay in her heart. There was tonight, but there could be nothing more.

Did disappointment flicker in his gaze? She wasn't sure. "At least, Mrs. Latham," he murmured, and there was a note of bitterness there, "be bold enough to keep your gaze upon the man you're bedding! My skin isn't blue, Lenore. It's just the color of the uniform."

Tears suddenly stung her eyes. She shook her head. "No," she said softly. "The color is the man. But you wear blue very well!"

His lip curled slightly. In a second, he had swept her into his arms and strode the few feet to the bed, where, so sweetly in this strange sanctuary, the scent of rose petals teased the air. Yet as he laid her down and came beside her, they both paused as her skirt and petticoat were crushed between them, and the lightest little clinking sound could be heard. The magic was brought to pause for a moment as once again those blue eyes stared down into hers. Then he arose, helped her to her feet, swore softly, and pulled her cumbersome black gown over her head and shoulders, then spun her firmly around as she stood in her wide-belled bone petticoat, all the numerous vials of medicine so very carefully tied to the horizontal strips of bone.

He turned her around again, found the tie on the petticoat, and freed it. She held her breath, but merely heard the grating of his teeth as he carefully lowered the garment so that she could step from it.

He gazed at the petticoat. For a moment, she felt a terrible shiver standing there in nothing now but her worn black shoes, darned hose, threadbare pantalettes, and spilled-open chemise. She felt the cold as she wondered what went on in his mind, but his gaze fell back to her suddenly and fiercely, and she was just as swiftly within his arms once again. "Nothing but medicines," he murmured quietly. "Mrs. Latham, you wear gray well yourself!"

"I might have carried arms, had I been asked!" she tried to warn him.

But he had set her down again, and his hands closed over her worn shoes, and tossed them aside. His fingers slid sensually along the length of her calf and thigh as he sought the garter for her darned hose. Then she felt his touch against her naked flesh as he peeled away the hose, and the room itself seemed to spin, the moon to glow within it more brightly.

His eyes met hers. His voice was husky.

"Lenore, at this moment, I might not care if you were smuggling a dozen long-range cannons!"

She felt a smile curve her lip, and the cold was gone, all gone. And it was very easy to meet his eyes when he rose, casting aside the blue he wore so swiftly, boots tossed, jacket thrown to the shadows, shirt wrenched over his head, Yankee trousers quickly discarded. Then she tried very valiantly to keep her eyes pinned upon his, but they fell, of course, and once again, she felt the shimmering heat take root inside her, and the moonglow was enchanting, almost surreal. It gleamed upon his bronzed, broad shoulders, the breadth of his chest, the flurry of dark hair upon a very finely honed and muscled structure. Whorls of hair tapered in a tiny cyclone to his waist and below, and despite herself, her eyes followed that fascinating trail, and once again the hair thickened, surrounding the length of his sex, creating a dark backdrop that seemed to enhance even further the sight of his arousal. She swallowed quickly, feeling a curious weakness, a shivering, and then the fiercest explosion of heat and excitement. She forced her eyes back to his, only to discover him quickly crawling over her. She reached for him instinctively, but he forced her gently back to the pillows. His lips found hers again, tarried there, then moved.

He kissed her throat, and her breasts. His tongue played upon them until she could feel each wet touch into the very depths of her. Her chemise fell upon his blue jacket. His fingers stroked down the length of a rib gently, brushed over her upper abdomen, and found the tie to her pantalettes. He slowly pulled the bow, and began to ease the last of her garments from her body. And as he slid the fabric away, his lips fell upon the flesh so suddenly chilled by the night air, and warmed it. In seconds, the pantalettes were cast away, and she felt his stroke upon her upper thigh. His lips brushed there again, then her lower abdomen, her thigh, the bared flesh everywhere except that very center of desire until...

Until she ached to feel him even there so intimately, and when she thought she would die already, he touched her there with his liquid caress, and she felt as if she exploded with the very stars themselves.

She still seemed to streak across the night as he came upward against her, taking her into his arms, finding her mouth once again with his own, finding her eyes. No words passed between them as he eased himself very slowly and surely within her, yet when she was filled, a cry escaped her lips, and she wound her arms around him, pulling him close, the thunder of her heart seeming to race with the rhythm of his. She felt his tension, his heat, the unleashed energy. Felt the night, the stars, the world begin to spin again, and all encased in moonglow as his hunger brought her crashing toward a wild, abandoned ecstasy once again. Her fingers dug into the smooth expanse of his back, needing him closer still, savoring each excruciating moment as they catapulted toward a climax. She thought very briefly that she should have felt some shame. She did not. She felt as if she had been born to lie within his arms, as if she had not lived in truth until now. Nothing had ever felt so right, so natural.

Or so explosively *good*...

He tensed, so rigidly above her. His muscles tightened to a glistening gold in the moonlight as he plunged deeply, deeply within her. The lava heat of his body flowed into hers, and she soared again to a new level, closing her eyes, seeing gold replaced by blackness for long seconds, then seeing the stars burst into the heavens all over again. Yet even with it over, she lay against him trembling, loath to move, afraid to speak.

"There are no colors in the darkness, Lenore," he said very softly at last, cradling her head against him, threading his fingers through the wild length of her hair. "No colors at all in the darkness and the shadows."

She lay silent.

"I love you," he said again.

Tears stung her eyes, but she remained silent, trying to bury her head against his strength.

But he would not allow her to do so. He gently tugged her hair back until his eyes met hers, cobalt, fierce.

"At least tell me that you love being here with me. Tell me that you love to have me make love to you."

That was easy enough.

"I love... for you to make love to me," she whispered.

"Thank God for that!" he muttered fiercely. "And for the night," he added more softly. "I pray the morning comes slowly, for I swear, I will make good use of the night, and make love to you throughout it."

She tasted his kiss again. Hard, demanding. And she rolled within his arms, eager to touch him now, and eager to be touched again.

And she, too, prayed that the morning would come slowly.

And she didn't even realize that in his arms, she had forgotten the strange whispering she had heard earlier.

She had forgotten the fear.

And the sense of...

Evil.

Chapter 5

Lenore winced as old Dr. Tempe drew back the flap of the trouser leg he had just slit on the young Georgia private's leg. She had helped out enough in surgery to know what Doc Tempe knew—the boy, barely able to shave, was going to lose the leg.

Then he would have a fifty-fifty chance at life.

"Thank the good Lord for that morphine you brought in on your last trip!" Doc Tempe murmured softly to her. The boy wouldn't have heard him, no matter how loudly he had spoken—he had passed out from the pain long ago. But the hospital quarters where she helped out were really nothing more than the center of the church, and beds lined the place one after another. Doc Tempe spoke softly so that none of his patients would hear his words— every man there dreaded losing a limb. Some were certain that death was preferable, and Lenore thought that maybe they were right, because so often, limbs were amputated, and then the men died anyway. They just went piece by piece instead of all at once, one old soldier had told her.

Doc Tempe set the scissors he had cut the fabric with back on the tray she carried. "Orderly!" he called out to one of the heavyset men assisting them. He inclined his head, indicating that this soldier was going to have to be moved out back where once, not long ago and yet in a distant world, the choir had practiced hymns.

"Are you assisting me?" he asked her.

Lenore bit into her lower lip and nodded. There was nothing she would rather do less. Watch the surgeon with his kit, sawing first the flesh, tourniqueting the stump to stop the endless flow of life from the blood vessels, then finding his bone saw next, and finishing off the grisly task. The orderlies would hold down the poor man and she would jump about as quickly as possible, having what Doc Tempe wanted when and where he wanted it.

Admittedly, she'd passed out cold herself the first time she had tried to assist in surgery. But that, too, had happened in a different, far distant time. Dr. Claiborne, the head of the Confederate medical team here, was a near neighbor, and long before the siege had begun, she had found herself helping out at his side. There weren't enough surgeons in Petersburg to handle the flow of wounded who constantly poured in now. But Doc Tempe was among the best of the men they had; old, grizzled, and white-haired, he was witty and bright, and ever willing to learn from the men. Most of his patients did live. He had told Lenore that the secret was in using sponges. The Yanks liked to sop up blood from wounds with linen bandages and use them over and over again. Some young surgeon had told Doc Tempe that using a fresh sponge with each surgery helped the boys live. "Be damned if I know why!" he told her. "But the boys are living, and that's that!" So, even in the worst of times, Lenore did her best to find fresh sponges all the time. If Doc Tempe even thought that they might help, then it was worth the effort.

A shell suddenly exploded close by. So close that the windows in the church rattled in their panes, and the structure seemed to waver on its foundations.

Doc Tempe shook his head, looking around his ward. "Damned Yanks are mighty close in today. Mighty close in." His eyes narrowed on her. "But then, you know that, don't you, Lenore?"

She shrugged, lowering her eyes. It had been just about a month since she had taken her last foray out to smuggle in medicine. There was darned little of it left, and the doctors were only using what remained of the morphine and ether when a man's pain seemed to be excruciating. Dr. Claiborne had been sending out messages to beg, barter, and steal whatever could be gotten, but when she had told him she was ready to venture out again at any time, he had merely looked at her worriedly and said no more.

That was because Nathaniel hadn't left her after her last foray until he had brought her right across the river from one of the defending encampments. And she had been seen there with a Union soldier, and even when she had tried to explain to Dr. Claiborne that it was all right, the Yank had been a friend of Bruce's before the war, Dr. Claiborne had been very worried.

"And what if he hadn't been a friend?" he had demanded, sighing. "What then? You might have wound up in Washington in prison!"

"The Yanks haven't done anything terrible to a female prisoner yet—" she began, but he had waved that comment aside.

"They *did* threaten to execute a few!" he warned her sternly. "I don't know, Lenore. I just don't know if you should be out there anymore. And it's not just the Yanks. It's the—" and he had broken off flatly, staring at her.

"The what?" she had demanded.

"The murders," he had told her softly. And she had known then that the Rebs were every bit as aware as the Yanks that some of the invading enemy were being slashed down before they could come to the battlefield. "I had some Yank friends before the war, too. And the letters have been flying back and forth from side to side on this thing. Something's not right out there, Lenore. Something's not right at all, and you shouldn't be out there!"

She swallowed hard. Nathaniel had told her the same thing. He had told her when they had awakened in the old abandoned farmhouse on a morning that now seemed like part of a distant world as well. He'd held her very tightly, and told her that he'd bring her home—or as close to it as he could—but that she'd best swear not to make any more nocturnal excursions.

She hadn't done so, of course, and he'd been angry with her, and she had wound up lowering her head as if she agreed with his warnings, and finally, in exasperation, he'd held her fiercely again and said, "You will not wander out again, do you understand, Lenore?"

"I never *wandered*—" she began.

"Dammit, you know what I'm saying. And you know why!"

And she did. He had stayed with her through the darkness, and oddly enough, it wasn't until morning's light that she had been afraid again.

And that had been when she had recalled the horrible whispers she had heard when she had been alone.

Lenore...

It had called her name.

Something evil had whispered her name...

She hadn't let Nathaniel see her fear. She'd tried to tell him that she was all right, that he must return to his own men. He had refused to do so, assuring her that he could leave her safely—and disappear before any Reb could think about capturing him. The North, he assured her, did have a few decent horsemen left, even if the Rebels did pride themselves on their cavalry. She'd even smiled then. Yet her smile had faded because it was time to go. And he'd taken her to the river, and watched while some of the Rebs had seen them and risen, and she had called out. And then he had proven himself right; he had mounted his bay, and ridden into the forest.

And she had been left to tell Dr. Claiborne something of the truth...

Of course, she had left out everything that had happened in the old farmhouse. The night had remained a secret she guarded well within her heart. One that she dreamed about in the darkness now, one so very sweet, and so very painful.

The war went on. Nathaniel besieged her city. She didn't carry arms, but they were enemies nevertheless.

All that she could have of him was the dream...

"You were the best smuggler we had!" Doc Tempe said now with a sigh. "If only..."

"If Dr. Claiborne finds anything out there that can be procured," she said softly, "I'll be going for it."

"Lenore, you don't seem to realize—"

"I realize perfectly well," she assured him. "I was terrified out there. But you forget, I have a brother—a fourteen-year-old brother—fighting on the line. And a grandfather. And every man who comes in here hit might have been one of them, and I never will know until the very end if or when one of them will wind up on an operating table. I'm not so stupid that I'm not afraid—it's just that whatever we can bring in, we have to!"

Doc Tempe shook his head. "It's a sad thing, eh, when we have to risk the very flowers of the South!"

She smiled at him. It was a gallant comment.

"Doc Tempe!" the orderly called out. They both turned. The orderly stood at the back of the church. "The lad's waiting on you, Doc!" he said very softly.

"We'll talk later if need be," Doc Tempe told her. "But I guess we're needed now. Sure you're up to this one?"

She shook her head. "I'm never up to them. But let's go."

They went. The boy awakened while the very brief preparations were being made. Doc Tempe was calm and reassuring while the orderly doled out a little of the precious morphine.

Lenore moved mechanically, trying not to feel the boy's pain and loss. It seemed a very long and hard day, even in the midst of so many other long and hard days.

She went home in the darkness that night, after the last of the day's wounded had been brought in.

131

Walking from the church, Lenore felt a strange breeze seem to creep around her. It was chilling, and she found herself hurrying through the streets.

She came to the big Victorian house where she lived alone now except for Matty, who had practically raised both her and Teddy. With Teddy and her grandfather on the lines, it seemed a lonely place. Matty worked at hospital locations throughout the long days, too, but just like a mother, she always tried to reach home before Lenore, and most often, when Lenore did come home, Matty was there, and when she could manage it, she had a bath ready for Lenore and something hot to drink—even if it was painfully weak coffee. Matty loved her, and Lenore loved Matty right back. The tall, slim black woman seemed ageless, and she seemed to carry all the wisdom of a dozen centuries. Lenore knew that her grandfather had bought Matty and her old husband when her last owner had been determined to sell them both off wherever he could, and that Matty had always been grateful that Lenore's grandfather had believed that slaves were human with human feelings and that no man had a right to split up a man and wife. Lenore was certain that Matty must want the Yanks to win—she didn't believe in slavery, and she had pointed out to Lenore often enough that many masters were downright vicious to their slaves, and Lenore had been forced to admit that it was true, even if she had pointed out in turn the goodness of some men. Right now, it didn't matter. They weathered the siege alone, seeing Teddy and Grandpa infrequently, and all of them eating at the old table in the kitchen on those few special nights when Grandpa or Teddy did make it back from the trenches.

When Lenore came into the house, Matty was sitting on the bottom step of the center stairway right behind the entryway. She was darning some old, worn socks, but she offered Lenore a smile. "In the kitchen, missy," she told Lenore, "there's a kettle of water over the fire, and the hip tub's drawn right to it." Matty frowned. "Good night for it? You look right worn down!"

"More so and more so," Lenore told her, trying to speak lightly and offer the woman a smile in return. She started through the door at her left to the kitchen, which took up much of that side of the house. "Then again," she called back, "the siege is a nightmare, but I've got you, and a bath sounds like a little brush with heaven!"

Matty chuckled softly after her. Lenore quickly discarded her

132

clothing, tossing it all over a chair by the fire. She poured the last of the water into the tub, smiling as the steam rose to her face, then she crawled into her bath. The good thing about a siege, she thought, was that it could make the littlest things seem like the greatest wonders in the world. A bath... hot, luxurious, causing the aches and the pains and even some of the heartache to seep from her body.

She leaned her head back against the wooden rim of the tub and closed her eyes. She opened them just a slit and watched the steam start to rise. For a few moments, she felt really deliciously oblivious to the world around her. Maybe she was just exhausted, so exhausted that she managed to make it disappear at will...

Maybe just dozed. She must have slept, must have dreamed. For she was suddenly back in the forest.

And listening while someone, *something*, whispered her name. *Lenore... Lenore...*

Chills swept around her—she could scarcely see, for the air was filled with a swirling mist and the black powder that prevailed after a battle. But she could hear, and feel, the evil.

Lenore... Lenore...

There was someone standing before her. She had to see; she prayed not to see. The mist was lightening. Any minute she would see his face, and she didn't want to see it.

She tried to waken.

She could not. She could only stare as the mist cleared away.

Then she saw...

Saw his face, his eyes, the evil in them. For a moment, it seemed that he was there, alive. Then it seemed that he was a walking corpse. A terrible corpse, caked with mud, long dead. She could see his skull, his eye sockets, staring, empty...

Bruce!

No...

Lenore... Lenore...

And he started walking toward her.

He didn't look at her, though; he looked beyond her. She knew that someone stood behind her, someone who meant to protect her, at the cost of his own life. Nathaniel. And the thing with the empty eye sockets was still whispering. *Lenore, Lenore. I'd never hurt you, just send you to hell with him!*

Her voice was locked in her throat. Then she managed to

scream. With terror, with vehemence. And, suddenly, she was out of the forest and the mist, and back in her own kitchen, and Matty was there, standing above the tub, her lean face lined with worry, her hands upon Lenore's shoulders. "Missy! Missy!"

"Oh!" Lenore stared at her. "Oh!" she said again, and buried her face in her hands. "Oh, dear God, Matty, it was horrible. You can't imagine..."

Matty stood and disappeared for a moment, then returned with a small glass that offered an even smaller sip of whiskey. It was about all they had left. But Lenore accepted it gratefully, swallowed the burning amber liquid, and leaned back again.

"A dream," Matty said.

Lenore nodded.

"You've had it before?" Matty suggested.

Had she? Yes, ever since she had been alone in the forest, waiting for Nathaniel to return that night, she had been haunted by the whispers she had heard.

She had seen the man standing in the mist.

She had never seen the mist clear before, never seen before that it was *Bruce* standing there. Nor had she seen that he was coming after her, and Nathaniel.

She shivered violently now, feeling a wave of heartsickness seem to wash over her with a vengeance. Bruce! He had never been cruel, surely never evil...

But it hadn't really been Bruce, not the man she had married. Rather, it had seemed to be some kind of a mockery of him, like...

Like the prisoner they had held in the Yankee camp. Even Nathaniel had said it. Yes, the man had looked like Bruce, but it hadn't been Bruce...

"Matty, have you ever thought that you had seen a ghost?" she asked softly, miserably. She realized how foolish she must have sounded. "Ghost! Dear Lord! Listen to me, how—"

"There are more things that prowl the worlds between the living and the dead than mere ghosts!" Matty said.

Lenore's eyes shot to those of the woman she thought she knew so well. Matty wasn't laughing at her, or frowning at her with concern. She didn't seem to think that Lenore was crazy at all for asking about ghosts.

"What?" Lenore whispered.

Matty smiled then, just slightly, taking the empty whiskey glass from Lenore's knotted fingers. "So many things prowl the world, missy, that we do not want to see! And when you were out that time, you ran into one, and you still do not want to see it."

"Matty, you can't—"

"I've listened to your nightmares, your cries in the night," Matty said softly.

"But—but it is all a nightmare!" Lenore said. "The war, the siege—"

"And the creature who murders the Yankee soldiers each month by the light of the full moon."

Lenore gasped. "You know—"

"Everyone knows. You have been gone scavenging too often to hear what's been going on. The Yanks had threatened to hang Rebel prisoners each time one was murdered, but even they know that it is nothing sanctioned by Southern generals. They no longer threaten, but still, there are whispers about what goes on everywhere, speculation."

"And what do you speculate?" Lenore asked her.

Matty shrugged, walking over to the kitchen window, parting the curtain slightly. "I think," she said, "that it is going to be a full moon again tonight. And then we will see."

"Matty, you can't believe—"

"I was born on the island of Haiti, Miss Lenore, you know that. We believe many things there. The moon is rising now. We will see very shortly."

Lenore's water seemed to turn very cold. She couldn't move. She sat within it shivering.

And she prayed.

Not for herself. She prayed for Nathaniel, and she longed for him. Yearned to be back with him, held in his arms.

To feel his heartbeat...

Until the long hours of night passed, and the sun burst through the darkness, and the nightmare, once again.

A deeper fear swept into her. Nathaniel was in so much danger. And he didn't know it. He hadn't believed that she had heard the whisper in the woods.

But it had been real...

Dear God, just what would the night with the full moon bring this time?

Chapter 6

The full moon had come again.

Nathaniel had watched it all night, watched it from a time when it had still been day, when the moon had been a ghostly sphere in the blue sky. Then it had brightened against the sky dusk, against the golden colors that had streaked the heavens. And finally, when full darkness had fallen, the moon was a white orb, glowing over the velvet black of the night.

His patrols were out, twenty men to a company. He had warned them to stay together, to watch each other's backs.

So the hours passed and the evening progressed. He took a guard shift himself, riding the perimeters of their camp. He sat with Lieutenant Green afterward, sipping coffee, trying to stay awake. He had marched through enough nights, so the long vigil didn't seem so deadly.

Yet, as the night went on, he found himself thinking far more about Lenore than about his own men.

A month ago. It had been just a month ago when so many of his men had been slain. When he had found her trying to get home with her precious vials of medication. When he'd dragged her into camp...

When he'd made love to her in the deserted farmhouse.

Thinking about her so made him ache. Burn inside, long for her again. Don't love me, she had told him, but he could never forget holding her, feeling her; the look in her eyes, the warmth that enveloped him when he touched her. Don't love her. He *did* love her. He had spent years dreaming of having her. Somehow, the war had delivered her to him. And now, if he survived the war...

If he survived the war, he would still be the enemy, hated even more once the South was conquered. And it would be conquered. Petersburg could not hold out much longer. Lee would be forced to abandon Richmond as well, and from that point on...

"I wonder where our boy is tonight?" Lieutenant Green said.

"Our boy?"

Green nodded, filling up his coffee cup, staring into the liquid over the campfire. "That strange prisoner, the Rebel boy. The one you said looked like someone you knew."

Nathaniel looked at Green quizzically. "I thought we sent him to Washington with the others a long time ago."

Green looked startled. "I thought you knew! But then, maybe it didn't get reported to you. You were gone with Mrs. Latham when it happened. He slipped through our fingers again. That very night, as a matter of fact. When they were being transferred. We're convinced we didn't lose him, but the unit we turned the prisoners over to came up a man short. It made me damned uncomfortable. There was always something about him. He looked wrong; there was something in his eyes... and he—he smelled bad. Like..."

"Death?" Nathaniel suggested, remembering the man and feeling a sweeping of cold seep down his neck. *Death.* That was it. The man had smelled like death.

And he had looked so damned much like Bruce Latham.

He stood, swallowing down more hot coffee, thinking he needed a good whiskey instead. Lenore had seen him, too. He had scared the hell out of her; Nathaniel had seen it in her eyes.

So what? What did it all mean? Maybe the Reb was their man. He was someone who looked a whole lot like Bruce Latham, someone who was damned evil, maybe maniacal. And maybe he let himself be caught just so that he could escape and be close at hand to murder his Yankee jailers.

Maybe. But how did he survive against so many? What man had that kind of strength?

"My turn to head on out," Green said, standing. He pulled out his pocket watch and flipped open the gold case. "Two a.m., sir! We're making it through the night."

"Just a few more hours to go," Nathaniel agreed. "I'll be out to join you again in another hour."

Green nodded and left him. Nathaniel sank down on one of the camp chairs before the fire. He stared into the flames, drank the rest of the coffee in his cup, and set the cup down. His back ached from all the riding he had done, and he was damned used to riding. The days were long ones. He closed his eyes, just resting them for a moment.

Lenore...

Where was she now? He prayed that she was safe. Sleeping, hopefully. Starving, probably.

Dreaming, maybe...

The flames snapped and crackled. He was vaguely aware that he had dozed, vaguely aware that he was dreaming himself. He saw Lenore, and it was a wonderful dream. She was running toward him. Yet, as she came, he saw her face, saw the terror in her eyes. She was trying so very hard to reach him. Trying to tell him, to warn him...

Then he saw through the mist. Bruce Latham—or someone very much like Bruce Latham—was behind her. He was laughing, and the laugh seemed chill, like the black hollows of his eyes. Dead eyes.

There was a glint of silver. Latham had a knife, razor honed, glittering beneath a full moon. And he was reaching out, grasping at Lenore's hair as she ran.

"No!" Nathaniel heard himself screaming.

He must have cried out aloud, and awakened himself. Lenore was gone; Latham was gone. The campfire was burning low.

And Lieutenant Green, dismounting from his sorrel horse, was before him again.

Nathaniel leaped to his feet. Green was grim. "The western perimeter, sir! We need you fast!"

He was up in split seconds, mounted on his waiting horse before half a minute had elapsed.

He followed Green hard for a full five minutes, then came to a clearing where two men were down, where their companions held and supported them, where others were rushing in. Private Haines, Company B, was the most coherent, quickly saluting Nathaniel and speaking. "All eighteen of us in the company were lined up, sir, near close enough to touch. Then Perry over there screamed out, struck down, and we saw *something*. We gave chase into the foliage, and both Jacobs and I fought, but we don't exactly know what we fought. Jacobs is injured there. I got away when the others started calling out, but, sir, I swear, I still don't know who or *what* I was fighting!"

Even as Haines spoke, they heard a shrill cry from down the line. Nathaniel spurred his horse, leaping down the trail. Three of his men were crying out, screaming, clasping at injured limbs. Nathaniel saw a shadow disappearing into the trees. He followed hard, his saber drawn.

He rode into dense foliage and a low ground fog. Mist, mist surrounding him. There was movement ahead. He jumped down quickly from his horse and made his way through the underbrush.

Suddenly, in the mist, the form of a man sprang before him. He could barely see, but then there was a strange glitter in the mist, and he saw that a knife was raised and that the man was ready to come barreling into him. He swung his sword in an arc just as the man lunged.

He caught the knife in his shoulder, but hit flesh as well himself. He felt his sword shuddering, felt it as it sliced into the man, a mortal blow.

But the man didn't fall. Nathaniel heard a strange keening, and his attacker ripped himself from the blade of Nathaniel's sword. Even as Nathaniel clutched his own bleeding shoulder, the man stumbled into the foliage. "No!" Nathaniel roared out again, and ran hard in pursuit.

But the man was gone, almost as if he had evaporated into the trees, become part of the mist.

Panting, Nathaniel leaned upon the handle of his sword. He started back to his men. No one, at least, had died. But a number of them were seriously injured.

As he spoke with the others, Green touched his shoulder. "Sir, you're bleeding."

"Flesh wound," he said.

"Still, sir, it's almost daylight now. You can have that bound up and then get some sleep."

The company surgeon saw to his wound. It wasn't serious. Nathaniel had been the one in good position to strike at an enemy coming after him too wildly.

He should have killed the man. Instead...

He closed his eyes, and he saw Lenore again. Running. Her beautiful hair streaming about her.

And there were cold white fingers reaching out to grab her. There was the glitter of a knife beneath a full glowing moon...

Tonight was the full moon.

The light was coming. He stared up at the canvas of his tent, and the urge to see Lenore was overwhelming. He had to know that she was safe.

And he had to demand to know what she knew!

Damn her! He groaned inside. He wanted to shake her, hard. He wanted to tell her that they were all in danger. He wanted to tell her...

That he did love her. And that they had to end this.

From somewhere, a rooster crowed.

It was daylight.

$* * *$

Lenore was in the makeshift church hospital, taking down a letter for a young boy from Georgia, when she saw one of the sergeants come in for Doc Tempe, and she saw Doc's face go just as white as the tufts of hair on his head. He wiped his hands on his apron and started out from the hospital in the sergeant's wake.

She smiled uneasily at the Georgia boy and asked him if they might finish the letter later. Then she hurried after Doc Tempe.

He was just outside, on the steps. A small company of Virginia infantry had brought two stretchers with sheet-clad bodies upon them. Doc Tempe lifted the first sheet, and a visible shudder ripped through the old man. He replaced it tenderly, then lifted the other. He spoke softly to the sergeant, and the company of men picked up their stretchers and moved down the steps. They were marching for the old office building up the street that was now being used as a morgue.

She hurried to Doc Tempe, who stared at the men as they left. "What happened?" she cried to him.

He stared at her, startled. He hesitated too long. "What do you mean, what happened? There's a war on out there, young woman!"

She shook her head wildly. "It wasn't the war, right? It was... something else."

He opened his mouth, ready to lie again. Then he sighed and shrugged. "Seems like it's our turn this time. Yes, Lenore, it was something else. Those boys were murdered. Nearly beheaded. Chopped right to pieces."

"Infantry men?"

"Cavalry. The infantry boys just brought them in. In fact..." He stopped, his eyes on her, his voice drifting swiftly to silence.

"What?" she nearly shrieked.

He shook his head sadly. "Now, Lenore, sometimes what we don't know—"

"Doc Tempe, tell me what you were going to say!"

He sighed deeply. "All right, Lenore. They were local boys. Boys who had signed up with your husband. Trenton Shaver and Harold McGilvey. They were troublemakers in the past, gave Bruce quite a

141

hard time, from what I understood. But I suppose that's all in the past now. God will judge them, and us all."

She felt ill suddenly. As if she were going to be sick there on the steps, or at the very least, pass out cold upon them. She fought the feeling, trying to concentrate on the breeze, the coolness of the day.

What did it all mean?

That her deceased husband had come back to life in some monstrous form and was now battling the Yankees in a different way?

Punishing his own men with a terrible vengeance?

"It can't be!" she whispered out loud.

"What can't be?" Doc Tempe asked.

She couldn't tell him. If she were to try to do so, she was convinced that Doc Tempe would say she had been working for the Cause for just too long, and needed an extended period of rest, perhaps locked away somewhere.

"What can't be?" Doc Tempe repeated.

"Uh... that it seems to be our men who are being murdered now," she said swiftly.

He shook his head, staring at her. "Go home, Lenore. Go home and get some sleep. You're done in."

"But—"

"Things are quiet enough this morning. Rest, so that you're ready if I need you later."

She couldn't argue with him at the moment. She nodded, then turned blindly toward the street. She wasn't sure she wanted to rest—if she slept, she just might dream—but perhaps she did need to be away for a while.

She hurried down the streets, deserted except for a few soldiers running here and there. By daylight, the buildings hit by cannon and mortar fire were painfully scarred, the air had an acrid taste to it, and the sun didn't even seem to shine properly down upon the city. She closed her eyes against the sight of one very badly charred wall and hurried on.

She burst into her own house, certain that she was alone, and leaned against the doorway. She heard a creaking sound and nearly cried out, then looked into the parlor and saw that Matty was sitting in the rocking chair before the cold hearth, staring at it as if she watched invisible flames.

"It's gotten worse, eh?" Matty asked her softly.

Lenore swallowed hard and nodded. "Southern men. Men out of Bruce's company, before he died."

Matty was silent. Lenore left the doorway and walked toward the chair where the handsome black woman was sitting. She came down on a knee before her. "Matty—"

Matty raised a hand to Lenore, then handed her an envelope which had lain on Matty's lap. "A soldier managed to hand that off to me this morning," Matty said softly. "I imagine it's from your Yank."

Lenore stared at Matty for a moment, then ripped open the plain white envelope. There were a few simple sentences upon it.

What's killing them, Lenore? You know, and we have to stop it. Help me. The old house. This afternoon, daylight. N.

She let the note slip through her fingers. "But I don't know!" she whispered aloud.

Matty rose slowly, stretching, as if her old back were sore. Then she turned around. And Matty's back and her bones might have been old, but her eyes were ageless.

"Don't you?" she asked Lenore.

"Matty, help me, tell me! Can a man come back? Why would Bruce kill like that? He wasn't a cruel man, he—"

"Forget any idea that that man out there is anything like Bruce!" Matty warned her.

"Then *what is he?*" Lenore cried out desperately.

"A shapeshifter," Matty said softly.

"A *what?*"

Matty sat again, folding her hands in her lap, staring at Lenore. "A shapeshifter. A demon. When Bruce Latham was shot and dying, the shapeshifter stole the body just as your husband's soul tried to escape it."

"Oh, my God!" Lenore breathed. "I can't believe this, I just can't! You're telling me that it is Brace's corpse—"

"I'm telling you that it is a demon. A shapeshifter."

She was going to fall, Lenore thought, and she leaned against the mantel as she stared at Matty, needing the support.

"I can't believe—" Lenore whispered again.

"Aye, miss, and don't believe!" Matty warned her. She waved a hand with beautiful long black fingers in the air. "So many don't believe, and so the demons live on! Men think they battle another man, and so they die! People will not believe what they do not see, and so they die! Lenore, where I come from, one often sees the walking dead. And you cross yourself swiftly, and if the demon seeks to do battle with you, you know how to fight back!"

Lenore gritted her teeth, walking forward again, coming down upon a knee once again before the old woman she had known all her life.

"How do we fight it?" she asked softly.

Matty's black eyes touched hers. "It will not die by gunshot or by a sword wound. The head must be completely decapitated, and then the head and body burned, and the ashes thrown wildly to the wind."

Lenore stood, amazed to realize how badly she was shaking. But then, she had to go. She had to risk a run through the city and across the river, and she had to reach the house. And she had to do so swiftly, because Nathaniel would be there, and she had to reach him before dark.

"I have to... behead... Bruce!" she whispered painfully.

Matty shook her head. "You have to kill a demon. And let your husband go free. He has already left life behind him."

"Matty, I'm so afraid."

"Good. You need to be afraid."

Lenore kissed the old woman on the cheek, then turned as quickly as she could. She drew her long black cape from the hall closet, and hurriedly left the house.

The streets were still very quiet. She passed a soldier here and there, and occasionally a denizen of Petersburg, trying to mend something destroyed by cannon fire or combing the street for anything at all that might be left to eat.

A Southern guard stopped her when she tried to leave the city. But another officer came up to him and addressed her as a friend. "Mrs. Latham! Another run out for medication? Jesu, 'tis a sorry day that we risk a lady such as yourself. Meyers, let her pass. She keeps many of us alive."

She wasn't on a medicine run. But then, she was trying to save Rebel as well as Yankee lives. The Bruce-demon had killed his own men last night. Maybe that would exonerate her for the lie she gave now.

"Thank you, gentlemen. I will return with what I can!" she assured them.

Then she was given an escort to the river and a small boat to silently bring her across it to a thicket of trees on the other side.

But once there, past her Southern guard, she found herself caught once again in the midst of a skirmish, soldiers running here and there, bullets flying. She sank back into the trees, determined not to die now from a stray bullet! She waited, and the shadows came before she could move again.

Then she ran, sticking to the trees, avoiding the fields where the skirmish had taken place, where Rebs and Yanks alike now looked through the ranks of the fallen, separating the injured from the dead.

She ran hard, seeing that the moon had risen against a still blue sky, but that the shadows would soon overtake the blue.

And then it would be night. Darkness, with only the full, glowing moon to light it...

She paused before the house, for it was dark within already. Shivers seized her as she breathed deeply, then started through the brush once again.

She paused. Something was moving behind her. She could hear the rustling in the leaves...

Stark terror held her still. Then she stared at the house. Nathaniel! She started to run again, blindly.

Something struck her from behind. She fell, and it fell upon her. She started to scream wildly and in terror, picturing her husband...

Deceased, all this time, the empty eye sockets...

"Lenore!"

A hand fell over her mouth. She heard the hushed whisper, and relief flooded her.

She saw his eyes above her own, blue as the sky, burning, very much alive. Nathaniel. Then he was pulling her up, and into his arms, and his words were angry.

"You shouldn't have come."

"You told me to come."

"You still shouldn't have come!"

He lifted her into his arms and began walking toward the house. She laced her fingers behind his neck, and for those few moments, she allowed herself just to be happy, to be glad to be with him.

He pushed open the door with his toe, then closed it, and slid the heavy bolt. Her eyes met the fire and the hunger in his. "I can tell you—" she began softly.

"No!" he murmured. "We've so little daylight left!"

She should have protested. She should have told him again that he could not love her.

That he must not make love to her.

But she didn't. She met his gaze as his strong strides and steps brought them up the stairway, and back to the bedroom where rose petals still cast their gentle scent upon the sheets. He laid her down upon the bed and gently disrobed her there, then cast aside his own clothing with less than subtle speed, and came down beside her. He enveloped her to the length of his body, touching her with his heat and fire from head to toe.

They could feel the last of a gleaming red sunset streaking in upon them.

It felt good upon her flesh. As sweet, as warm, as the feel of his lips upon her. Lips that tasted, savored, traveled. Caressed her naked flesh, teased her breasts. Caught her lips in an endless kiss. Roamed with a fiercer, more savage hunger now, upon her body. His mouth, searing, suckling. Touching her, all over her. A line of fire, created by the tip of his tongue, streaking from the valley between her breasts to her belly, lower, beyond. She cried out, writhing, waiting. Clutching him, her own lips burning into his shoulder, tasting his throat, seeking his chest. Her fingers, closing around him, feeling the pulse, feeling the deep, deep shuddering within his body.

Then he was atop her. Within her. Moving, whispering. Bringing her swiftly toward ecstasy.

Whispering...

That he loved her.

And she loved him. Loved when he pulled from her. Kissed her lips again, teased her thighs. Came between them.

Brought her higher and higher until she was crying out.

Swept her with his need, and brought them both at last to a place where time stood still, to where the world exploded, where only splendor existed...

She held him to her as she drifted back to a realm of peace.

"We have to talk," she whispered softly.

"I know." Held upon his elbows, he rose slightly above her. "I love you. And I know that you love me."

She fought the tears that glazed her eyes. "We've got to talk about—"

"Yes." He hadn't really expected a response on personal matters from her. His face was tense and grim now. "I've got to know what's going on, Lenore."

She nodded. "And you've got to try to believe me, Nathaniel. You wouldn't before—"

"Tell me, Lenore," he whispered.

She nodded, then frowned.

The daylight was gone. The red sunlight no longer shone upon Nathaniel's hard-muscled shoulders, making them gleam a copper-bronze. The world was muted now, touched only by the white glowing light of the moon.

"I—" she began.

And then she saw him. Past Nathaniel's shoulders. Coming into the room. He walked, but his footsteps made no sound. It was as if he had shifted into a human shape out of the mist and fog that darkness so often brought.

Bruce...

Not Bruce.

This creature was evil. It had Bruce's face, but not his face. The flesh was white, the eyes were black and glowing. She blinked. Dead eyes. There was nothing there except for the gleaming black. Nothing there but evil...

And he was walking straight toward them, a blood-drenched knife held high in his hands. He walked, no, floated, toward them, ready to rip his blade into Nathaniel's neck.

"Dear God, no!" she shrieked. Nathaniel twisted.

And the blood-coated knife began to fall.

Chapter 7

Nathaniel saw the blade just in time. His arms wound around her tightly, he rolled the two of them to the side in a fierce gesture.

The blade plunged into the pillow, sending goose feathers flying.

The Bruce-demon let out a cry of rage, wrenching the knife from the pillow. But by that time, Nathaniel had dragged Lenore from the other side of the bed. He had shoved her fiercely from him, and leaped to the ground to swiftly wrestle his sword from its scabbard, cast there so haphazardly in his haste to be with her.

He scarcely had it free when the Bruce-creature swung on him again, the knife raised. *"Colonel, sir, eh?"* it hissed. It was horrible. It was Brace's voice; it was not Brace's voice. It was a mockery of it, making something so horribly evil of the man she had once loved. *"Colonel, sir, eh?"* it repeated. A whisper, sibilant, horrible. The very sound of it brought chills streaking down Lenore's neck.

"So you're sleeping with my wife," it continued, staring at Nathaniel with its evil black eyes. It seemed to smile. *"It's been good to kill Yanks. It's been all right to kill Rebs. It's going to be ecstasy to kill you!"*

"You don't have a wife. Bruce Latham is dead. You've seized his body, but I'll be damned myself before I'll let you touch his wife!" Nathaniel responded swiftly.

"I'll have her, and you will be damned!"

It started to move. Nathaniel had his sword raised, his knees slightly bent, shoulders squared, eyes sharp. Naked, he was somehow exceptionally splendid at that moment, and her heart surged, because she knew that he would face down any danger for her.

Or die trying.

"No!" she shrieked. Nathaniel couldn't face this enemy. He didn't know how to kill it.

She started walking inward from the corner of the room, staring at the demon. She dropped down to the ground, keeping her eyes on the creature, searching for the knife Nathaniel kept in a small sheath—usually at his ankle.

But the creature smiled at her, and whispered her name. *"Lenore... I never meant to hurt you, Lenore. I just long to touch you again..."*

"You bastard!" Nathaniel shouted. "Bastard, I swear I'll kill you this time, I—"

"*Lenore!*" Now its voice was soft, almost tender. "*You're my wife. You wouldn't kill me. You couldn't kill me.*"

He started walking toward her. To her horror, she found herself nearly frozen by the power in his black eyes. She needed to be moving away. She needed to find her weapon, to run, to fight...

"*Lenore...*"

"You're not Bruce!" she cried out. "You're not Bruce. You've stolen his body, and you've kidnapped his soul. But you're not my husband. My husband was never cruel, never, never evil. *You're not Bruce!*"

The thing stopped then, and hissed in fury. But then its lips cracked into a dry smile again. "*Kiss me, wife. Join me. Be with me now, damned through eternity. Let my lips touch yours, let my blade caress your throat...*"

He had taken a step toward her again. "Before God, no!" Nathaniel cried out, taking a swift step before her, and slashing with his sword. He caught the creature right across the belly, but there was no blood, and the thing barely staggered back. "Damn you, you'll not touch her!"

But it came forward again, closer and closer. It struck out savagely at Nathaniel with a wicked punch, throwing him back against the wall as if he weighed no more than the feather pillow. Nathaniel slammed hard into the wall. Lenore heard the hard crack of his head against it. He fell to the floor. For a moment, Lenore thought that he was dead. Oh, so nearly! His eyes opened. He tried to rise. The demon was approaching him. He shook his head, fighting to clear it. Any second, and the creature would be upon him once again with its fierce, inhuman strength...

There would be no chance again.

"Dear God, Nathaniel, don't pass out! Live! It's a shapeshifter!" Lenore cried out. "It has to be beheaded and burned. The head, Nathaniel—you have to sever its head."

The creature paused, its eyes pure black fire and fury upon her.

"*You!*" It pointed at her. "*I'd not have hurt you, Lenore. Now you will feel my kiss, oh, yes, wife, I swear it...*"

She wrested the knife from the little sheath and raised it at the creature coming so swiftly toward her. She backed away, terrified.

"*A kiss, my love...*"

149

It reached out a hand. Like icicles, his fingers curved over her naked flesh. He drew her to him. Closer. She tried to raise the knife, but he slapped her hand with such force that the bones were nearly shattered. Her feeble weapon fell to the floor. Closer. She could smell his fetid breath. Like death. It swept over her. His eyes, blackness, seemed to consume her. Any second now, his lips would touch hers with their rancid whisper of the grave...

"Demon bastard!" she heard in a rage. The creature was tapped on the shoulder. Icy fingers eased from her flesh as the Bruce-demon turned to meet this new aggressor, come back to life.

"Ah, Yank! You'll die so slowly..." the monster began, straining back to pitch forward with its deadly blade, its whisper still so sibilant and chilling.

But it wasn't to be. Not this time. Nathaniel was ready. His sword was up and poised even as the demon finished its turn. The silver cavalry blade began to whip through the air, catching the creature right at the throat with a sound.

The head was nearly severed.

There was no blood to fly...

Lenore screamed as the thing set its hands to its head, trying to steady it. She crouched down on her knees, hugging her arms to her chest as she screamed again.

It steadied the head for a moment. It stared at her.

"Lenore..."

For a moment, it was so achingly Bruce's voice. For a moment, it seemed that the evil left the eyes.

"Lenore, Lenore, Lenore..."

The tenderness was gone. The evil lit like fire in the eyes.

The thing was reaching for her again...

"No!"

It was Nathaniel, roaring out the word. And his sword swung again, hard and sure.

And this time, the head came loose from the creature's throat. It flew across the room to strike the wall.

Head and body fell. Still. Dead.

Lenore screamed again and crouched on the floor, shaking uncontrollably. Nathaniel's arms came around her, and he hunkered down, engulfing her with his tenderness. He held her for long moments, whispering to her. Then, when her shaking began to ease at last, he spoke softly.

"You said—we have to burn it?" he asked.

She looked up at him with her tear-streaked face and nodded.

"Come on. We've got to get our clothes on. And we've got to get a fire going and cremate this thing before someone finds us here. I can just see trying to explain this to a Confederate officer!"

She rose swiftly, her terror and shock abating with the realization that if she didn't move, she could still cause great danger for Nathaniel. She dressed mechanically, and he did the same.

"Throw me that sheet!" he told her, and she did, and she turned her back to him while he picked up the head. A great sob shook her.

"Lenore."

She turned. He had the head wrapped. "That was not your husband, not my old friend," he told her.

She nodded, saw the pain and empathy in his eyes, and nodded harder. "I know that, Nathaniel. Matty told me that the only way the real Bruce could ever rest would be for this creature to die. I'm all right. I'm really all right."

He nodded, pulled out a blanket, and wrapped the other half of the body. He hefted the trunk over his shoulder, then strained to reach down for the wrapped head.

Lenore gritted her teeth and hurried forward to get it for him. He looked at her.

"It isn't Bruce."

She followed him down the stairs and listened carefully to his instructions so that she could help him get a good fire burning quickly. She gathered the driest kindling she could find, lots of it. He built three fires, then found a plank and some bricks so that he could stretch the torso out over the flame. Finally, he placed the head in the center, and struck matches to his boots to light the flames.

The kindling caught quickly. A massive blaze arose very fast. His eyes, blue, penetrating, met hers across the flame. She ran to him, and he set an arm around her. He kissed her deeply. She tried to pull away from him. "You've got to go!" she whispered frantically. "Rebs will be all over in a minute!"

"I know," he told her regretfully. "I love you, Lenore."

"Don't love me—" she began.

"But I do. And I want to hear that you love me."

"Nathaniel, no—" she began softly again. But she broke off

151

because he was suddenly spinning around, the soldier, ever wary, so quick to hear movement, so quick to draw his sword from its scabbard again.

He'd waited too late. A very worn and ragtag group of Reb soldiers had drawn around them.

Their leader, a lieutenant, dismounted from his horse and walked toward the blaze and the two of them. Lenore felt her heart leap. It was Jim Sawyer, tall, slim, a once-handsome young man with curling blond hair and lean features, a native son of Petersburg, a neighbor, a longtime friend. Maybe there was hope.

He looked at the blaze, and he looked at the two of them. He tipped his hat to Lenore, and nodded to Nathaniel, and she realized that Jim had known Nathaniel before the war, too. Of course, she thought. They had both been West Pointers, military men.

"Before I take you in, Colonel McKenna, I'd be willing to listen to an explanation for this."

Nathaniel lifted his hands. "I wish there was one I could give you, Jim. I really wish that there was."

Lenore escaped Nathaniel's arms and rushed to Jim. "It was the murderer, Jim, the—the demon."

To her relief, he stopped dead cold and stared into her eyes. "The murderer?"

"The boys! who were killed last night were killed by this—man," she said.

To her surprise, he smiled slowly. His eyes shot to Nathaniel's. "You managed to kill...the murderer."

Nathaniel nodded stiffly.

Lieutenant Jim Sawyer cocked his head, still grinning. "Boys!" he called out to the small mounted company behind him. "This fire needs to burn good. Real good. We've got to keep it going, all right?"

His men dutifully dismounted and came to the fire, poking the kindling to keep it alive, adding more to it. They all watched as it blazed.

"Thank you!" Lenore told Sawyer, staring at him curiously. "Thank you, you can't realize how many lives you might have saved by not stopping us. You—"

"I've known about this a long time," Jim Sawyer told her, and smiled. "And I've got some good friends out of New Orleans. The tales they can tell you on a winter's night are incredible, of course. A man or a demon, this fellow belonged in the fires of hell, he may as well start taking the heat here on earth."

Jim Sawyer turned and stared at Nathaniel and saluted. "You'd better go, sir. Quickly. While these men are busy."

Nathaniel nodded, and extended a hand to Sawyer. "Thank you," he said.

Sawyer nodded gravely. "Time might come real soon when you might be returning the favor for me."

Nathaniel lowered his eyes for a moment, then met Sawyer's stare once again. "It would be a privilege, sir, to help you in any time of distress."

Sawyer saluted once again and turned away. Nathaniel kept staring at Lenore. She came to him, clutching his hands. She looked into his eyes. "Go!" she urged him.

"As soon as you tell me you love me," he whispered.

And he meant it. He wouldn't move. "Damn you!" she said softly. "Damn you. I love you. Now go away! Please, God, go away!"

And so he turned. And while the fire burned, he became one with the darkness.

The terror was over.

And he was the enemy, once again.

Epilogue

Petersburg, Virginia June 1865

The war had taken its course. It had all been painfully very much as Nathaniel had said it would be. Petersburg could not withstand the brutal beating it had taken forever. Lee realized that he would have to abandon the city, and it fell.

And for the South, it was then a swift downhill slide to defeat. Lincoln came to Petersburg after the city fell. He was greeted by a tomb of quiet. Union soldiers marched through the streets.

Lenore waited, but she didn't see Nathaniel. He had been sent in pursuit of Lee's army, she heard.

There was no way then for the Army of Northern Virginia to hold Richmond.

Lincoln walked in the streets of the Southern capital.

Then, at the beginning of April, Lee came to the sad conclusion that there was nothing more that he could do. He was beaten. And so he surrendered his army to the Union General Grant, and he said farewell to his troops. There were still some Southerners on the field. But the war was, for the most part over.

Then Lincoln, who had claimed "Dixie" to be his favorite song, the tall gawky man who had fought so hard to keep his Union intact—and who just might have been, in the end, the true hope for a dignified peace—was assassinated at Ford's Theatre in Washington, D.C.

It was over. Truly over. The last men surrendered on the field. Andrew Johnson took over as president, trying to rule with a Northern Congress who had many members hell-bent on revenge.

And so Petersburg, like the rest of the South, began the long struggle up from her knees.

Dr. Tempe was still in town, and Lenore spent many long days with him. They were somewhat easier now. They saw expectant mothers and children with runny noses as well as men trying to adapt to peace with whatever injuries they had sustained.

She had been blessed in the end, she thought. Both her grandfather and her little brother had made it back in from the trenches. Teddy had turned fifteen at the end of May.

And Lenore had to admit that he was older than his years; the trenches had made him old. He had been left at an inn right in the center of the city by a dying friend, so he and their grandfather worked on righting the place, and she pitched in whenever she could. She had been with Doc Tempe a long time now. She wasn't ready to leave.

Matty was still with her, too, of course, and on a Friday late in June, when Lenore returned from her hours at the hospital, Matty had her a very hot bath waiting. Lenore sank into it, and closed her eyes. Defeat was bitter, but life was sweet, and she was learning to enjoy it again. If only there weren't the awful aching...

The loneliness that nothing could quite cure.

"You need to find that Yankee soldier of yours," Matty told her, laying out fresh clothing before the fire for her and eyeing her with her stern dark gaze. "Find him, and leave the past behind."

Lenore lifted a hand. "Can we ever really leave the past behind?"

Matty paused, folding a bright towel over her arms. "Some things, yes, we leave behind. Nightmares. Things that are lost to us, that we cannot bring back. Bruce Latham is gone, peacefully now. He was a good man. By God's grace, he rests in heaven."

Lenore watched Matty, and sighed. Matty was right. Some things, you had to let go. The war was over. She had almost convinced herself that her meeting with the shapeshifter that had stolen her husband's form had been a dream. That Nathaniel seizing her had been a dream...

That falling in love had been a dream...

Dreams were gone. Faded with the bugle calls that no longer sounded. She had to look to the future. Here, they needed to rebuild.

"I can't leave home," Lenore said softly. "I'm needed here."

Matty shrugged. "As you wish." She stopped speaking, staring out the window to the rear yard behind the kitchen. She frowned, then she looked at Lenore. "Maybe fate will give you a hand."

Lenore sat up, staring at the woman. "What—"

Matty was smiling then. "Indeed, missy! Sometimes, it seems, the good Lord will step in even for those who haven't the good horse sense to help themselves!"

"Matty—"

"Get dressed, Miss Lenore. You've got company."

Matty disappeared. Lenore leaped from the tub as fast as she could and stumbled into her clothing. She was struggling to do up the little buttons at the back of her dress when there was a knock at the kitchen door.

"Hold on!" she cried out. "Matty, where in the devil—"

But the door opened, swung in.

And he was standing there.

He looked different. He wasn't wearing his blue anymore. His face was drawn, certainly worn, and yet his eyes were beautifully bright. His hair was neatly trimmed, and he was wearing a handsome red vest, a very attractive dark frock coat, and fawn breeches. For a moment, she couldn't believe that he was standing there.

"Nathaniel?" she whispered.

He strode into the kitchen, looked from the bath to her flushed face, and smiled. Before she could move, he had come to her. Hands on her shoulders, he swung her around and started doing up her tiny buttons.

"Seems I was always trying to undo these things when I was with you before," he said softly. "But then, I understand that I'll have to be going through your grandfather and a very grown-up brother if I want to have things my way, so I guess I'd better fight against instinct and make sure this dress is on you instead of off you."

The buttons were done. She swung around, staring at him.

"Nathaniel—"

He dropped to a knee. "Lenore, marry me."

"Nathaniel, I can't leave Petersburg—"

"Then I shall move into it."

"The people will hate you—"

"They'll learn to love me. That is, if you do." One of his dark brows arched over his eye. "You do love me. You told me that you did, that night before the fire."

She nodded. She dragged him to his feet. "Nathaniel—"

His turn. He drew her into his arms. Kissed her.

Tasted her lips, savored them, kissed her more and more deeply.

"Marry me?" he whispered at last.

"You'll really stay here?" she asked him incredulously.

He nodded. "The war is over. Our demons are all laid to rest. I love you, Lenore."

She threw her arms around him.

"Say it!" he whispered.

She leaned back and met his eyes. "I love you, Nathaniel. With all my heart. Yes! Yes, I'll marry you!"

Once again, his lips touched hers.

Exhilaration filled her. Happiness, excitement.

Indeed, she loved him.

And he was right.

Their demons were all laid to rest...

AND I WILL LOVE YOU FOREVER

Prologue

Glenraven
Isle of the Angels
The Land of the Scotia
The Year of Our Lord 897

The massive wooden door to her room in the highest corner of
the keep was suddenly slammed open and he stood there, the breadth
of his shoulders nearly blocking all light from entering. Yet the light
glittered behind him. It fell upon his shoulders, making them bronze,
making the ripple of muscles on his arms all the more apparent. It fell
upon his hair, which was blond like the sun, blazing with hints of red.

The day was not so warm, yet he was not heavily clad for the
battle he had fought. Leggings barely covered the length of his thighs;
a sleeveless tunic, trimmed in fur, fell to his hip.

His sword, held ever ready at his side, dripped with blood.

His eyes, bluer than the deepest sea and colder than the ice of
winter, fell upon her own.

And he smiled.

"The day has been won," he said simply. "I have won it."

Fire seemed to dance upon her. Little sparks of searing fire
darted along her spine, sweeping up and down. Her heart began to

pound, and she met the blue triumph in his eyes.

Indeed, he had come this far. He had won the day.

"I have won the prize, lady," he added softly. "And the prize is you."

She could scarcely breathe. As battle had waged here between the various factions, as she had seen the contenders time and time again—as she had fought them off!—she had felt that curious sizzle in her heart and blood and body whenever their paths had crossed. Aye, they were enemies, for he was of the heathen scourge who had sailed across the seas, and she had been born here, on the very bed that stood between them. Before, they had fought their battles with words.

And now they would fight with their fists. She *had* to fight him! She could not give up without a battle herself, for she was the lady here, and they called her the princess of the Isle of the Angels. "Nay, my lord! I am not a prize! And you have won nothing, for you've not won me!"

His blue eyes looked angry. "Brave talk, my princess!" And he gave her a deep, mocking bow. "But indeed, you are the prize, and you are won. And this very night, you will be my bride."

"Never!" she promised fervently.

"I am the conqueror, lady. And now the king of all that I see."

"Then I shall blind you, and you will see nothing."

"Too late, lady. For I have seen you. And you are mine. Aye, mine. Now. Tonight."

The door closed behind him with a heavy slam, kicked shut by his foot.

"Don't you dare think to touch me! I will call upon what men I have—"

"I dare anything, lady. And any man knows that to disturb me now would mean his death. Would you still call upon your men, lady?"

She held still. Dear God, she'd have no more men die over this isle!

The cold steel of his sword clattered upon the floor.

And he strode into the room.

She could not let him touch her. Reaching wildly, she found the earthenware water pitcher and hurled it across the room. He ducked, and it crashed over his head, and suddenly his laughter filled the room. It was deep, rich and husky, and it caused the cascade of fire to leap within her again. He came toward her once more, his strides incredibly long. She leaped on top of the bed, a mattress of down on tight-wound ropes, and tried to escape by way of the other side.

It was not possible to do so. His hands closed around her arm. She cried out, swinging hard with her free hand to strike him, to free herself. Her fingers swept across his ruggedly handsome jawline, touching the red and gold fire of his beard, but doing little damage. She lashed out frantically then, trying to strike him again. She heard the sound as her hand at last caught his cheek with a slap which reverberated in the stillness that was only softened by the rush of their breath.

His eyes narrowed. None dared strike this great Northern jarl in the face. No man, ever, had done so.

And now she...

Thunder crossed his brow. Thunder that seemed to shake the heavens; thunder and darkness. There was a great trembling, and it was seconds before she realized that it came from her heart.

"Nay!" she cried, for his hand was raised against her, and she was suddenly afraid.

Afraid...

For he towered over her. His thighs were twice the size of her own, taut, rippled, looking stronger than oak. And his shoulders, laden with scars, were so hard, rippling bronze once again as she stared down at him, as still as the air around them for split seconds as her eyes locked with his, the green of the earth locked with the blue of the sky and the sea...

"Now, my lady!" he repeated.

And even as she stood poised to flee on the bed, she shrieked out again, for he had jerked her arm and she was falling, falling on the softness of the down bedding. She screamed again as he fell on her, for once he was over her, there could be no escape. Arms of steel embraced her like the bars of a prison. Thighs of rippling, fevered muscle locked her in more securely than any walls of earth or wood or stone.

"Nay!" she shrieked again, her head tossing from side to side. "I am the trueborn lady here, and you, sir, are base and vile, a heathen cast upon the sea—"

"An adventurer, my lady, indeed," he responded, his thumb and fingers pinning her jaw still so that her eyes were forced to his once again. "Base, lady? Never. I am the son of a grandson of a great jarl, and born not a morning's swim distance from this place. Someone was destined to take this isle. Someone was destined to hold it. That someone, lady, is me!"

"The isle is mine—"

"But you, lady, are mine, spread now beneath me, and nothing more is fact," he said simply. Then, staring down at her, he smiled slowly.

It was a wicked smile. Full, sensual lips beneath the vivid gold of his beard drew back to display white, perfect teeth. Teeth as strong as the man; handsome, compelling. Fire flashed in his eyes. Blue fire. Tempting, searing fire.

Then his hand was at her breast, ruthlessly ripping the beautiful blue linen of her garment.

"Oh!" she cried out, and she struggled again, furious, terrified...

Excited.

"Nay..."

She tried furiously to strike him again. His lingers wound around her wrists. His hands joined together, and he held both of hers with one of his.

Then his knuckles moved slowly, sensually over her cheek. His eyes burned into hers, taunting her. And he lowered the mane of his blond hair slowly against her. His mouth closed over one of the full, tempting breasts he had just bared to his pleasure.

She shrieked out again, writhing madly to free herself.

The heat of his laughter touched her flesh where his kiss had just been. His tongue moved over the delicate bud of her breast. The feel of it hit her mercilessly. She wanted to hate him. She wanted to fight him unto death...

She wanted to still the fever that he created. Oh, to her horror, she wanted him to find her lips, to kiss them, to touch her.

"I will fight you forever!" she swore to him passionately, tears of fear and fury and frustration threatening to spill from her eyes.

"Fight me, lady, but fight me well." And then his lips did find hers. They found them pitilessly, and with no mercy. They swept down on them, full, hot, openmouthed, and demanding. Beneath the onslaught, her mouth parted; she felt the searing heat and fire of his mouth, of his touch, as his tongue entered into her mouth, deep into her mouth Oh, so suggestively into her mouth. Sweeping, warming, stirring...

And somehow warning her that he would enter her. As ruthlessly and as completely.

She tried to toss her head. She tried to fight the kiss. His free hand held her, forced her to remain. His tongue grew more gentle, more cajoling. More lulling. And then he was still.

And she was suddenly motionless herself. Waiting. Her eyes half closed, her body... alive.

Then she opened her eyes once again, and saw his. Saw the triumph within them.

He had won again...

"Nay!" she screamed in outrage.

But it was too late. Oh, far too late.

For every warning, every promise, was made good. Ere she could begin to move, he shifted, grasping her slender limbs. She fought, but no mercy was asked, and none was given.

She did not cry out again. His eyes caught hers, and his powerful body irrevocably parted her legs. She felt the brazen touch of his fingers, moving lower over her belly.

Then she felt the pain, and she screamed.

"Nay, lady, nay..." It was he who protested then. The sweetness, the husky fever and the moist warmth of his whisper against the sensitive area of her earlobe and her throat. His lips touched her flesh again and again. His whisper continued. Then his mouth found hers and caressed and seduced it, his tongue plunging into her slowly and erotically.

Like the great movement of his body, like the rhythm of his desire. He held her first in his arms, letting her know him, letting her body embrace and accept his own. Then he was slow. Filling her until she thought she would split, until she was certain she would die, until she could bear it no longer...

Then slowly, so slowly, he would near be gone. Until he came again. Deeper and deeper, wedging his way into her body. Into her soul. Into her life. Everlasting.

Then suddenly it seemed that the storm within him broke. He cried out himself, some primitive cry of his ancient, heathen gods. Clouds and thunder seemed to cascade upon them. He moved with fierce speed, engulfing her in his great rhythm. The pain was gone, for it could not combat the speed. They might have ridden a dragon ship over a black and tempestuous sea. It did not matter, for his arms held her. Indeed, she no longer felt the pain.

Just the heat. A wave of it. Rippling down on her. Dancing along her back. Entering into the center of her, to that very secret place when his body entered hers, reached up, and touched...

The storm exploded, into the heavens, into the fall of the night. It seemed to sweep over her and through her. He shuddered above her, fiercely.

He rose above her, his captured prize. His princess.

His love.

For, aye, he loved her. Loved her more passionately than he had ever loved any land, coveted her more than he had ever imagined coveting a woman.

They had been enemies afar.

But now...

She would be his bride. He had won the land. He had fought his rivals, and he had won. And he would have his love.

He smiled and looked down on her. Her eyes were halfway closed. There was the most curious curve to her lips.

For she loved him, too. He was sure of it. She'd had to fight that last battle. She'd had no choice.

But now...

"Now, lady, you are mine," he told her.

By all the gods, she was beautiful. A wealth of blonde hair spilled around her on the linens and furs that covered the bed. Her face was pure and beautiful like alabaster. Her high cheekbones were ivory and pink, her nose was fine and straight and perfect. Her lips, swollen now from the force of his kiss, were still the color of a summer rose, while the rich wealth of lashes that half covered her eyes were honey dark. Her brows, delicately arched and fine, were that same deep color despite the golden-blond array of her hair.

Her eyes...

They opened now to his. Ah, but they were green! Greener than gems, greener than the earth! Greener, deeper, more beautiful than any shade or hue of life.

Color stained her cheeks. A soft, lovely blush. "I am lady here!" she vowed to him. But her voice was husky and sweet. "I will fight you—"

"And I will love you, my lady, forever." He smoothed back her hair. "Forever, and ever, and ever."

Her lips trembled.

"But you cannot—"

He touched his finger to her lips, then softly stroked the length of her beautiful hair. "I have watched, and we have battled, and I have waited. And as I waited, I dreamed of a day like today. Of touching you. Of kissing you. Of feeling your fair body entwined with mine. Of laying my hand against your breast. I am the man meant to have you, my love, and the time has come. Would you have preferred that dark lord, Egan, or the Dane, Radwald? Nay, lady, I see your smile. I think not. Indeed, I come from the heathens, far across the seas. But, lady, I love this island, as I love you. And come what may, I will have you both. And heathen though they call me, I will love you, and honor you, and cherish you, love, from this day forward."

She touched his cheek in wonder. The fierce, sweet fire tore through her once again.

"Can it be true?" she asked him. "Will you really love me so?"

"Aye!" he vowed fiercely. He held her close to his heart. "Aye, I will love you. Forever." He laid his cheek against her breast. "Forever. No storm shall ever sway me, no man, no woman, no beast or creature of any heaven or any hell shall stop me. Indeed, not even death shall sway me. I do love you. And I will love you forever."

Her fingers curled around his. She smiled the rose-sweet smile that truly captured his heart.

"Forever," she agreed softly.

And forever it would be.

Chapter 1

The Fortress Glenraven Isle of the Angels 1746, after Culloden

It was her birthright, but she had not wanted to come here.

It was beautiful, men said, but surely that was their interpretation of beauty, for to Marina, this was not beauty.

This was darkness, this was foreboding—rugged and sparse. This was bare rock and jutting cliff. Marina was certain that if she could fly, and look down, the Isle of the Angels would appear like one great ragged rock, tossed down by an even craggier coastline.

Sometimes, when the tide was low, a tall man—or a mounted man—could ford the distance from the island to the shore. But sometimes, when the winds whipped and storms came, the sea between the island and the coast became deep and wild, drowning the unwary, clutching them up and swallowing them whole. Ships were sometimes fooled, and captains were caught on the cliff and rocks today, just as they had been since the Scotia tribes had first come from Ireland to settle this coastline, giving the country its name.

Looking up at the solid rock wall of the island, Marina shivered. The Isle of the Angels had become home to well over five thousand men, women, and children. They raised their surefooted sheep here. They kept fields of wheat and corn in the expanses of land made safe from the sea by the great stretches of rocks that rose to the sky. It was her home. They were her people.

But she hadn't wanted to return.

"You must come and reside in the palace," her cousin Kevin had written. "Uncle Fraser is dead in the war with the German, and all here is dependent on you. I am still in control of our forces, and of our family, but as you are the MacCannan in truth, you must now come home. God bless us, Marina, but they've taken the best of the Highlands, they've cut us down and sliced off our heads. They've stripped us of our rights to our tartans and our colors, and they seek to strip us of our honor. We can hold this place. If only we've the colors to rally round. Come to the palace..."

He had called the family castle a palace.

Now, that stretched anyone's imagination. And, as usual, he had referred to King George as "the German." Well, that was much the way he was thought of here, for right or wrong. No matter what the religious differences, the Highlanders still looked to the Stuart line as the true kings of Scotland and England. A Stuart hadn't ruled since Queen Anne died in 1715, when the very Protestant English government had ignored James, the Catholic son of Anne's father, the deposed James II, and sent across the sea to the House of Hanover for another great-grandchild of James I—George. The first Hanoverian king had never bothered to speak the English language, but to a nation where the reformation of the church had been strong and firm, the idea of a Catholic—and a foundling!—on the throne had been unacceptable. Those who supported the Papist James had taken on a title for the Latin of his name. They were Jacobites.

And continually, so it seemed to Marina, they lost.

James was no longer for the crown—it was his son, Charles, the Young Pretender, as the English called him, who had fought at Culloden Field. In the Highlands, they called him Bonnie Prince Charlie. He was a charming man—Marina knew him well— dedicated, intelligent, and handsome. But his quest had brought great grief to many, and for that, Marina was heartily sorry.

Just as she had been sorry to leave France.

There had been no hopeless causes in Paris, no sheer rock cliffs to rise above the sea—and no thousands of clan members to shield from the wrath of the English. Two years ago, her Uncle Fraser had determined that she must be sent to Paris while the battles raged here. She had been weary of the constant tug between those supporting the Protestant causes and those championing the handsome young prince. She had been weary of the battle cries. Were any men more argumentative than the Highlanders? More determined to wage battle after battle?

But she was back. She had been ordered home by her family, and so she was here. Watching the rising stone appear closer and closer as her dinghy from the mainland neared the shore, Marina bit lightly on her lower lip. She would not let Kevin and Darrin have the best of her, she swore it. As Kevin had written to her, she was the MacCannan now. They were not going to press her into any action that she did not deem fit.

She did not want to be here...

But even as the dinghy came closer and closer, sliding smoothly through the shallow water at the practiced command of a Glenraven oarsman, she felt a trembling, as if a shivering had begun in her heart. It echoed throughout her limbs with a hum, and to her surprise, she felt a growing sense of excitement.

Yes, she was home.

She loved the sheer and brutal rise of rock—

She hated it!

No, rebel as she might, this was her home. She loved the fields on the spit of rock, and she loved the wind when it came. She loved the westwardly view out to the seemingly endless Irish Sea, and she loved to turn her eyes to the east, the craggy rise of the Scottish mainland.

"We're nearin' shore, me lady," Howard, the oarsman, informed her cheerily. "I kin see yer cousin, Sir Kevin, awaiting ye there. And the clan, lady, see, there! One by one, they be coming to the dockside, all to pay ye tribute!"

Indeed, they were coming. Men, women, and children, flocking down to the docks. A cheer had rung out, and people waved, from the sheepherders in their simple wool garments to the merchants and soldiers with their more fashionable wives. Yet even the women with their embroidered bodices and boned skirts were oft wearing some piece of their colors, a scarf in a plaid, a swatch of wool across a chest here or there, a band for a hat.

And then, of course, there was Kevin.

"See, lady, there be your cousin, in the midst of them."

"Aye, I see him," Marina said. And she lifted her hand, gesturing toward her tall, proud cousin. *Kevin, ye knave!* she thought, feeling a sinking in her heart. For more so than any man or woman there, he was dressed still in his colors, kilted in the MacCannan plaid of heavy blues and greens and cross weaves of brilliant red. He wore a white ruffled shirt as well and a handsome black frock coat. He was dressed in formal wear to greet her, she saw, but she knew him well, and knew that he would ride into battle much the same.

We press our luck with the German king! she thought.

"Marina!"

The small dinghy thrust hard against the shore. Marina prepared to step carefully from the dinghy to the dock, but Howard quickly rose and handed her over from boat to shore.

As she stepped on the wooden dock, a chill suddenly swept through her, hard and fierce. She looked up. Far up. The sun was nearly out this day, breaking through the clouds. She stared up to the tower, to the oldest section of the fortress. It was surrounded by the cliff that formed a natural barrier to the island, but the structure itself had been crafted of hardwood hundreds of years ago. The very first laird of the isle had begun its construction, holding tenaciously to his little kingdom with it.

A high, narrow window looked out from it to the sea below, to the spot where she now stood.

And someone was watching her. She was certain that someone was watching her.

She raised her hands, trying to shield her eyes from the uncanny touch of sunlight that had suddenly seemed to stream down on her.

"What is it, lady?" Howard asked her.

"Why, I think—I think someone is watching me."

"Hundreds are watching ye, lass."

She shook her head. "Nay, Howard. From up there—"

Howard shrugged, releasing her hand as he watched Kevin coming toward her. "A servant perhaps, but not likely, Lady Marina, for that be the laird's room—rather, the lady's room now, eh? Kevin will have seen that it be set for yer arrival. Perhaps the sun, playing tricks..."

Nay, someone was watching her...

She still felt the curious warmth, the heat that sailed down her spine. Did she see... something? Nay, nor could she give it any more thought, for cheers and waves were going up. "'Tis the MacCannan, Lady Marina, home at last!" came a cry.

Then there was a shrieking sound, one she hadn't heard in a long time, one that truly wrapped around her heart.

The pipers were playing. Playing a tune to welcome the MacCannan back to her home.

Marina smiled and waved broadly to the players. *Jesu!* she thought. For those men, too, were proudly dressed in their kilts, and if she had heard right, the pipes had been outlawed along with the colors.

Ah, but the Highlanders had never felt themselves bound to other men's rules. They had reigned supreme in their rugged hills and cliffs too long. The war that they really understood was the battle waged between clans.

But we must take care, for this is a different world, and this German king a hard man! she thought. And she raised her chin, for she must lead them to fight, if the English thought that they could take a single man from the MacCannan clan a prisoner. Yet if peace could be met by lip service, then she would agree that the colors must be banned.

The men would wear them when they chose, the moment the English threat was gone.

"Marina!"

Even as Howard released her and she waved gaily to her people, Marina was lifted from her feet, swept into her cousin's arms.

"You've come!" he announced with pleasure.

"You summoned me," she reminded him.

He smiled, shaking his head, a man with hazel eyes when hers were green, with dark blond hair when her own was a startling, sun-drenched blond. He reached down, grabbing a handful of sandy shoreline and rock. Then he took her delicate hand and transferred the earth to it.

"This summoned you. Our home. Our land."

"This is cold sand," she said lightly. But the warmth had begun to sweep through her again, the excitement. Yes, this was home. She did love it, and she would fight for it' Like every fool man here, she would risk her head on a block to salvage it—and their right to their own way of life.

Kevin waved a hand in the air, dismissing her words. He grinned broadly at her, then lifted her high and spun her around again. "Ah, Marina, 'tis glad I am to have ye home once again! And home safe through the lines. Walk with me to the fortress. We have the closest lads coming to dinner in yer honor, cousin, but ye'll have a minute to wash and change, if ye so wish." His whisper moved nearer her ear. "Look around ye, Marina. Feel them! They've been waitin'. Waitin' fer the true MacCannan to lead them onward! Feel the love they bear ye!"

She felt breathless, unequal to the task. She had come home from France where the people had looked upon the plight of the Jacobites with some fair distance, though many French soldiers had risen to fight with the displaced prince. The French and the Scots had often been careful allies against the English.

But they could see, as the Highlanders could not, that the

English were completely and determinedly set on their German king. There would be no mighty revolution within the English kingdom itself.

George was there to stay. Marina was certainly sorry for Charles, but the Bonnie Prince was doomed to wander his days away from foreign court to foreign court.

"My lady!" cries went up. Kevin smiled to her and offered her his arm. She took it while servants scrambled behind her to bring her bags.

They walked through the crowds. Children rushed forward to touch her skirts. The men jockeyed to offer her the deepest bows; the ladies strove to touch her hand. Aye, it was home, Marina thought. She spoke to Conar, the blacksmith who had always cared for her ponies, and she laughed, hugging the baker's fat wife, the woman who had sneaked her marzipan candies when she was a child. There was Gunther—named for a distant, Viking relative—aging now, but once the head of her father's guard. There were Elizabeth and Joan, her closest childhood friends, and Dame Margaret, her tutor. She hugged them and swirled around again to wave to the others. Exhilaration filled her. The wind suddenly picked up, wild and cold against her cheeks. Yes, she was home!

She came at last through the crowd to the entrance to Fortress Glenraven. Built of brick, continually mended and altered through the centuries, it now had a gothic appeal, with tall slender spires and gargoyles, some handsome, some hideous, to stare down at her. Men-at-arms awaited at the entrance, all bowing to her as she came through the large doorways. She saluted in return and paused on the last steps to turn around. She addressed the people with a strong voice that carried well to all of them.

"My dear friends, relatives, and all who live beneath the banner of the clan MacCannan, thank you for this welcome. Thank you for your loyalty to our island, and for your faith in me. We will survive this storm, as we have survived those storms that came in years past!"

A vast cheering went up. It was wonderful. The sun touched her face, her people believed in her.

She had not wanted to come...

Because she had known. Known that she belonged here. Known that she was the MacCannan now, and that she was letting herself in for danger and tempest. But she could not shirk the duty. It was hers.

Suddenly, again, she had the curious sensation that she was being watched.

How very strange. Of course she was being watched. People were standing before her, cheering her on, in the hundreds.

Nay...

Someone was watching her from afar. She could almost feel the heartbeat, almost feel the danger.

"Marina, come in now. I'll see ye to the lady's chamber, and Peg will see to yer needs, and then ye'll come down to dinner and a meeting with the chieftains."

And so he escorted her in.

As Kevin had promised, Peg was there to greet her, bobbing a quick curtsy and, to Marina's dismay, catching up Marina's hem to kiss it almost reverently. "Ye're home, m'lady, home!" Peg told her.

"Indeed, yes," Marina said, lifting Peg up by the shoulders. She was a thin, pretty woman, with salt-and-pepper hair and bright, light blue eyes. Peg had been with her since Marina had been a little girl, and Marina hugged her gently. "I've missed you, Peg," she said sweetly. "Please, quit acting as if I'm royalty."

"Ah, but ye are the MacCannan now, lass," Peg whispered. "Near enough to royalty here."

Marina refrained from mentioning that true royalty might soon be seeking the heads of their finest young men. "Come up with me, Peg, tell me about your family. I must wash off some of the dust from travel and gather my wits about me for this evening." She grinned engagingly at her cousin and continued, "Kevin will have the lesser chieftains chewing my ears off with their proposals and complaints, and I must be ready for them."

"That you must," Kevin agreed.

Peg nodded, "Aye, lass, 'twill be a long night."

Peg had already seen to it that she would be ready for the night. The big wooden hip tub that sat between the wardrobes in the great tower master room had been filled with steaming water. Sweet-smelling salts—French salts—had been left for her. The bath was the first thing that Marina saw when she entered the chamber. After she expressed her appreciation, she paused to look around.

The master's chamber, the room for the MacCannan. Until her uncle's death at Culloden, he had resided here.

Marina's father, the second eldest of the previous generation, had been killed in a minor skirmish with the troops of George I. As their Uncle Fraser had left behind no children, Marina came next in line for the inheritance, for Kevin's father had been the third and last of the sons of the generation. He had died in a border feud. Their grandfather had been killed at the uprising of 1715.

It was a pity that Kevin had not been next in line, Marina thought, for he was a fine young man and would have done well as Laird Glenraven. But the people here were incredibly strict about tradition, and since the days of Mary, queen of Scots—no matter how it might be seen that she had failed as queen—the MacCannans had followed the direct lineage for their leader, be the new MacCannan a laird or a lady.

So it was her chamber now. "And perhaps it is for the best," she murmured softly. She would not face any of the British commanders in battle. When it came time to negotiate, she might stand in better stead.

She gazed around the huge room. When the first laird had claimed this land, his men had often gathered here to plan their battle strategies. There had been nothing but a rope bed against the far wall, and mats for all the lesser chieftains. And there had been the windows. The circular chamber was surrounded by windows, so that the laird might see every angle of attack.

The windows remained. The mats were gone. A handsome Tudor-style bed, big and comfortable with massive posts and a high flat canopy, was positioned between two of the windows. The dressing section was set on a dais. A large full-length mirror stood to the left of the stairway, and numerous trunks and a very handsome dressing table accompanied the wardrobes. It was a beautiful chamber, no matter how old—and drafty upon occasion!—it might be. It was beautiful because, at those rare times when the MacCannans were not embroiled in some war or another, the windows looked upon scenes of startling, wild magnificence, the sea in all its splendor, and the rugged, wave-slashed cliffs of the mainland far beyond.

"Indeed, I am home," she said softly.

"What, lass?"

She shook her head. "Ah, for that bath!"

Peg helped her with her fashionable French skirts and bodice, corset and petticoat. Down to her silk stockings and soft chemise,

Marina sat on a small chair to peel the stockings from her calves. A curious sensation stirred within her once again, that sensation of being watched. She looked around uneasily, wondering if things were not even worse than she had imagined, if some nearby clan had not chosen the English side of the issue and come to spy on her.

Here, in her own chamber!

Outraged, Marina rose and looked around the room. Peg, carefully laying out a fresh gown from the traveling trunks that had been delivered, looked over to her, startled.

"What is it?"

Pressing a finger to her lips, she threw open the door to one of the wardrobes. Nothing greeted her but rows and rows of the family plaid, white ruffled shirts that had been her uncle's, and a fine array of gentlemen's frock coats and boots.

"There is someone—watching me!" she whispered.

"Nay, lady!" Peg protested. "Ah, Marina, do ye think yer cousin Kevin would allow fer ye to come to danger? Nay, lass, the wolfhounds were brought here; I set the flowers on the stand meself. There is none to harm ye here!"

Marina had to agree with her. Ruefully, she smiled. "It must be the travel."

"It must be the king's reckoning," Peg muttered. "'Tis said he's sworn to behead the whole of Scotland if he don't have what he wants from it."

Maybe that was it, Marina thought. Indeed, the days that loomed before her were threatening ones.

She cast aside her chemise and stepped into the tub. The heat of the water seemed to sink deliciously into her body. She had not realized just how chilled she had been from the boat trip across the water. Maybe it was the cold that had given her the shivers.

"Ah, I could die here in delight," she said softly.

"Nay, Marina, don't say such things!"

"You've just assured me that there are no king's men awaiting me in the wardrobe!" Marina said, laughing. "It is wonderful, Peg, the water. I could lie here forever, that is all I meant."

Peg sighed softly. "I'll bring you tea here, then, lass? Some hot, sweet tea, laden with cream and sugar. That will warm ye more."

"I'd love it," Marina assured her.

Peg left her. She leaned her head back against the wooden rim of the tub, her hair creating a pillow for her. She closed her eyes. The steam rose all around her like a gentle, encompassing blanket.

It was a wonderful, comfortable feeling. She tried to luxuriate in it. She tried to forget that Lord William Widager was still in the Highlands, seeking out the troops who had fled Culloden, seeking to cut them down, slay them all, or bring them to London to rot in the Tower and die at the whim of the headsman's axe.

"Tea, lass, is at your side."

She dimly heard the words. "Thank you," she told Peg softly. What could she do?

They would have to fight again. If not, as Kevin had written her so urgently, she would be forced to turn over Kevin as well as the lesser chieftains. Oh, God...

If they could not hold the island...

But we will hold the island...

She almost started, for it seemed that she had been answered in the softest whisper. It wasn't Peg, she knew.

It was in her own mind.

She sighed softly, leaning forward, burying her face in her warm, wet hands. Her hair cascaded damp around her shoulders. Then she felt it lifted.

Felt a touch on her flesh, a gentle but firm touch on her shoulders, kneading against them. Ah, the touch was both strong and tender, easing away the little aches. She kept her eyes closed. Peg was so good. So quiet and kind a servant. So talented! Ah... it was good.

Lean back...

It was a whisper. A whisper in her mind. Peg hadn't spoken.

Nay, this whisper was...

Husky. Masculine. Seductive.

I am losing my mind! she thought briefly.

Lean back, it said, yet she felt as if she were floating. Ah, it was the mist, and the comfort, in a world of tumult.

Illora...

She could have sworn that she heard the whisper then again, in a curious gathering of syllables. She hadn't the strength to raise her head, though. The feel of her massage was too compelling. Too sweet to her weary heart and soul. Too...

Tender. Seductive. The fingers moving over her flesh with such expertise. Like a masculine touch, not Peg's at all. Sensitive, sensual,

175

sweeping over her nakedness...

It was suddenly gone. She felt bereft, cold.

And startled.

"Peg?"

Her door opened and closed. "Ah, sorry it is, m'lady, but I went down fer a brick to be warmed by the fire fer yer bed tonight, lass. I didna mean to be gone so long."

Marina started violently. "You haven't been here?"

Poor Peg seemed very concerned. "Nay, I'm sorry, I didna mean to distress—"

"Someone was here!"

Peg shook her head. "Marina, by the cross, I swear to ye, lass, none has come here. I left young Thomas at the door, knowin' how ye were worried. Now, young Thomas be a scamp of a boy, but a lad more loyal to the MacCannan clan, I cannot imagine."

Marina took one look at Peg's pale but passionate eyes.

No one had disturbed her here.

Then...

Had she dreamed it all? Had she been far more exhausted than she thought?

The water suddenly seemed to go cold. Icy cold. A shivering set into her.

"Ah, lass, I'll bring yer bath sheet," Peg cried, and she hurried to Marina, ready to wrap the large linen sheet around her. Her teeth nearly chattering, Marina gladly stepped from the tub, thanked Peg, and hurried over by the fire, kneeling down beside it.

"M'lady, are ye all right?"

She nodded slowly. Nay, she was not all right. She was weary, she was worried...

She was losing her mind.

Ah! This was home.

"I am the MacCannan," she whispered softly to herself.

"Lady—"

"Peg, I am still Marina. Just Marina. Please, call me by my name."

"Aye, then, lass, if that's what ye wish."

"It's what I wish," she said. She turned and smiled at Peg. "And I'm really all right. I need some privacy, though, if you don't mind. A little time for myself."

Peg nodded, but she still seemed worried, as if Marina had gone to France and become quite daft.

Well, maybe she had.

"Young Thomas will stay just beyond the door, should ye need him."

"Thank you," Marina said.

Peg left her. She laid her head down on one of the needlepoint chairs that faced the fire. "I am the MacCannan. I, in truth, alone."

She closed her eyes. She was weary. She felt she was ready to doze even as she closed her eyes.

She did sleep, she thought. Yet if she slept, could she still think?

But she must have slept. Long, powerful fingers touched her hair. Cradled her head.

Nay, not alone, lass. Never alone. Illora...

She could see him, coming toward her. He was tall. Taller than the sun in the sky. He was like the sun, for his hair seemed to be a blaze of golden fire, and likewise his beard. And his eyes... they were brilliant blue, a startling blue, the deepest shade of blue that she had ever seen. He walked with long, arrogant strides, as well he might, for his shoulders were broader than those of any warrior she knew, his limbs were longer, muscled like oak. He came toward her, walking through fog and mist...

A log cracked in the fire.

With a violent start, Marina awakened.

There was no one with her. No one striding toward her. She leaped to her feet and swirled around.

And still, she spoke aloud to calm her own fears.

"I am the MacCannan. I—alone!"

Her only answer now was the lonely wailing of the wind beyond the fortress walls.

She was, indeed, alone.

Chapter 2

They were all arrayed before her at the grand dining table in the great hall.

Like the tower bedchamber, the great hall had been there since the first crude earthworks of a castle had begun. Then, the flooring had been dirt, the table had been rough-hewn oak, and the surrounding chairs had been stiff and graceless.

And no matter how the English—and perhaps even some of the city dwellers of Scotland—liked to mock the Highlanders, they had come far from those days. The laird's table in the great hall now was a masterpiece of polished mahogany. The twenty-two chairs that surrounded it were made of the same wood, yet all seated and backed with hunting scenes in a fine needlepoint. Great, plush chairs, covered in deep purple velvet, were arrayed before the fire, and the buffets and cabinets that held the family plate and silver were polished to a high and beautiful shine. Hospitality was prized here as greatly as it was across the sea in Ireland, perhaps because the people had been emigrating over the centuries from Ireland to these outward isles, bringing the name Scotia along with them very early in Scotland's recorded history.

As she looked at the lesser chieftains seated down the length of the table, she was reminded of the many peoples who had come here to form the devoted and loyal natives of the Isle of the Angels. There were Lairds Cunard, Gunnar, and Ericson—proof of the Viking sweep of the island. Lairds deMontfort, Montpasse, and Trieste gave credence to the fact that some Normans had decided to travel forth from England, and brave the rugged mountains and coastline. There were seven men at the table carrying the family name, seven fine Sirs MacCannan, her cousin Kevin among them, then her second and third cousins, Jamie, Ian, Geoffrey, Gavin, Angus, and Magnus. The six other chieftains at the table were still members of clan MacCannan, though they bore other family names, for the island was their home, their forefathers having come to settle here by choice. Each gave his sworn loyalty to the MacCannan, and sitting at the table as all the great warlords had done before her, Marina felt overwhelmed.

Uncle Fraser had had no right to go and get himself killed, she thought wearily. Then a deep-seated pain seemed to sweep through her, for she had loved Fraser MacCannan. He had been a father to her since her own had died, she had been bounced on his knee, and he had even told her wonderful fairy tales many a night to get her to sleep.

But maybe he hadn't planned on dying himself. He had prepared her to manage a household, and he had seen to it that she spoke French and Latin and Spanish as well as English and Gaelic, the last well enough to deal with any Scottish or Irish dialect. He had seen to it that she could play the piano, the harp, and the violin, and that she could sing like a lark. He had taught her to dance with the wildest of the Highlanders, and with the most gracious gentlemen of Europe.

He hadn't prepared her for this—this line of men staring down at her, awaiting her words for their own salvation.

Kevin would have been the better leader, she thought.

But even as dinner was served, Angus, second in command now, beneath Kevin, stood and addressed her. "As ye are well aware, Marina, we of clan MacCannan chose to fight for the Bonnie Prince, our Laird Charles, now a-running in sad and bitter defeat. The English gave no quarter then, chasing after the men who left the battlefield, weary and wounded and sore of heart. They still seek us out for vengeance's sake, and their orders are no quarter, no mercy. But we've a stronghold here at Fortress Glenraven. And though they seek the blood of the chieftains who led our men against them, no MacCannan can turn over his men to the likes of the English horde."

"We'll fight, of course," Marina said. "But are we strong enough to do so?"

Angus was much older than Kevin, silver-haired, gray-eyed, dignified—a survivor. He had fought during the uprising of 1715 and lived to tell of it.

"We're strong," he said. He gazed down at Kevin, who shrugged. "We've a few marriage offers on the table to make us stronger."

"What?" Marina said, pausing with her wineglass halfway to her lips.

Angus cleared his throat. "Marriage offers, my lady." He rushed on. "The MacNamara of Castle Cleough has asked for ye. He's a mighty host of forces beneath him, and he'd then be honor-bound to fight fer our cause."

Marina sat there in silence. The MacNamara of Castle Cleough was also nearing sixty if he was a day.

"Go on," she said.

"Aye. Then there's Geoffrey Cameron, laird of Huntington. He's made it known that he's willing to battle the MacNamara fer yer hand."

"For the island," Marina corrected sharply. Lord! Geoffrey was not old. Some even said that he was handsome with his fire-red hair and dark eyes. Perhaps he was handsome. He also had a reputation for cruelty that had spread far abroad. Even in France, the young women had heard that his first wife had died mysteriously, yet it was suspected that the mysterious cause had been Geoffrey himself.

"Why not the English lord general, my fine counselors?" she demanded lightly, her bitterness barely touching her words. "That might give the English host pause before decimating the island."

She had spoken in ironic jest, of course. She was astounded to see that Angus seemed to give her words grave concern.

"Nay, ne'er an Englishman! 'Twould not do," he responded, after pondering the question.

She gazed down the table at Kevin. Her wine seemed to have formed a knot in her stomach. He wouldn't look at her.

Well, then, they might have been just as glad to rule the clan themselves. She wasn't so important for who she was. She was important for who she could be married to.

She hadn't protested; she knew where duty lay. Yet they obviously knew what they were doing to her, for Angus suddenly spoke passionately, and from his heart. "Lass, lass! None of us would ever do ye ill, ye must know that! But how many men can we lose before the hangman or on the block? How many women must weep and wail?"

And why hadn't they thought of that before rushing out to do battle for a fool prince? she wondered, feeling a pounding in her head. Not a one of them, she was certain. They were Highlanders, impetuous, and passionate to a fault.

She rose, her meal untouched. "Do I have time to think about this?" she asked.

"Aye, Marina!" Kevin said, rising, finding his tongue at last. "Surely we've several days, I think."

"Days," she murmured. She stiffened her shoulders. "All right.

Then I will think. My lairds..." She inclined her head. The men at the table stood quickly to a man, bowing in return. She swept from the dining hall, shaking.

She hurried from the hall to the stairway and swept fleetly up the steps. But when she reached the second level, she paused before going the next set of steps to her tower room. She wandered into the gallery that sat above the dining hall. Once, guests had been received here. When she had been a child, entertainments had often taken place here. Numerous narrow windows looked down on the rocky cliffs below. A minstrel's gallery was at the far rear, and a set of large regal chairs stood at the opposite end—one for the laird, one for his lady.

There were paintings here, too. Paintings that traced the history of Fortress Glenraven, from the first laird to travel over with the Scotia to the uprising of 1715, and all the wild and reckless border wars and feuds in between.

Candles burned in sconces along the wall. Marina walked slowly along. There were the portraits with which she was very familiar. Her Uncle Fraser on horseback, the proud Scot, kilted in his colors. There was the portrait that had been done of her parents together, down in the great hall below. There was the one of herself that Fraser had ordered the summer before she left home. She was different now, she thought. Perhaps she had changed just today. The girl in the painting was young, with clear, passionate green eyes that seemed to believe in love and life and magic.

Marina kept walking, pausing before a painting of a great battle that had taken place during the time of Mary, queen of Scots. Those had been treacherous times indeed, for it was said that the young queen's husband had one of her favorites murdered, and that Mary was involved in the plot when Lord Darnley was murdered in turn. Soon after, Mary married Bothwell and fled to England, but the Scots fought one another then, too, some wanting to bring back their queen, some wondering why it took so long for Elizabeth Tudor to sever her cousin's head.

The battle painting, though, was intriguing. Marina moved closer to it. There they were, the clan MacCannan, riding forth. They were dressed in their colors, many in half armor, some just in their kilts and shirts, their legs bare against the flanks of their horses. At their head was a blond man with a red-gold beard. Like the others, he was kilted, standing high in his stirrups as his sword swung above his head. He was young, he was indeed passionate—a strikingly handsome man. And his battle cry could almost be heard on his lips. *He could nearly leap down from the painting,* Marina thought, he was so very real. A tribute to the artist.

She kept walking, smiling as the paintings and artworks took on a far more medieval flair. She paused before a grave etching of Angus James MacCannan, laird in the early 1300s. He wore armor and held his sword stiffly at his side. His eyes closed, he seemed at peace— even if his jaw and body were just a bit disproportionate.

There was a beautiful gold leaf drawing of the hall with the Latin descriptions beneath it from the twelfth century.

Then there was a painting of a blond woman at one of the tower windows up above.

And then there was...

Him.

Marina paused, forgetting that her own life was in awful turmoil. This painting was by far the most intriguing of the many in the room. She couldn't tell the time, or the place, for he stood against the blue sky, one foot planted on a rock. He looked to the sea, and the wind swept by him, catching the gold of his hair. Face forward, he met the wind. His features were handsome, strongly crafted; a hard, determined jawline met with high, wide cheekbones. He stood as if he defied the world and would meet any threat with that same arrogance and defiance.

He was dressed in some sort of short tunic. His arms and most of his legs were bare, the taut, hard muscle of his calves crisscrossed with sandal straps. Whatever laird he was, Marina determined, he had ruled here long, long ago.

"Ulhric, the Viking," Marina heard. She didn't need to turn to know that Kevin had come to find her here.

"Ulhric, yes," she murmured vaguely. She'd heard the name before. He'd been born on the Scottish mainland, but his father had been one of the Norse invaders to settle the area, so they had called him the Viking. He'd been fierce and heroic, so she had heard. All manner of legends surrounded him. He had stormed the fortress and taken it for himself, and then saved it from a more hostile clan.

"I'm sorry, Marina," Kevin said.

She turned to him, forgetting the portrait for a moment. "Kevin, is there no other way to turn?"

He opened his mouth, shut it again. "I think not, Marina." He paused again as she stared blankly at the pictures before her. "With such men as those you have chosen, the MacCannan name will die out on the isle."

"And worse," Kevin agreed glumly. He set his arms around her like a brother. "Ye should have married that French marquis when he asked, Marina. Ye'd not be in this position now."

Aye, she should have married Jacques St. Amand, and she would have been a marquise now, residing in his fine palace outside Paris. He had been charming, with his dark eyes and flashing smile, and he had loved her. And she should have said yes, and heaven help her, she had certainly flirted enough with the young man, but in the end...

Had she known that she wanted to come home? As barren and wild as the rock might have been, as backward as their society was compared with that of the elegant French, had she been unwilling to spend a lifetime away from it all?

Or had it been Jacques himself? Had she liked him tremendously, but not loved him well enough? Something had been lacking. She didn't know what right now.

But she had made a mistake. Jacques would have been decidedly preferable to either of the men set before her now! And if she had been married already...

"The one doesn't have any teeth, and the other comes laden with fangs," she said sorrowfully.

"Now, ye don't have to marry either of them, Marina—"

"Right. We can lose even the fortress itself, and the English can carry away half of my clan, and slice off their heads on Tower Hill. Aye, Kevin, I will live with that easily enough!"

"Perhaps..." Kevin began.

"Perhaps what?" She was ready and willing to leap on any form of hope.

"I shouldn't have spoken."

"Well, you did, so continue."

"Perhaps, before they come against us here on the isle, seeking the king's vengeance, some other form of rescue will arrive."

Her heart seemed to fall. What other form of rescue could there be? Only another Highlander would so recklessly place himself in battle against men who already—and with proof of their triumph behind them!—claimed victory.

"What we need is a hero."

"Indeed," Marina murmured. She was exhausted. She wanted to hold her shoulders square and her chin high. Both were drooping.

"Stranger things have happened here, for clan MacCannan," he said. He was staring at the battle painting that had so caught her attention earlier. The scene in which it seemed the horses' hooves moved in truth. The scene with the kilted blond chieftain waving his sword high in the air.

Kevin seemed caught up in the painting. Marina stared at him.

"Eric MacCannan," he said, pointing to the blond giant on the horse. "They were coming once before to decimate the island when he came riding in with four score horsemen. They fought off an army of near to five hundred alone, pushing them back to the sea."

Marina stepped forward, staring up at the blond man. "'Tis a pity we've no long-lost cousins to come our way now," she said with a sigh. Then she frowned. "Look Kevin! Look at the resemblance! See, there, Ulhric the Viking, Eric the chieftain. They are incredibly alike!"

Kevin studied the paintings, then smiled in agreement. "Perhaps the artist of the later painting borrowed from the artist of the first. This battlescape was surely done after the fact."

"Aye, I suppose," Marina murmured.

"Speaking of likenesses, little cousin, come here," he said. She frowned and followed him down the gallery. They came upon a scene of a far earlier time in which a woman sat before a fire, her hair hanging in long plaits behind her, her fingers held lightly over the strings of a small instrument that resembled a lute. Rich lashes fringed her eyes, but their green color was still apparent, as was a curious twist of sadness in them.

"She could be ye," Kevin said.

Marina did not see the striking resemblance here as Kevin did, but she shrugged. "I suppose they are our ancestors."

"Ah, but so far removed!" Kevin said. "Generations upon generations!"

Marina shrugged. "Why do you suppose she looks so sad?" She shook her head. "Perhaps she was given a choice similar to mine for a marriage partner—one with no teeth at all, and one who has fangs as long as a wolf's!"

"Nay, lassie!" came a voice from the entryway. Marina spun

around. It was Angus, and the sorrow in his eyes as he studied her
was so deep that she promised she would never let him see how
dismayed and horrified she was over her own future.

"That fair damsel, so they always told me, was the Lady Illora.
And the sorrow in her eyes was for her laird, the Viking Ulhric."

Marina tried to smile for Angus. "But he was a great warrior. He
fought for the island, and for Illora, and saved it from the upstart
nobles who would have kidnapped her and flattened the fortress."

"Aye, but those very barbarians came back. Illora was threatened
once again, and Ulhric was forced to ride against them. Dying, he was
placed up in his saddle, and there he commanded his men. Even as
he died, he carried with him any number of the enemy. He had been
betrayed, so it was said, by those within his own house." Angus
walked closer to the picture. "He was cast out to sea in his funeral
bier, as was the Viking way. The bier was set afire, yet as it drifted
into the sea, it did not burn. Legend has it that Valkyries, Viking
goddesses, appeared at either side of the bier. And some say that they
came to the Lady Illora at night and swore that he would come again,
in times of darkest need."

Well, the way that Marina saw it, they were in the midst of
darkest need now. If a dead Viking was going to rise from his funeral
bier, now was the time for him to do it.

"'Tis a wonderful legend, Angus," she said lightly. She kissed him
on the cheek, for he was still studying the painting, that haunting
sadness in his eyes. "I am exhausted. Perhaps I shall better be able to
choose between the two lairds by morning!" She tried so hard to
speak lightly.

"Perhaps we should all turn ourselves in to the English
authority," Angus said.

"Never, Angus, never!" she told him passionately. "Don't you
fear. No man shall ever have the best of me, I promise you." *Brave
words*, she thought. But no man would do so, she decided. Fortress
Glenraven was her birthright—that was why she was now
condemned to defend it and her people.

"Good night to you both," she said, determined that she would
still be cheerful. She waved to Kevin and left the gallery behind her,
then climbed the remaining steps up to the tower room that had now
become her own.

A fire was blazing comfortably. Peg had fallen asleep before it, awaiting her. Marina patted her lightly on the shoulder. "Peg, I'm for bed now. You must go and get some sleep yourself."

Peg's eyes only half opened. "Let me aid ye, lass—"

"Nay, I've no need of any aid. And you just as weary as you might. Go on now, for I will need you in the morning."

"Aye, lass, I'll bring ye yer tea early. With a big pitcher of cream and big lumps of sugar and the very best of me scones!" Peg assured her a bit sleepily before she left.

Marina began to disrobe. Peg had unpacked her belongings. Her dresses were hung, her dainty French underthings had been neatly placed in drawers and trunks. She had to look about for a nightgown, and as she did so, she discovered that the room had been well stocked with the MacCannan colors in various forms for her to wear: a floor-length skirt, a sweeping sheath for a banner across her chest, and several scarves. A tarn sat high atop the wardrobe! cockaded back with a MacCannan pin bearing the coat of arms and a parcel of the wool plaid.

She sighed. These were proud people. And she was their leader. She needed the courage for the task, and she suddenly and fiercely prayed that she had it.

Despite the fire, the room seemed cold to her. She found a long white flannel gown and slipped it over her naked shoulders, then plunged into the laird's large bed.

She had never felt so alone, so tired, so uncertain.

She swallowed hard, moving her hands over the expanse of the bed beside her. Who would come here? She shuddered fiercely. The MacNamara? God spare her! No teeth, no hair—

No way to judge a man, she warned herself fiercely. But he was old and shrewd and cunning, his tanned face like leather, his old eyes frightening when they fell upon her.

He was a deadly old warrior. That was why the clan would be wanting him.

Then there was Geoffrey...

She shuddered again. Aye, now there was a deadly man, too. He looked like a wolf. He had beaten Mary MacGregor, his first young bride, Marina was positive. And she had heard worse. She had heard that he practiced what were whispered to be "perversions of the harshest kind."

Oh, God. She inhaled sharply. Her clan members would let no

harm come to her. She was sure of it. But once she had been married to the man...

She twisted over in the bed, slamming her fist into her pillow. Sleep. She just had to have some sleep.

But for the longest time, sleep seemed to elude her.

And when she did sleep, she dreamed.

It was so very strange, for she was not sure when wakefulness and restlessness gave off, when she entered into the dream.

She was suddenly in a field of mist. And she saw him.

He was coming toward her. Riding hard, but in a slow, slow motion. She could see each rise and fall of his horse's hooves; she could see the mud and the earth torn up and flying beneath the great beast.

She could see him. Study him, long and hard.

Blue eyes blazed into hers. Keen, sharp. The wind caught his hair. Sun-gold hair, brilliantly blond. He rode the horse bareback, and he was nearly naked himself, clad only in some form of short pants or leggings. A silver bracelet curled around his forearm in the image of a snake. An amulet hung around his neck.

His bare chest was bronzed so deeply it was near to brown in color. He did not seem to feel the cold. The closer he came, the more she could see the sheer ripple of the muscles in his chest and arms and shoulders. The sun played down on his chest, hard corded, riddled with short, coarse, red-gold hairs.

And as he came...

She felt a thrill rising within her, an unprecedented excitement.

She wanted to fight with him...

She wanted to touch him.

The horse came closer. Came close to running her down where she stood, waiting. But she would not falter, she swore it. She would stand before him, she would best him.

The hooves continued to thunder, closer and closer.

She could almost feel the stallion's breath. She could feel the blue fire of the man's eyes, searing into her, warming her from head to toe, lighting some secret fire deep, deep within her.

In seconds, the mighty hooves would fell her.

She could feel the quaking of the earth.

Feel the hooves rising, parting the air...

He reined in, the horse reared, and the forelegs fell, just inches from where she stood.

"Surrender to me now! Spare the isle from battle!"

"Surrender? To you?" Her voice was imperious. She was riddled with the sweet fire that he had brought. "To you, a heathen? Never!"

The great hooves of the war-horse pounded beside her. She stood her ground. Then she heard the thunder of his laughter, and before she knew it, she was swept up into his arms, and she was flying through the mist.

"But you will surrender, because I will have you."

The words were bold, determined. The huskiness of his voice rang with laughter.

The mist swallowed them up.

She tossed in her sleep. She dreamed, and she knew that she dreamed.

But then she saw him again.

Out of the mist, he walked to her like a stalking beast. More than his chest was uncovered then. He came to her naked as a panther, his long strides equally as sure as those of a great cat intent upon its pursuit. And like a great cat, he was completely, supremely confident in his nakedness, in the agility of his movement, in the ultimate victory of his quest. He came out of the silver of the mist, to the place where she lay...

In her own bed.

It was not real. It was a dream.

She should scream. This was her bedchamber. He could not be here. No man had a right here. She was the...

She was...

She could not remember her name, nor could she remember quite why men would leap to her defense, why they would fight for her, why they would die for her.

She only knew that he was coming closer and closer, her golden panther in the night. And his eyes were on her, raking over her, ravaging her even as they traveled her length, creating fire.

A scream rose to her lips. She closed her eyes. She dreamed...

Dreamed... erotic, fantastic dreams.

He crawled atop her, sleek, blatantly masculine. "Bastard!" she cried, and tried to fight him.

But his lips touched hers. The softness of the mist swept around her, and she was sinking, sinking into the mist, into the downy softness of the bed.

His mouth...

It was not tender, but neither was it cruel. It demanded, it ravaged. It formed over hers, parted her lips to his. Hot and thirsting, it brought wildfire to her. Her temper soared with indignation and fury...

Her body burned.

His kiss went on, his tongue tempting, teasing. Breaking the barrier of her teeth. Thrusting evocatively into the very deep recesses of her mouth.

His lips parted from hers. The fever of his kiss moved against her, discovering the pulse at her throat. She found some strength, and slammed her hands against his chest. He caught her wrists. She opened her eyes and saw him again.

Saw the eternal, sky-blue blaze of his eyes. The handsome curve of his taunting smile.

His fingers entwined with hers, bringing her hands flush back against the bed.

And his kiss moved downward against her throat. Found the thundering pulse that beat there. Moved downward again, his mouth forming over fabric, over her collarbone over...

Her breast. His mouth was so hot, so wet, just against the hardening peak of her nipple. She arched back, ready to scream, yet his kiss was suddenly on her lips once again, swallowing the sound of her cry.

She was looking at him again. Meeting those eyes

Eyes she knew.

"Tonight, lady..."

Was it a whisper? Was it the wind? Had she gone mad'? Did she dream?

His rakish grin deepened. "Tonight!"

With one swift movement, he caught hold of the edges of her gown, and with a rending sound, they were ripped asunder. Shocked, she sprang to action, trying to rise, trying in all earnestness to strike him.

She was no match for him. No matter how she flailed, he caught her wrists again. She swore savagely and did not understand her own words. She did not sway him. Once again, his lips moved over her, flesh now naked and bared to him. His kiss traveled the long column of her throat. He breathed hot fire against the rise of her breasts.

His mouth closed around the nipple; his tongue slowly traced erotic circles around it.

Somewhere in the mist, she ceased to struggle. Somewhere in that same mist, she felt the soft, exotic movement of the clouds, of time, of night. She felt him, sweet and tender and savage.

A kiss that would not be denied. A body fierce, hard-muscled, proud. Sliding against hers. Causing her to lose her breath.

A kiss, a touch, that wandered places she'd never dared imagine.

That brought sensations she'd never dared dream.

Ah, but they were there. The feel of molten lava streaking through her body. The rippling fire dancing along her spine, centering in her middle, arousing, wicked, fantastic...

Then his eyes were on her again. Bold, blunt, demanding. And she cried out sharply as he knelt before her, sweeping up her knees, parting her thighs to his pleasure and scrutiny.

She gasped, stunned, shocked... protesting, as his kiss so boldly seared flesh so intimate. But her protest fell to a series of gasps as the sensations burst into a miraculous climax that swept her breath away.

She struggled against it. It was a dream! A dream, no one felt this from a dream...

But even as she fought the feelings, a new one descended on her. A quick moment of startling pain. And she realized that he had become one with her. That her dream lover had entered her. That she was filled with the startling size and heat of the man, that bold strokes were seeming to tear her in two...

She bit his shoulder. She tasted salt and blood. He whispered to her. She did not hear the words. The pain ebbed. Slowly. To her shock and embarrassment, the fire began to wind within her again. Brilliant, wicked, wild, rising and rising...

Bursting in a shattering of stars, sweeping through her, filling her again with a touch of sheer mystery and magic and wonder...

She drifted down in amazement. Slowly, sensually. The mist crowded in around her. It billowed and deepened and darkened, despite the whisper of the wind.

Mist...

And then darkness.

It had been a dream.

She slept peacefully.

* * *

When she awoke in the morning, she didn't remember the dream at first. She felt so very groggy.

She was worn, nearly as tired as she had been when she had gone to bed after the wearying days of travel.

Perhaps it took a day or two to recover, she told herself.

But light was suddenly streaming, and Peg was in the room with her. Peg had drawn back the tapestries over the eastern windows, and sunlight now touched her with its brilliance and warmth.

"Tea's here, Marina," Peg said. "Angus and the others will await ye in the great hall this morning. Ye must ride and see the ranks of the MacCannans."

"Are they ready for me yet?"

"I don't know, but ye must take yer time, luv."

"Nay, I'll hurry!" Marina said. She started to throw her covers back and stopped, her eyes widening in horrified amazement.

She was naked.

She quickly drew the covers around her. A misted remembrance of her dream rushed back to her, and she frowned with growing panic and confusion.

"Marina—"

"I—I'm fine, Peg," she said quickly. She jerked the covers back around her and tried to smile at Peg.

Nay, she was not fine! She was losing her mind, and doing so damn decadently.

"Peg, there's no way for anyone to reach this chamber in the night, is there?"

"Indeed not, m'lady! At night, why, the hounds guard the door with one of the lads, and the men of the household sleep just down the next level!"

Marina moistened her lips, fighting for a sense of sanity. It could not be. She had tossed and turned. She had imagined a hero, a man young and bold and beautiful because she was so very afraid of what was to come. That was it, surely.

"Peg, see for me, please, if the chieftains are in the hall yet. Quickly now, I beg you."

"But, m'lady—"

"Now, Peg, please?"

"But I told ye—"

"Now!"

Peg sighed, shaking her head. "Aye, m'lady."

The second that Peg was gone, Marina leaped up to dress. She dug into a trunk quickly and slipped into a long cotton chemise, determined to be decent at the very least before Peg could return.

She looked at her hands. They were ceasing to shake. She breathed deeply.

Was she losing her mind?

She ran her hands under the sheets, looking for her discarded gown. Her fingers curled around it. She sank down on the foot of the bed.

Well, she hadn't lost her mind completely. She had gone to bed dressed.

But as she lifted the garment to fold it, she started to shake all over again.

The garment was torn, wrenched cleanly in half from the bodice downward.

Chapter 3

She had scarcely dressed and come downstairs before she heard the sudden clamoring of the church bells, bells that pealed out an alarm. Rushing straight into the great hall, she discovered everyone scrambling to his feet and heading from the fortress, as stunned as she that they seemed to be under attack at that very moment.

One of the tower guards burst into the room even as Angus swore and Kevin leaped to his feet, buckling on his sword.

"Be it the English?" Angus demanded swiftly.

"Nay, it's Geoffrey's Camerons!" the young guard told them swiftly. "He's riding hard, demanding surrender, swearing that he will take Marina MacCannan and hold this fortress by nightfall!"

"Why, the bloody wretched bastard!" Angus exclaimed.

"He couldna' wait to negotiate; he would come and blast us all down when what we seek is strength?"

"I think, cousins," Marina said calmly, "that Geoffrey Cameron does not want negotiations. He believes he can have the fortress unconditionally, and then perhaps better negotiate with the British himself."

"By the Lord Jesu!" Kevin breathed to Angus. "She is right! Best us quickly, and he shall have everything! And he can use MacCannans as his own blood sacrifices in atonement to the German king!"

"Then we had best fight him, and swiftly," Angus said, striding for the door. He paused, a gallant old warrior, before Marina. He took her hand in his and bowed low over it. "Fear not, Marina, for every man here would die ere letting this upstart come near ye by force!"

She smiled and tenderly touched his graying beard.

It was fine for the upstart to have her—if she had agreed. But they were under attack, and the Highlanders here would fight.

The men were swiftly gone from the hall. Marina paused, watching from the entry as they mounted. Peg stood behind her with a silver tray and cup on it. "Fer Angus, luv; he be leading," she whispered to Marina.

Aye! She had forgotten the proper way to see her men to battle. She smiled her gratitude to Peg and hurried out. Angus was mounted, at the front of the troops. She hurried to him with a smooth and dignified pace, offering up the cup as he sat his horse. "Godspeed, Angus MacCannan!" she called out. He raised the silver cup in a salute to her. "Aye, Godspeed! Hail the MacCannan."

A cry went up, half cheer, half battle cry. Then Marina could hear the sound of the invaders. It was coming louder and louder, a sure pounding of horses' hooves.

The tide was low, and Geoffrey Cameron knew it. He was riding across the shallow sea to take them.

"We ride!" Angus called out. His sword flew into the air, and Marina stepped back as his huge war-horse reared into action. Behind him, Kevin, jaunty in his kilt and feathered and cockaded bonnet, saluted her with a promising smile. His horse followed Angus's, and then hundreds of men were racing on by her while the people waited behind, cheering on their warriors.

Marina hesitated, then hurried to the stables. She found a young groom there. "I need a horse, and quickly. A mount who will not panic at the sounds of battle."

"And what do ye think ye're doing?" came a voice behind her. She swung around. Peg was standing there with her hands on her hips, her eyes worried.

"I'm riding behind the troops. I'll stay clear of the danger, Peg, I swear it, but I'll be there to support them as they ride."

"Marina, ye cannot—"

"Peg, I am the MacCannan!"

That she was. The groom did not intend to insist otherwise, and even as she argued with Peg, he brought her the mount she desired.

Perhaps she had never really prepared for war, but she had learned to ride. Any child of clan MacCannan knew how to ride the wild Highland ponies as soon as he or she could walk.

She leaped onto her mount, and as she looked down at Peg and the young groom, she was every bit the vision of both a fine lady and the MacCannan of Fortress Glenraven. She wore a fine white ruffled blouse beneath a deep blue jacket, and one of the long skirts in the family plaid made from fine wool. Her small black bonnet was adorned with a brooch bearing the MacCannan motto—"God and courage shall lead." A jaunty feather danced above the pin, and both were held in place by a thin band of the plaid.

Beneath the bonnet, her hair was free, a golden banner

streaming down her back. Her chin was high, and the emerald of her eyes sizzled beneath the rising sun.

"I am the MacCannan!" she said to Peg. Waving, she set her heels to her bay horse and followed behind the racing trail of men.

Perhaps it had been a fool thing to do. Angus would have told her so. But she was determined that she should be seen.

If men were to die for her, then it seemed only fair that she should, at the very least, ride with them.

Yet as they plowed down the fields from the fortress, she saw that the forces were already engaged in the shallows. Marina led her horse back upward along the slope, looking for a vantage point from which to watch the proceedings. Her heart seemed to fall into her stomach and there burn, for seeing the battle was a horror. Gunfire roared, and men fell into the water, men in the green and blue and red of the MacCannan, and men in the Cameron colors. Together, they fell within the shallows. Swords were drawn, swords were slashed. Battle cries ripped the air.

It was then that she saw their enemy, and saw him splitting his troops.

Looking far across the shallows, she saw Geoffrey Cameron. He was far from the battle, as she was herself. He sat his large black horse and viewed the carnage. Dark and deadly, he lifted his arm, splitting his forces so that they would ride around the MacCannans and take them from the back.

"Nay!" Marina cried out. Without thought, she rode down from her slope, crying out the warning. Her mount raced far across the fields and toward the shallows. Moments later, the salt water ripped up and flew around her as she began to pound through, seeking the attention of the chieftains.

"They come around. Form ranks! Take heed!" she screamed.

"Marina! Get ye far from here!"

It was Kevin, racing up beside her. A sword flew—too close to her! Kevin slashed and fought, his horse dancing beneath him, the sea water foaming and flying. "Ride, lass, we see the bastard's cunning now!"

He slapped her horse's haunches with the flat of his sword. The animal leaped, bearing her from the twisted melee of fighting men.

Yet even as she came free of it, she looked up to see that a horseman was riding down on her.

Geoffrey. Geoffrey Cameron.

She spun her mount about. She could not head back toward the island. She was cut off by the bulk of the Camerons. She could strive for the cliffs of the mainland to the south.

Her horse reared, and she gripped her reins tightly, holding dear to the mount with her thighs. Her heart sank as she caught a brief sight of the battle.

Camerons were surrounding them.

Yet, unarmed, here in the midst of her men, she endangered all of them. She had come, she had given them warning. She had done all she could do.

Now she had to ride south, out of their way.

Even as they were slaughtered there...

Her mount's forefeet landed hard into the shallows. She urged her horse toward the south. Leaning low, she raced from the pursuit she knew was coming.

She was startled as the sound of a new chilling and savage cry suddenly rang out on the air. Ducking low against her horse, she turned.

The wind whipped her hair around her face, nearly blinding her. Her eyes stung. Yet, coming from the mainland now, bringing with him that awful, bloodcurdling cry, was a new combatant.

Marina could see little of him, for she rode so fast and the spray of the sea cast up by the horse's hooves was all around her.

But he was dressed in the MacCannan colors.

Indeed, he was dressed very much as she was at the moment, in a frill-ruffled shirt, dark jacket, and kilt, his long limbs encased in tawny leggings, a cockaded hat on his head with a band of the colors, a brooch, and a dark flying feather. A sporran lay against his waist beneath his scabbard, and a swatch of the colors was looped over one shoulder and held in place beneath that scabbard, too.

Beneath his plumed bonnet, his hair was gold, a fierce, reddish-gold, a color that caught the sun like a banner.

And his face...

He was a clean-shaven man, striking. His features were rugged, as threatening now as a storm, wild, challenging, proud, and ever defiant.

The enemy seemed to fall back, even as he rode. The stranger's cry itself seemed to promise death.

Much as the sword that he swung above his head in a mighty arc as he rode into the battle.

She did not know if he rode alone or with others, but somehow he was bringing about a turn in the tide of the battle. He entered into the melee with that awful cry still on his lips.

She cried out herself, nearly unseated as her mount bore her out of the water and onto the rugged shoreline. Here, dangerous cliffs and rocks jutted out to catch the unwary. She reined in on her panicked horse and fought for her seat while the animal danced.

She heard the sound of hooves crashing behind her and turned quickly.

Geoffrey Cameron was behind her. Dark; a slow, evil smile curling his thin lips, he watched her. "So ye'd ride into battle, me pet!" He laughed. And his voice deepened. "And into me hands, lass!"

There was nowhere for her to go on horseback with the cliffs before her.

She knew them well. She had climbed them often enough as a child.

She leaped down quickly, not bothering to give him an answer, and raced along the rock-strewn beach to the first slim trail that led upward into the cliffs and caves.

"I'll have ye yet, Marina MacCannan! And at me mercy, it will be!" he shouted furiously.

Panting, she ran. He would be fleet behind her, she knew.

He was familiar with these cliffs and caves, too.

She had to be fleeter. She had to know the terrain better.

She ran nimbly, swiftly. She knew a place where the rock seemed to jut as one piece, but where there was a narrow space that led into a cave. If she could but reach it...

She could hear his sword, clattering over the rock. She moved even more swiftly, gasping, inhaling desperately for breath. Her path grew harder and harder; the ground became more treacherous. Her heart pounded fiercely, and she scarcely heard anything else for the sound of her breath rushing from her lungs and the sea pounding against the rock.

She found the opening and slipped within it, then leaned back against the rock, gasping. She held still for a moment, regaining her breath, then started forward.

"So there ye be, Marina! Did ye think that I'd not know the fool's gap here as well as ye?"

She spun around. Geoffrey was there, standing before her, legs spread apart, hands arrogantly on his hips.

"What in the Lord's name is wrong with you, Geoffrey Cameron?" she demanded haughtily, tossing back the mane of her hair. "Your offer was on the table; it was being considered—"

"Ah, but I knew ye, lass, and I knew ye'd choose that stooped-o'er old fox of a MacNamara long before ye'd choose me. And I've coveted the island, girl, just as I've coveted ye!"

"Well, you'll not have me, or the isle, Geoffrey Cameron," she vowed bravely and indignantly. But who was there to stop him?

He knew the thought that ran through her mind, for he stepped forward. "The MacCannans, bah! Always with their noses in the air, and now ye've come home with yer Frenchie ways about ye, lass. Well, I'll have them tamed out of ye, I will."

"I'll never marry you, Geoffrey Cameron. The clan will not have it now."

He started to laugh. "We need no blessing from the clan, lass. We've the rock we stand on, and when I've had ye beneath me, bearing a Cameron heir perhaps, the clan will be quick enough to agree to a wedding."

She tried not to show the least fear to him, yet she felt the color flee from her face, and the thunder of her heart began to roar once again. By God, he meant to rape her, and she had little help to stop him. If only she had remembered to strap her little dirk to her calf, but she had dressed so quickly this morning, and with no thought of danger.

The laughter left his face. Dark eyes narrowed as he strode forward with sudden urgency. "I'll have ye now, me great and fine lady!" His hands landed on her shoulders, wrenching her toward him. She was quick and furious and desperate, and she lashed out at him with her nails. She caught his cheek with them and drew thin lines of blood across his cheek, bringing a howl from him.

"Bitch! Wretched, arrogant bitch!" he exclaimed in amazement, losing his grip on her in his astonishment as he touched his face. She turned instantly to flee, determined to escape now through the rock.

His hand landed like a vise on her shoulder, throwing her back. She stumbled, then tripped and fell backward to the ground. Her head struck rock. Stunned, she lay motionless for several seconds.

For a moment, he didn't move. Did he think her dead?

Nay! Nor did he seem to care if she was dead or alive. His feet straddled her waist, and he started to lower himself down to her. "Bloody bitch, Lady MacCannan, ye'll pay now, and dearly."

"Nay!" she shrieked, flailing at him. But he caught her wrists. He stared down at her with dark malice and evil intent, coming ever closer. Then, even as the blood seemed to freeze and curl and congeal within her, he suddenly yelled out.

As if picked up by a giant's hand sent down from heaven, he was plucked off her and cast hard against the wall of rock to his right. Marina was able to see the incredulity and fury that touched his eyes.

"Lay a hand on her again, Laird Cameron, and forfeit said hand! Threaten her with any other piece of your anatomy, and said anatomy will likewise be forfeit, sir!"

Marina struggled to rise on her elbows, staring at the deep-voiced savior who had come to her aid. At first she saw only his back, the deep blue jacket, the wild head of sun-gold hair, the massive breadth of his shoulders. Then he turned, and the most awful and curious rush of fire seemed to rip into her and through her.

Blue eyes, bluer than the sky, deeper than the sea, piercing, endless, stared into her own. His was a clean-shaven face, harsh and rugged, yet handsome, strikingly handsome in its cleanly defined planes and angles, the high-set cheekbones, the firm, unyielding jaw, the generous mouth, the high-arced honey-deep brows. She knew him...

Nay, nay, she'd never seen him before.

Not before this day.

He was the warrior who had ridden across the shallows, come to their aid when the house of MacCannan was near to a fall.

"Who the bloody hell are ye!" Geoffrey Cameron demanded, pushing off from the wall. Careful now, he circled the stranger. He stared at Marina, still on the ground. "Who is this impostor wearing yer colors, girl?"

The stranger bowed in a mocking, courtly gesture to Geoffrey. "No impostor, sir. The colors are mine to wear, for I am a MacCannan; a cousin, if a very distant one at that."

"And ye'd refuse me!" Geoffrey swore, staring down at Marina. "This man would have yer place, yer fortress, yer island. He's probably come from the king, come to steal into yer place and have at the brave MacCannan lads who fought against him fer the Bonnie Prince!"

But the stranger was offering a hand, a hand with long, strong fingers. They touched hers and entwined with them as he drew her to her feet.

"Nay, I've not come for her fortress or her title, Laird Cameron. Only for her defense." His ice-blue gaze shot to Geoffrey Cameron again. "And I say again, sir, touch her once more, and your life might well be forfeit."

"Why, ye bloody rogue!" Geoffrey swore. "Ye'll not speak so cocky, man, once I've sliced the tongue from yer mouth!" And so saying, he drew his sword, already bloodied from his day's work.

Yet there was no contest. Even as Marina gasped, stepping back, the stranger drew his own weapon, a heavy broadsword that he swung as lightly as if it were a thin rapier. Steel clanked against steel, sparks lit the air. But ere the swords could clash again, the stranger whipped his up with a strength that sent Geoffrey's weapon flying into the air and clanking down harmlessly on the rocks.

"Why, ye bastard—" Geoffrey began again.

But the stranger was angry, and angry in a way that brought a shiver even to Marina's spine, though he was supposedly on her side.

His voice did rise; it deepened. It seemed to shake the earth, it came forth with such fury and such command.

"Have done with it, my Laird Cameron, have done with it! I've let you live, you callous swine, for the sheer fact that you, too, need fear the German king, and 'tis likely you'll need to fight beside us for your own salvation when the English seriously come against us. So for now, Laird Cameron, I'll not kill you. Not if you can get from my sight within the next few seconds!"

"I'll kill ye yet, I will!" Geoffrey swore in a rage. But he took no step toward the stranger. "By my word, ye rogue bastard, I'll find ye, and I'll kill ye yet! Take heed. And ye—lady!" He swung suddenly and fiercely on Marina. "Ye will suffer fer the both of yer sins!"

Then Geoffrey was swiftly gone, pausing only for his sword. He gave no backward stare and left as quickly as he might.

Yet when he was gone, Marina felt no greater comfort. She found the stranger far more frightening than Geoffrey, for she didn't know at all what she felt in his presence.

"My lady—" he began, extending his hand to her once again.

She stepped back warily. "Aye, my laird rogue! I'll have the answer that you failed to give Geoffrey Cameron. Who are you?"

He hesitated, shrugged, and dropped the hand that he had offered to her.

"Does it matter?" Brilliant blue eyes rose to hers, eyes filled with laughter now. "I came when I was needed. I fought well."

"Are you a MacCannan?"

"Oh, aye, a distant relative, surely."

"I've never seen you before," she snapped out quickly.

But she had seen him. Where? "Are you from the island?"

"Nay, lass, not from the isle, but from this very mainland."

"But—"

"I have been away a long, long time," he stated softly.

That was it, she knew. The end of it. She could question him until winter came and the snow fell, but he was done with giving her answers now.

"All right, sir, so you've no intention of telling me the truth about yourself—"

"I have told you the truth, my lady!"

She waved a hand in the air. "But you haven't—"

"My lady! I had somewhat expected a thank-you rather than this barrage!"

She felt as if the tiny gold hairs at her nape rose, and she gritted her teeth. "It is not that I am unappreciative, it's just that I am surprised to learn of the existence of a distant relative, and I'm even more surprised to find myself rescued by him. How did you know I was in danger?"

His handsome mouth quirked upward in a grin. "I simply knew you needed me."

"But how—"

Taking her arm, he interrupted, "Come, my lady, let us join your men on the beach."

Marina's eyes blazed at him, but she said no more as he led her down the cliff. Just before they reached the rocky beach where the MacCannan clansmen were gathering, staring curiously up at them the blond stranger turned to her. "Allow me to introduce myself, my lady. My name is Eric. It's an old MacCannan family name."

Chapter 4

Eric.

He was another Eric MacCannan, like the bold Highlander in the picture above the stairs in the gallery. His name—she knew that at least, for though he managed to avoid any of her determined questions, he had been quick enough to answer Kevin and Angus and the others.

But then, they were treating him like a conquering hero.

It was difficult sitting in the main hall that night, for naturally all the men who had not been injured in the battle were gathered around the table, intent on getting to know the man who had come to their rescue.

Eric.

At the swift rise of her brows when he had mentioned his name, he had smiled serenely and informed her it was a very old family name; that if she were to delve, she would discover any number of Eric MacCannans in their history.

Somehow, she didn't doubt him.

His explanations to her clan were no more satisfactory than any words he had given her, but not a man among them seemed to care.

He had changed the tide of battle. He had ridden out, and the Camerons had been bested. That was enough. And he seemed to have proven that he was an extraordinary man in battle, for in the midst of the meal, Kevin and Angus and the others were forming maps of the area, pointing out their weaknesses and their strengths, and planning ways to fight off a larger army indefinitely. And they hung on his words as he explained why both the Camerons and the MacNamaras would fight with the MacCannans when the British came, for in their numbers they would find a strength that they had never found before.

It had been one thing for the English horde to defeat them at the site of the previous battle. Now the Highlanders would be in a position to weary the Englishmen, for the enemy would have to come after a sheer wall of stone, time and time again, taking great losses for very little gain. Once they had done this, a negotiated settlement could be achieved, and that was all the Scots sought at the moment.

The prince was still in the Highlands, but he was not at Fortress Glenraven, and his cause was lost, truly lost, in the bloody field at Culloden.

Marina maintained her place at the table, listening to the man and watching the faces of the others around them.

She was at the head of the table. She was the MacCannan. And despite the fact that he seemed to know very well what he was doing, she was determined to question him sharply at every turn.

Angus and Kevin, it seemed, had been ready to hand the fortress over to him the moment they saw him climb from the cliffs with her safely in his company. But then, they had already fought with him. And they were men. Show them a good warrior, and they would ask no other questions, just gladly accept him.

Marina was not so certain. She sat out the meal, and she was careful to keep her tone level and her words civil as she spoke with the blond intruder. But there was something about him...

Something that both angered and excited her. Something that made her want to lash out at him...

And something that made her want to touch the handsome, clean-shaven lines of his cheek. The mere sound of his voice still created a slow-burning fire within her. The flash of his eyes on her could make her feel a simmering in her blood, a fire deep within her center.

And each time he looked at her, it was as if he knew her so well. As if he could read her mind. As if he saw into her soul, and even into the secret, intimate places where she burned and wondered. And he was amused, so it seemed.

With the meal barely over, she rose in a sudden and swift determination to be away from him. She stared straight at him while she excused herself, explaining that she was bone weary.

As she left the room, she could hear Angus complaining that she had entered into the battle herself and must not do so again.

She could also hear the stranger answering Angus.

"Oh, aye, she'll not do anything so foolish again, Angus, I shall see to it, I promise."

He promised, did he? Well, he had best learn to take grave care regarding his promises!

She had thought that she was exhausted, but when she reached the second level, she did not proceed up the steps to the laird's—or lady's—bedchamber. Rather, she found herself in the upper gallery again, striding along the length of the room, idly gazing at the pictures.

Aye, he might well be a distant MacCannan, an Eric MacCannan at that. With his eyes so fierce a blue and his hair so bright a reddened gold, he might well fit in with many a MacCannan male.

She had walked down half the length of the hallway when a curious feeling crept over her.

She knew that she was being watched.

And she knew by whom.

She spun around. Just as she had suspected, he was there in the doorway, arms crossed idly over his chest as he watched her.

"Aye, what is it?" she demanded sharply, staring at him.

He strode into the room, gazing over the portraits and paintings.

"'Tis a long and restless history we've made, eh, Lady MacCannan?"

"The 'we' of it I most certainly still question," she told him coolly. The closer he came, the faster the blood seemed to race through her body. She must not allow him to see his effect on her.

She backed away from him.

Poorly done! she warned herself. She mustn't let him see the weakness in her movement.

But he smiled and seemed to sense her unease. Her temper soared quickly. "MacCannan or nay, sir, you are unknown to me, and you are a guest in this house, and I do not remember inviting you here. I do, in fact, specifically remember saying that I was weary, and that I was going up to bed."

"But you're not in bed, are you, my lady?" he queried softly.

"Where I choose to be is none of your concern!"

Despite her words, he walked toward her. She backed away again, her eyes widening. "I am the MacCannan!" she began indignantly.

But he had come before her then, directly before her. And she was backed against a wall, and his hands were on either side of her face, and the muscled length of his body was like the wall of a dungeon about her. "My lady—"

"How dare you!" she breathed furiously. "Leave me this instant!"

He was not about to leave her. She saw the wild challenge and defiance in his eyes, and she knew she had merely piqued his interest in their battle.

"I dare anything, lady," he assured her.

She slammed her fists hard against his chest, trying to pass by him. She might as well have chosen to push by the wall of stone that formed the fortress.

"I shall have you thrown out—" she began imperiously, her green eyes flashing.

"I think not," he advised her softly. The blue of his eyes burned into her. Burned like a swift and secret fire, igniting her anger, igniting a raw and reckless stream of excitement. How could he know what she felt?

She lifted her chin again. "I am the MacCannan, and you mistake the gratitude of my menfolk if you dare to harm me in any way—"

"Had I thought to harm you in any way, my lady, I had the opportunity in the cave and on the rocks earlier today. And not to disillusion you, for your menfolk do love you, lady, but those same menfolk have already and eagerly offered you in marriage to me for the strength of my sword."

Marina gasped, amazed. They couldn't have done such a thing! They hadn't even mentioned such an arrangement to her!

"I don't believe you!"

He shrugged. "As you wish."

Her eyes narrowed sharply. "If that is the truth, Eric—if that is really your name!—why aren't you down below now, completing those arrangements? You are intending to be laird here, are you not?"

"Oh, aye!"

She hit his chest furiously again. "Arrogant oaf!" she gasped. "Then—"

She didn't complete her words. Before she knew it, her fingers were entwined with his, and his head was lowering to hers. And even as she cried out, trying to twist aside, his lips found hers. Found and seized them, his mouth parting hers beneath it in a wild, reckless onslaught of heat and searing fire. For a dazed moment, she remained there, awed by the masculine command of his lips and mouth and tongue, knowing the feel of him, the taste of him, and the wonder of the sensations that burst and shivered and grew within her.

Then she realized that she was but a pawn in his expert hands.

She was the MacCannan. He was a stranger with much more to prove.

She twisted from his kiss at last, shoved against him, and tore free, spinning around. "Ah! So you are better than Geoffrey Cameron, eh? You'd choose a gallery instead of a cave of rocks!"

He moved toward her, his eyes narrowing sharply. "I haven't that much time, my lady, else I would take greater care. But, aye, lady, I am better than Cameron. I am better than any man you have known."

"And more humble, too!" she exclaimed.

"Nay, I am better, lady, because I love you. And I've no intention of forcing you. I seek only to make you remember."

"Remember what?" she exclaimed in exasperation. She was free of him now. She could run if she chose.

But she was trembling, watching him. Waiting...

He bowed deeply to her. "I'll bid you good night, Lady MacCannan. I am here to obey your every command."

"Indeed!" she said incredulously.

"Aye," he said, stepping by her and heading out. He paused, looking back. "You shall command me to love you, and that, as you know, I do."

He was gone then. She wasn't even sure that she really saw him leave the room. She only knew that he was gone.

She let out a long oath of extreme aggravation, slammed a fist against the wall, and started out herself.

But there was something wrong, she thought as she left the gallery. She had seen something that wasn't quite right...

She turned around and studied the pictures. She could almost see it, almost touch it...

But it eluded her.

She hurried on, determined to sleep.

* * *

That night, she dreamed again.

He was there once more, the man who had come before, the tall, striking blond.

And she was expecting him.

Nay, she was glad of him. She heard her own voice, welcoming him, the soft sound of her laughter as he came around to her. Her arms stretched out to greet him, she was so glad of him.

She heard his voice, husky, tender. Heard her own.

She felt the hot rippling of the muscles beneath his shoulders as she touched him. Felt the ripple of sheerest, softest fabric as the gown she wore slipped from her shoulders, caressing her flesh as it fell.

She felt him...

Felt his arms, felt his kiss. Felt the fabulous eroticism as he touched and stroked her. Caressed the length of her body.

Covered it with the powerful strength of his own.

The movement began. The slow, seductive movement. His eyes touched hers. Their fingers entwined. The slick warm feel of his body sliding against hers, stroking in and out, the wondrous sensations building and building.

His fingers, tightening around hers...

His facial muscles constricting...

The tempest coming faster and faster, and the call to ecstasy building. It burst on her suddenly. A cry tore from her throat and was swallowed up in the sweet fever of his lips as they tenderly caressed hers once again. Falling by her side, he swept her into his arms.

Arms that were so powerful, so warm, so strong, so real.

It was a dream...

A dream with strange shadows. She heard laughter then, and the laughter was hers. And there was comfort, and wonderful security. There was being with him.

Loving him, being loved by him. There could be no greater glory, no sweeter happiness.

But the darkness was still there. Waves of it, washing over them, leaving only glimpses of the happiness between rushes of black. Then she realized that the darkness was a shadow, the shadow of a man, reaching over them. She could see the shadow then, see it plain. His hand was raised, and a dagger was in it.

The dagger was falling down toward her.

She screamed, she raged—and she waited for the blade to pierce her flesh.

But no pain touched her, for he was there. Within seconds, she was swept beneath him.

She heard the fall of the dagger, heard the awful crunch as it connected with flesh.

His flesh.

He did not cry out; he fought the assailant as the blood poured over them both. He leaped from the bed, and she screamed again, calling for help.

It didn't matter. Even stabbed and bleeding, he could wage a one-man battle. The assailant lay on the floor, and her love was over him, demanding to know the truth of the attack.

She was up herself, staring down at the man who would have killed her. She gasped in horror. "We are betrayed!"

The guards were there, dragging away the offender. And her love was up, shouting to her, clutching his side where the crimson tide of his life's blood came through the barrier of his fingers.

He was rushing out to do battle.

It was a dream...

She rose and walked to the tower window, and she watched as he mounted, and his men mounted with him. His sword swung high in the air. She heard cries, and the riders thundered out to the mainland.

It looked as if they rode on water, phantom warriors able to fly, waging their fantastic battle, the sounds on the night air bloodcurdling.

"Nay!" she whispered and touched her cheeks. His blood on her fingers now mingled with her tears. "Come back!" she whispered. "Bring him back to me. Bring him back. Let me staunch the flow of his blood!"

Indeed, they brought him back to her.

He had fought bravely, and he had fought well. But the wound in the side was deep. No dressing held back the blood. He winced, helped by two others, as he returned to her by the morning's light.

"I will heal you."

"Nay, I cannot be healed. And..." He paused. "I have to go out again. Their forces are stronger. The men will only rally if they see me."

Tears streamed down her face. "You cannot go out there! You cannot lead an army! You bleed like a stream. My laird, my love, you must stay with me!"

She gazed down at her hand. Where she had touched him, her palm was now covered in blood again. She stared at him, newly, horribly alarmed.

She had tried so very hard to deny what had happened.

But then she realized the truth. He was dying, and he knew that he was dying. And he knew, too, that he must lead their forces, or they would falter and fall.

"My love..." she breathed. Her words choked off. "Nay, you cannot leave me..."

He found the strength to set his hands on her. His fingers curled around her shoulders, and then he paused, lifting her chin so that she met his eyes. She could scarcely see him, she was so blinded by her tears.

"Nay, you mustn't fear for me, you mustn't weep for me. It will be well, my wife, for I will love you forever."

For I will love you forever...

She looked up. Into the blaze of his eyes. Into his heart. "Forget me not," he bade her. Then his lips closed over hers, and the taste of tears and blood mingled in that kiss. "You must remember me, love," he whispered.

But then he was gone. And when she tore from the tower, she discovered that he was tied into his saddle so that it could not be seen that he slumped.

"Come back to me!" she shrieked to him. And as the horses pounded away, she fell to her knees, defying the Christian god and all the gods. "Bring him back to me! Please, bring him back, for we were betrayed! It should not have been, we deserved life, bring him back!"

And he came back again. Still tied upon his horse.

But the fierce blue eyes were never to open again. The handsome face was ever still in repose.

With his body laid before her, she shrieked and covered it with her own, weeping.

They could not take the body from her, or her from the body.

Nor did she even care that the isle had been saved from the attempt to overtake it.

She closed her eyes, and darkness descended.

She stood on the shore. The distant shore. She was still at last.

The body was laid out at last.

Dressed in his finest, clad in linen and leather and fur, his sword stretched out above his head, his belongings around him, he was ready for his bier to be set out to sea and set afire.

The smoke would carry him to Valhalla.

She stood, cold and alone, for ice now seemed to weigh down her heart.

One last time, she kissed his lips. She tried to breathe life into him again.

But his lips were silent, his body cold.

Then his eyes flew open. Blue as the sea. His lips moved. One word touched her.

Remember.

"Wait!" she cried, but the bier had been set free, the torches had been lit. The bier was set adrift, and the flames should have risen in seconds.

They did not. As the people lined the shores and watched in wonder, it seemed that two white-clad figures formed on the bier.

They were clouds, they were fog...

Whatever, the fires ceased to burn.

The bier drifted into the clouds of eternity.

Her tears fell. "I will love you forever," she whispered. "Forever."

* * *

Marina awoke, shaken. She touched her cheeks. They were soaked with tears.

She was shivering, and she leaped up and found a warm robe at the foot of her bed. She wrapped it around her, breathing deeply as the details of the dream began to fade.

"I am losing my mind!" she said aloud.

Perhaps she was.

She needed a drink.

With her robe around her, she hurried downstairs to the great hall. A fire still burned there. The fortress wolfhounds lay about the hearth one big nose laid on another as even the hounds sought companionship. Marina patted a dog and made her way past the table to the buffet and the bottles of liquor there. She didn't read any labels, but selected one and poured herself a long drink.

She had barely taken a swallow before she heard a crackle in the fire and knew that she was not alone. "Oh, nay," she moaned and spun around.

And indeed, he was there.

"What is it, sir? Must you plague me every waking moment?" she demanded.

He smiled and shook his head. "I did not mean to plague you, my lady. Only to guard you. I heard that you were up and about and came only to see to your safety."

"Well, I am quite all right."

"Just thirsty, eh?"

"Aye, just thirsty." Defiantly, she cast back her head and gulped the glass of whiskey she had poured. It was too much. She coughed and choked and started coughing again, and before she knew it, he was behind her, laughing, patting her on the back.

"You're shaking," he said. "You're cold."

She wanted to protest. The searing blue of his eyes was on her, and no words would come. He lifted her up, fur-lined robe and all. Cradling her in his arms, he carried her to one of the deep chairs before the fire and held her there, gently.

Firelight touched his eyes. They were the most extraordinary blue. Really, she couldn't deny the family resemblance, no matter how he infuriated or disturbed her.

She reached up and touched his chin. "Who are you?" she demanded softly.

"Does it matter so much?"

At the moment, it did not. She didn't understand him, nor did she understand her dreams.

But somehow, he was the lover in them. The tall, blond giant who came to her, haunting her sleep.

"I keep dreaming..." she whispered.

"We all dream."

"But you know what I'm talking about, don't you?"

He didn't reply at first. His eyes were on the fire. "You needed help. I was here. Why must you question these things?"

"You came back—from where you will not tell me—just in time to save us in battle. How is that?"

He smiled. "My lady, we are always at battle, so it seems. It is not hard to come upon a battle here at the Fortress Glenraven."

"You know the family history then," she murmured, studying him.

"Aye."

"Tell me about the Viking."

"The Viking?"

"The Viking Ulhric."

He shrugged, but his arms were warm. The blue steel of his gaze traveled from the fire to her eyes, and then back to the fire once again. "He wasn't a true Viking, you know. He was born on the mainland—his father was a Viking jarl. He had known Illora all his life, watched her from afar as she grew. As she watched him. Those were tempestuous times indeed. The Danes raided, the Norwegians raided, and the host of Picts and Scots and Gaels had waged constant war on one another."

"And what happened?"

"Well, he went to war for her, and for the isle," he said softly. "Radwald, a mainland chieftain, planned to take the isle, and Illora. She hadn't enough men to fight off an invasion herself, so it was a matter of the two fighting over her, and the island. To the victor went the fortress—and the princess."

"Then he was a cruel and brutal conqueror, no more!" Marina exclaimed.

His gaze claimed hers once again. The fire was reflected in the sheer blue color of his eyes as he spoke. "Oh, nay! He had watched her for years, he had loved her for years. And she did love him, you see. No matter what words she said at first, she loved him. Women are like that, so it seems, my lady. They fear a man— not his strength, but the weakness that he may bring out within the lass herself. So they fight. They say nay when they truly want nothing more than they want him."

She suddenly felt the pressure of his arms and the intimacy of their time together.

And looking into his eyes, she saw the eyes of a dream lover. Of a man who had come to her... somehow. She saw the tattered remnants of her gown on the bed, and she felt the salt tears of her terror and anguish on her cheeks.

She pushed away from him, leaping to her feet. "Nay, sir! When I say nay, indeed I mean the word. If you'll excuse me, I will retire once again."

He did not try to stop her. She did not hear a sound from him. When she was halfway up the stairs, she had to pause to look back.

He was standing by the chair by the fire, noble, striking,

212

handsome. He was still clad in his battle regalia, his frock coat over his kilt, ruffled white shirt, and cockaded bonnet with his feather. He seemed eight feet high there, golden as the sun, regal and glorious.

And her heart began to pound, so fiercely. Her mouth felt dry. Dear Lord, she wanted him. Not a dream. She wanted to touch this man, in the flesh. She wanted to give in, surrender to desire.

Nay...

"Marina!" he said suddenly, striding to the base of the stairway, looking up at her.

"Aye?" She tried to keep her tone imperious, regal.

"Just... remember," he said softly, watching her with a sudden, dark passion. "Remember..., love."

A tension suddenly seized her. "What happened to the princess?" she asked.

"What?"

"The princess. Illora. In your fine family tale. What happened to the princess? I understand that he died. What of her?"

"Ah, well," he said with a shrug. "It was hundreds of years ago. She died, of course."

"But how, when? You know, don't you?"

"Aye. All right. She died nearly nine months later. She gave birth to the son and heir of the fortress, and passed from this life. Crying out her lover's name."

"You do embellish, I am certain. Good night," she said determinedly.

She was certain she heard his laughter as she hurried up the stairs.

When she would have turned to her bedchamber, she paused once again, wondering why the hall and the pictures and portraits had so disturbed her before.

She walked in among them. She looked from painting to painting.

Then she halted.

She went back to the battle scene. The one in which another blond Eric MacCannan had led his forces into war, his sword flying, his passion so great that it could almost be felt from the canvas.

Only... no more.

It was just a painting now. The man leading the charge was scarcely visible.

The life had gone out of the painting, so it seemed. She walked backward, questioning her sanity in truth. Then she looked at the painting of Ulhric the Viking.

And she started to shiver.

It, too, seemed to have changed.

A handsome man was still portrayed, but he was different. He no longer seemed to look on her with burning blue eyes.

Again, the passion, the very life force, seemed to be gone.

"Nay!" she cried out softly.

Illora. She needed to see the painting of Illora.

Nay, nay, not this night! No more dreams, she could not bear the dreams!

She turned to flee the gallery. She took the steps two at a time to her room and slammed the door behind her. She bolted it.

Then she began to laugh and cry, and sank down beside it. A bolt meant nothing to a man, to a lover, who came in a dream.

"Nay, no more dreams!" she cried aloud.

And then she realized that, merciful God, she would have no more dreams that night.

The sun was rising in the eastern sky.

Chapter 5

Marina was in the upper hall by midmorning, having spent the early morning hours trying to make up for her lack of sleep in the night by finding some rest in the daylight, but it was difficult even then to sleep when she was so very determined not to dream.

By ten, though, Peg had come to warn her that a number of the MacCannan men were waiting to see her in the upper hall. She attended some of them there. It was the chieftains that the British wanted, she knew, but few of the men who stood sorrowfully before her then were chieftains. They were farmers who had sprung up with the excitement to do battle at Culloden, and now they were sorely afraid. They were anxious to take their chances in the New World, having heard that there was a ship leaving the countryside soon, and that the captain was asking few questions of the men who were ready to sign on. She listened to them all, reminded them that the English were not anxious to hang farmers, but gave them her blessing when they seemed determined to go.

Angus was with her then, and as the men filed out, she found his eyes on her, heavy and sad.

"What would you have me do? Command them to stay?"

He shook his head. "Nay, lass. But ye must do something, and soon. It seems as though ye wish no more to do with the Cameron, and as he saw fit to attack us, demanding an answer, I'd not be inclined to give him the time of day, much less the hand of the MacCannan in marriage. That leaves the MacNamara, or..."

"I've heard. This Eric MacCannan."

Angus shrugged. "Well, lass, ye did ask fer a fellow with a full set of teeth, ye know."

Was she doomed to pay forever for her foolish comments? She sighed softly.

"What are our losses, Angus, from the battle waged with the Camerons?"

"Thirteen wounded, and all have survived the first night, though young Neall was bashed severely in the head and faces a grievous fever now."

Still... no losses. Yet thirteen men who could not fight when the

English came against them.

"Ye must decide, Marina," Angus warned her.

She nodded. "By tonight, Angus," she promised him. "This morning, I think that I will ride."

Angus must have told Kevin her intent, for her cousin was awaiting her down by the stables. "I'll accompany ye, Marina."

"Nay, Kevin, I've a wish to ride alone today." She smiled. "To survey my domain."

His frown assured her that he worried for her safety. "I'll not leave the isle," she promised.

She didn't know if he was relieved or not, but she didn't care. She simply wanted to be alone.

The groom brought her the same small bay that she had ridden into battle, and Marina was glad of it; she was coming to know the mare. She left the ancient tower behind her and started to race across the open fields that faced the mainland straits, then turned westward and finally began to climb the cliffs and jags that faced toward the Irish Sea.

She had slowed her frantic pace, of course, for she could not run the bay here lest she break the horse's slim legs. But the bay was from local stock; she was surefooted and accustomed to the rugged landscape, and so they quickly climbed the rock until they were on a precipice, looking far down to the sea.

It was beautiful here. Wild, barren, with heather growing in sparse clumps from cracks in the rocks. The wind seemed stronger here, it seemed to whistle, and the sea today was dark and deadly and dangerous, and as tempestuous as her mood.

The urge to walk the beach struck her, and she lifted her reins, prodding her small mare to take her down the rock to the cliffs and the stretch of beach beneath. When she had arrived on the narrow border of sand, she dismounted and left the mare to chew on the weeds that grew by the rock. She started to strip off her shoes and stockings when she noticed an old woman in a long black dress and a black shawl wandering the sands nearby. She finished with her task, feeling the sand beneath her toes, then rose and wandered to the water line.

The woman came closer and closer.

She seemed ancient, with flesh like wrinkled leather. Her black shawl covered incredibly thin strands of gray and pure white hair, and she stooped as she walked, as if weighed down by the years. All that seemed young in her were her eyes. They were gold eyes, not brown or green but gold, and they were sharp as a blade as they studied Marina.

"So ye're the MacCannan come home, all growed up."

"I am Marina MacCannan," she told the woman.

The woman smiled, a toothless smile. She clutched Marina's arm. "And ye'll stay, and it'll be all right. This time. The fields will grow rich, fer ye'll know now, ye'll take heed, ye'll take care."

Marina shook her head, growing alarmed at the woman's desperation. "I've come home, aye. I'll not be going anywhere—"

"Ye'll marry him! But that canna be all. Ye must listen to me!" For a stooped old thing, she had tremendous strength. She swirled Marina around, and her fingers seemed to dig into her arms. "Treachery come from within, Mora; when will ye learn?"

Marina freed herself, her teeth chattering. This was an old crazy woman, she told herself. She had to be kind but firm.

"Listen to me, please," she said and clutched the old woman's wrists lest she try to take hold of her again. "I am Marina MacCannan. My name is Marina. But I will stay here. Things will be well. You mustn't worry. The English will not hurt you."

The woman looked at her as if she were the crazy one. Then she broke away.

Heedless of the cold waves against her feet and ankles, she walked out into the water. "'Twas from here that they set sail to the bier. But it would not burn. For it was said on that very day that he would return. Why, 'tis on Illora's tombstone. 'He will come again, this lion among men, and stay when love meet him, not die if love will greet him.'"

"That's, er, lovely," Marina said. Could she leave this daft old woman here alone? Would she drown herself if Marina did so?

The woman spun around. It seemed that she moved in slow motion. That her black cape took flight around her like the wings of a giant raven. Water flew from the long hems of her sleeves and shawls, catching the sunlight in magical droplets.

"Nay, listen to me, lady, heed the warning this time! Fer he has come afore, yet the treachery made mockery of love. Ye must take the blow, lady, ye must take the blow. Know that it is coming, and do not let him perish again! 'Tis up to ye, Illora, 'tis up to ye!"

"I am not Illora—"

"*Cuimhnich!*" the old woman shouted. For a moment, Marina did not understand her. Then she recognized the word. *Cuimhnich.* It was Gaelic for "remember."

Then the old woman turned away and started running toward the cliffs that curved inward from the horizon.

"Wait!" Marina called to her.

But for a hunched-over old woman, she moved extremely well. It seemed that she raised her black shawl, and, almost like the giant raven she resembled, took flight across the sea and land. Marina ran to catch up with her, but she could not.

Exasperated, weary, panting, she wandered back across the sands. She looked up at one of the dunes. A man there sat on a horse. A huge black horse, a war-horse with thighs and flanks as muscled as those of the warrior who sat his back.

Eric. Even at a distance, she could feel the blue of his eyes. Feel their touch on her.

His thighs nudged against the great black horse. The animal walked her way until man and beast were right before her, dwarfing her.

She stared up at him, suddenly very tired and very confused. He had appeared from nowhere. Had he stepped down from a painting? Or had he returned from the dead, as a prophecy had promised?

Had he come before, riding in his clan colors at the head of an army when the forces turned against Queen Mary and came here to battle MacCannans then?

She was losing her mind. And to think of it, she could have remained safely back in France rather than coming here where the clans fought one another just as swiftly as they fought any alien foe.

Back in France...

His eyes touched hers. The warmth spread through her. Nay, she could not be back in France. She knew why she had not married the marquis. She had liked him, aye. But she had never felt this. Never known this fever, this excitement, just because a man's eyes fell on her. She had never wanted to touch a man as she wanted to touch this one. She had never felt the passion, the fever... the need to be wildly, wickedly loved; to be held and treasured and caressed.

Taken, as a ghost lover touched her in her dreams.

Nay, nay, this cannot be, she assured herself quickly. *He is not the*

Viking laird returned, for I am assuredly not his Mora!

Nor had he come to speak to her of love. "The British have gathered on the mainland, in some few miles. They'll take their stand against us this day," he said.

She gasped, coming nearer, taking hold of his saddle as she looked up at him in dismay.

"So soon? I thought there was time—"

"You need no time, Marina. I've come to tell you, I will lead your army. And I've come to demand you, too. Marry me, Marina."

Command, indeed! "But the battle—"

He pulled back on the reins, and his great black war-horse moved away from her touch. "Be it then as you wish, Marina MacCannan. I'll fight the battle again. And I'll take the prize as I see fit."

Fury instantly rose within her, but with it, a rich flood of excitement. Aye, let him win, let him have what he would. She did not know what she was fighting.

"My dear sir—"

"My dear lady! I could be tender, I could be coercive. I could demand that you marry me because you do love me, but perhaps I cannot convince you yet that it is so. I can command that you marry me, for I will be the victor; I will prevail. Then, too, I can suggest that you wed me because I have all my teeth, and all my hair, and my limbs are sound and strong. It will not matter. I will return tonight. The threat to you, and to the isle, will be done with, and this night, lady, you will lie with me!"

"How dare you—" she began, hands on her hips, her temper flying. But he meant to have none of it. The great black reared and turned, and soon the sand was flying beneath its feet.

And he was gone.

The battle, the big battle, was nearly joined. They would make their stand. They would find peace, or the clan would be decimated.

And he would lead...

She moistened her lips, fearful of the longing, the shivering that began within her. He seemed determined that he would have her that night...

A slow smile touched her lips.

He did have all his teeth, and all his hair.

And, indeed, he was sound in limb and body!

Marina turned, forgetting her shoes and stockings, and raced along the shore to her bay. She leaped astride the mare and gave the horse free rein to hurry her back to the fortress with all speed.

She returned to the courtyard just as the men were preparing to march out again. She rode into the middle of them, her hand raised high in salute, a cry on her lips. She rode to the very entrance of the fortress, knowing that she would find Peg there with the stirrup cup of wine to be offered to the leader of the forces.

Marina leaped down and took the tray from Peg with a nod of silent thanks, then made her way through the horses with their riders to the very front of the ranks. She passed by Kevin, and by Angus, and proceeded onward. "Laird Eric!" she cried.

His eyes fell on hers, yet betrayed no emotion. He was a warrior, prepared for his battle now.

She offered up the cup. "Godspeed, sir!"

He took the wine. She thought that a small smile played on his lips. He drank the wine, then raised himself up in his saddle, his great sword swinging.

"*Cuimhnich!*" he cried out.

And en masse, the great horses began to move, and in seconds, there was a thunder that seemed to split apart the land as they galloped onward.

Marina stood alone where so very many had been. *Cuimhnich...*

Gentle hands touched her shoulders. Peg was there. "Come in, lady, now, come in. Ye're wanderin' round with no shoes upon yer feet, and ye'll catch yer death."

Marina didn't move. She stared after the riders.

"There's naught we can do here, lass. Naught at all. Messengers will come. The guards will keep sight on the horizon, and keep shelter on the fortress itself. Come in."

Marina went with her. She climbed to her chamber high up in the fortress, and she put on new stockings and shoes. Restlessly, she wandered back down to the main hall, but it was so empty. She went back up to the second-story hall and wandered along the paintings and portraits.

Today they told her nothing. They were just as they had been the night before. Paintings. Color on canvas.

She stared at the Eric MacCannan who had come in the time of Mary. Take away the beard, and...

She felt a presence behind her. Peg, come after her to see that she was all right, she was certain. "What happened to him, I wonder?" she said aloud. "Did he rule wisely and long? Did he die an old man, with a full score of grandchildren about his feet?"

"Eric MacCannan?" Peg said softly. "Nay, lass, he did not. Why, he was stabbed in his bedchamber in the middle of the night, and died in the morn. 'Twas said that the blow was intended for his lady, for she was the heiress in truth, if legend serves. But he couldna' let her die, ye see."

Cold—severe, eerie, icy—swept down her spine. "Like Ulhric the Viking," she said. And her voice grew bitter with the fear that raced through her. "And I'm sure that he rode against his enemy, bleeding though he was. And that he bested his enemy. But he died. And his wife bore a single child. And she died, too. And perhaps he was Ulhric come back."

"Ah, legend. Stuff and legend." Peg sniffed. She was quiet then. Marina did not turn. She swallowed hard. She walked down the gallery to the painting of Illora.

Surely it had been done at a later date. The artist must have guessed at the way Illora had looked.

But she had been a woman with emerald-green eyes, with long blond hair flowing down her back. And her head was bowed in the greatest sorrow...

Go to the tomb, Marina. Go to the tomb.

"The men are at war!" Marina protested. "I must await every word. And there is good reason to expect that I may be called to meet with the English general, if all goes well and peace is to be made. I cannot go running around believing in legends and tales—"

She broke off, for she was alone in the room. Peg was not with her.

The chills that assailed her then were awful. She couldn't bear being in the gallery a second longer. With a startled cry, she tore down the length of it.

She did not pause until she had run down the stairs, and come to the great hall beneath.

"Peg!" she called, her hands gripped by her sides.

From the pathway to the kitchens, Peg ran out.

"Where is it?" Marina demanded.

"Where is what?" Peg asked, mystified.

"The tomb. Mora's tomb."

Peg frowned, wiping her hands on her apron. "Why, 'tis in the cliffs by the sea. Down by the strip of beach that looks outward toward Eire."

Marina swung around. She was going riding again. Peg followed after her quickly. "Where are ye goin', lass? Ye must stay now, ye must listen fer the messengers, ye must be ready to meet with the Englishmen."

"That's exactly what I just told you," Marina snapped, and ignoring Peg, she hurried out.

Behind her, Peg frowned more deeply, terribly concerned. "Ye didna tell me a thing, lass, not a thing," she said, but she spoke to herself.

Marina made it back to the cliffs, climbed the rocks and shale on her bay mare, and trekked down toward seaside once again. She dismounted and led the bay until she came to the connecting maze of cliffs and caves. She had come here often enough as a child. She and Kevin had played here. She should have remembered the tomb. Someone in the family had always cared for it. The ancient rock had been protected. The inscription had been rechiseled time and time again.

She'd never even glanced at it. She'd had little time for the past then. Fraser had led the clan—she'd had no call to worry about it.

The crypt had been dug high against the wall of the cave, protecting it against any encroachment of the water. A massive stone had been set before it, and marble had been brought and a massive cross created of it.

Then there were the words. They were in Gaelic, and despite her knowledge of her native language, the spellings were very old and difficult to read. She touched the words "Our fair princess here shall sleep. One day with destiny, her tryst she'll keep. For he will come again, this lion among men, and stay when love meet him, not die if love will greet him."

Marina stepped back, biting her lower lip. It was madness. All madness.

"I am not Illora!" she cried out. She said it again, loudly, letting her words echo in the caves. "If that tomb were opened, her bones would be there; her flesh would have rotted, but her bones remain! I know that they do!"

She closed her eyes, clenching her teeth. She was so afraid.

And then she was not afraid. It was as if tender, gentle arms had embraced her. He was there. In some presence. He was there—holding her, caressing, assuring her. It was going to be all right. He loved her.

Cuimhnich...

Remember...

"Nay!"

She swung around, suddenly as desperate to leave the cave as she had been to leave the gallery. He was not with her, he could not be with her. He was flesh and blood, and he was out on the battlefield.

She tore through the caves and found the mare. She was so frightened that she fumbled trying to remount the horse, and had to try again and again.

Finally, though, she was mounted, and, once again, she gave the mare free rein, anxious to return to the fortress with all possible speed.

She came back just as a messenger in her colors raced in from the opposite direction. The tide was rising, and he was soaked from the waist down, and his horse gave a mighty shake, throwing off a rain of sea water. Marina did not care. She urged the bay toward him.

"What news? What has happened?"

"My lady! Battle was quickly engaged! The English meant to have us by surprise, but my Laird Eric was the one to surprise them. And by heavens, my lady! They all rose as one! When the force of Laird Eric's troops was seen, the MacNamara came into the battle, too, with his own. As did Geoffrey, of clan Cameron."

"Go on, go on! Quickly!" Marina urged him.

"The fighting was fierce and furious, lady. The English wanted to have no quarter with us mountain heathens, as they call us. But as they began to fall like slaughtered sheep before our onslaught, their general sent a messenger to Laird Eric, and a halt has been called. I've a parchment now for your approval as the MacCannan of the Isle of the Angels. A truce will be signed. The MacCannan men will be granted their freedom and their lives, all who fought at Culloden pardoned. We will abide by the rules set down for the Scots, forsake our colors for the time, and live in peace. 'Tis all there, lady. It needs but your signature."

Marina read over the long parchment she had unfolded carefully.

223

It had all been laid out, step by step, in neat and legible script. Everything that they wanted would be granted them. Once this was signed, she had managed all that could have been hoped for after the dreadful defeat at Culloden. Her clan would survive. They would be left in peace on the Isle of the Angels.

She had not managed it. Nay, he had done so.

Did it matter who had done what? she asked herself furiously. Angus would live, Kevin would live. Her kinsmen had bravely and heroically found their way.

"Come into the hall. I will set my hand to it," she told the young messenger.

Thirty minutes later, the deed was done.

And as darkness fell, the triumphant warriors began to return.

Marina had prepared for them. There would be a feast in the fortress that night, one the likes of which the Isle of the Angels had yet to see. Lambs and sheep and cows were slaughtered; fowls lost their heads by the dozens and were stuffed with breadcrumbs and seasonings and prepared with fine sauces. Barrels of ale were brought up, along with the best wines in the fortress.

And when the men returned, Marina was ready to greet them. She had chosen to wear a rich taffeta gown in the family colors, with a fine black velvet jacket over a soft chemise in white silk. She was very calm, greeting the lesser chieftains with handshakes and kisses on their cheeks. Angus she hugged fiercely, and Kevin she was loath to let go.

Yet all the while, she knew that he watched her. And that he waited.

And she felt his eyes. Felt the searing blue send fire into her.

She would not fall to him. Nay, she must take care, must keep her distance. Indeed, he had been triumphant. But this was the eighteenth century. Their courtship would be slow.

She had to know him. She had to understand.

"My lady," he greeted her, when it was his turn at last. And he offered her the deepest, most civilized bow.

"Eric MacCannan. Laird MacCannan. 'Tis a title that you deserve in truth, sir, and one I readily hand to you," she told him regally. "The table is set, gentlemen. A celebration is in order, and so it will be!"

"Oh, it will be more," he told her. "Much more. Where is the

Reverend Sean Hamilton? Come forward, sir, and let the wedding come now." His steely gaze set upon her. "Then we may celebrate in truth!"

A great cry went up from the chieftains all around them. Marina gritted her teeth, trying to keep her smile. "My dear laird, I am not ready for this!"

"I am the victor, I have won the prize. The prize is mine. Not a man here would deny me."

"But I am a woman, sir. And I deny you."

"This wedding will take place. I will be laird in truth tonight."

"But—"

"I fought, my lady. I gave you all that you desired. Would you have so little honor that you would deny your own word now?"

Marina gasped, furious. He was whispering, but the chieftains— her chieftains!—were all beginning to look at them. "Fine!" she snapped. "Have the wedding then. But my dear laird—almost husband!—remember that I deny you still!"

"I am the victor," he repeated softly. Then his voice rose again. "Sirs, the wedding shall commence, and then the wedding feast!"

Again there were roars of approval. And the reverend stepped forward, and before Marina knew it, Angus was at her side, and everyone was looking on, and Sean Hamilton was reading from his prayer book. Eric gave his vows in a loud, strong voice. He had to squeeze her fingers to get her to give hers at all.

When it was over, when she was pronounced truly his bride, he kept his grip on her fingers. And they sat at the great table together while everyone ate and raved about the battle and celebrated in good stead.

As soon as she could, Marina escaped the table. She hurried upstairs, leaning against the door to her chamber.

Then she was half thrown and half leaping away from the door as it suddenly slammed inward. Her heart beat furiously as she spun around, staring at him as he came in, shutting the door behind him.

"How dare you! How dare you come here like this. You know that I am not ready for-for-you!" she stammered.

He smiled, slowly, wickedly. "Lady, were I to wait for you to bid me ready, I might well lose all my teeth, just like the MacNamara."

"Oh! Joke then, sir, if you will. I still don't know who you are, or where you've come from. Or why so many seem to ride to battle with

225

you when you are alone. I don't know anything about you. I don't—"
She left off with a short cry as he started toward her. The pillow was
on the bed. She threw it at him. "Stop now! I mean it, my laird, I
swear that I do!"

He had nearly caught her on one side of the bed. She tried to
leap over it. His fingers wound tight around her upper arm, and
rather than flying away, she was being lifted up, and then thrown flat,
and before she knew it, her conquering warrior was straddled over
her.

She tried wildly to strike him. He simply caught her wrists.
"Mine the prize," he whispered softly.

"Bastard—" she began.

But his lips found hers. Found them, caressed them, parted
them. Brought sweet magic to them. Her heart began to pound. The
rampant thunder of longing began to weave throughout her. A
cascade of rich, ardent crystals of fire danced throughout the length
of her as she tasted the rogue's demand of his tongue.

She ceased to struggle. She had wanted him. Wanted him so.

"I am not a prize!" she whispered as his lips rose just above hers.

"You are a prize. Cherished, beloved," he whispered in turn.

His hands were on her. And her clothing was leaving her. A
rustle of taffeta. A whisper of silk. The fire of his lips touched her
bare flesh.

"A man in truth, tonight, my lady. Flesh and blood. No longer a
creature of dreams..."

She did not dwell on his words. His lips lowered against her
flesh. Her fingers played on the heat and ripple of his muscled
shoulders.

"A man in truth. Flesh and blood..." she repeated.

"Tell me to love you, my lady," he commanded her.

"Love me," she whispered.

"Aye, I will love you." Again his lips seared hers. Traveled down
the length of her throat. Brushed and burned and fed on the
hardened peak of her breast. Cries left her lips, soft cries of longing,
of desire.

He rose above her, naked, determined. A golden warrior of any
age.

"I will love you," he vowed softly. "Forever..."

Chapter 6

The waves rushed out into the sea with the pull of the tide, and Marina laughed, running out with them, then running in again before the cold water could wash over her bare feet. She turned and saw that Eric was stretched out on the linen sheet she had laid on the sand. Leaning on an elbow, he watched her, a slight smile curving his lip as he idly gnawed on a blade of grass.

Marina left the waves behind, compelled to be at his side again. She lay down on her stomach, propped on her elbows, too, her chin held up by her knuckles as she met his gaze.

Why had she ever, ever thought to deny this man? she wondered. In the days after their wedding, she had come to know him so much better. They had laughed, they had talked, they had spun dreams for themselves and dreams for the clan. She had learned that he was hard, but fair. She had seen that men followed him instinctively.

She had discovered that she was sensual and passionate herself, just as she had discovered the fire and passion in him. Dreams faded away as reality eclipsed all else. He was a demanding lover, a demanding man. But he had his quirks of humor, too, and he could make her laugh. And when she was weary, the strength of his broad chest was marvelous. No man could be more tender, she thought. No man could hold her quite so gently, sleep with his arms curled around her quite so protectively.

And still...

"Where did you come from?" she asked him.

His eyes met hers with their startling, deep blue color. He rose up, walking out to watch the waves. "I was born on the mainland, not far from here," he said.

"Then where have you been?" she pressed.

He turned to her, a smile curving his lips. Then he walked back to her and sat at her side, smiling. "Ah, my love. I know what you're hinting at. That I rose up from the sea. That I came here first as the Viking Ulhric, and perished on this shore. That the gods were merciful and kind and sent me back last century. And that now, while the isle and my princess lay threatened again, I returned."

She flushed. "That's absurd, of course."

"Aye."

"But is it true?" she appealed.

He didn't answer for several long moments. Then he turned to her, and she felt a chill snake along her back. "Would it matter if it were true? Would it be so horrible to discover that you were Mora?"

"I am not Mora," she said flatly. "And..."

"And what?"

She stood suddenly. "Aye, it would be horrible if it were true. For if it were true, it would mean—" She broke off abruptly.

He stood, too. "It would mean what?"

"It would mean tragedy," she said. "Ulhric died, that Eric died, their wives died," she added quickly. "And I can't begin to understand—"

"Understand what?" he demanded, waiting, watching her.

She was suddenly cold. She hugged her arms about herself. "I don't know."

"Marina—" he said softly.

He was going to come to her. He was going to put his arms around her and hold her, and she wouldn't care anymore.

She had to care. She had never been so desperately happy, or so desperately afraid that she was going to lose the happiness that she grasped.

"Nay! Come no nearer!" she implored him. And backing away, circling, she let the words spill from her. "I knew from the moment I came back that I was being watched. Someone was in my room with me. Someone came at night."

"Dreams," he said, meeting her eyes.

"You're lying!"

He threw up his arms. "Marina, let it be—"

"I can't! There was more. The paintings in the gallery. They are part of this, too. First the Viking was so real. Just as the portrayal of Eric at battle. And now you can scarce see the color of the eyes in the pictures."

"Marina—"

"Then there was the old woman."

"The old woman?" His voice hardened, his eyes sharpened narrowly on her.

"I met her here. I came to Illora's tomb, to read it. You were supposedly in the midst of battle. But I felt, I felt as if you were behind me—" She broke off, closing her eyes, now so very, very chilled. "Are you real?"

She opened her eyes. He was still standing there. And standing there so silently.

Cry out! she wanted to command him. *Tell me that I am mad, that of course you are real!*

"I ask you again, Marina, does it matter? Not because of the past, but because of the present. If you love me, truly love me, what difference does it make?"

She did love him. She loved him with all her heart.

Not because of any legend.

She loved him because he had swept her off her feet. Because he had stormed across the sand on a giant black war-horse and saved her kinfolk and her world. Because he had kissed her and stolen her soul. She loved him because he could make her laugh, and she loved him because she never felt as wonderful as she felt in his arms.

"I am not Illora!" she whispered fiercely. "So you tell me, my laird. Do you love me?"

He moved at last, striding for her. And though a protest formed on her lips, he would not allow her to speak it. He caught her arms, drawing her close against him. "I love you. I love you, Marina. Before God, I love you. For now, for this life, for always."

She started trembling, and could feel the chattering of her teeth. "She said that I must take the blow."

"What are you talking about?" he demanded harshly.

Marina shook her head. Now she was losing her mind in truth! She couldn't tell him the words of a madwoman. He would think someone in her household meant to betray her. He was just, but he could also be merciless, she was certain.

"Marina! What—"

"Nay! Let go of me! Perhaps you are laird of this fortress, of this isle now, but I am lady here still!"

"You're my wife," he declared, his jaw locking. "Tell me what is troubling you now."

"I'm afraid."

"Nay, nay, don't be afraid, my love," he told her softly. "Marina, think on it. If I were this ghost you claim me, then perhaps the promise is that of happiness. Twice he has come, twice he has awaited his love. Now, this time, perhaps he is to be given life."

"You said—"

"Marina! I'm trying to make you happy, nothing more. Give us a chance."

Give us a chance...

Nay, she could not think of it so simply. The old woman had warned her. She must take the blow.

But that, too, would separate them. She would be the one to die this time.

Dear Lord! She was losing her mind.

"Marina, my love." He tried to pull her close, tried to set his arms around her. But she was so torn now that she could not bear it, and wrenched away from him hard. Startled by her force, he let her go. Barefoot, she raced across the sand for her horse and leaped on it.

"I am going to have her disinterred!" she called to him.

"What!" Hands on his hips, he stood watching her in amazement.

"Illora. I am going to have the rock moved away, I am going to have her dug up. I will know whether she truly rests in her tomb or not."

"You'll not do such a thing," he protested, eyes flashing. "Mora's story is legend here, and I'll not have it."

"I am the MacCannan!"

His eyes narrowed. "You were the MacCannan."

"Oh!" she exclaimed in fury. He was coming quickly toward her, ready to stop her, she knew. She waited until he was nearly before her, then shoved her heels against her mare's flanks. Sand spewed behind her as her horse gave flight.

Men! she decided.

Yet he could catch her. Catch her so easily, if he desired...

But when she reached the cliffs and looked back, he was still standing on the sand. His hands remained on his hips. His chin was high; his golden hair shimmered beneath the sun like a banner.

If he had wanted to, he could have caught her. He had chosen to let her go.

She returned to the fortress, her heart in a whirl. In the great hall, she peeled off her gloves and stood before the fire.

Peg hurried in. "Lady Marina! Why, I thought that ye and yer laird were out fer the day. What can I bring ye, lass?"

Marina spun around. "Nothing, Peg. Wait, no. I'll take tea upstairs. In my room. And a steamy hot bath, please. Set the lads to it, if you will."

Peg nodded, as if she had decided herself that the best thing for her mistress's tempestuous condition might be a soothing cup of tea and the even more soothing feel of a long hot bath.

Within minutes it was done, and Marina was upstairs, her body warmed by the water, her eyes closed, her head resting on the rim.

Once, she had heard whispers when she rested so.

Whispers. As if he called her name...

She heard no more whispers. Because he was a ghost no longer? Because she now held him in the flesh?

But he had called her Illora.

I am not Illora! she persisted to herself. *I cannot be Illora.*

Because the old woman said that I must take the blow.

The battles are over. We are at peace with the British. Things have gone as things should have gone. Who would seek to harm me?

No one. No one at all.

And so she was dreaming, after all.

"Marina!"

Again she heard a whisper. Soft. Sensual. She turned. And she smiled slowly. He was with her again.

He walked across the room to her. He knelt by the tub. He kissed her elbow, licking away a drop of water. He kissed her throat. He took her into his arms.

"I love you," he said.

"I love you, too, and it is all that matters," she said.

And for a spell, she might have dreamed again. As darkness came, they dallied as lovers, nothing more and nothing less. A flesh and blood woman, a flesh and blood man, with no darkness near to haunt them. Again and again he made love to her. Again and again she returned his kiss, and made love to him in kind.

Night fell. Peg tapped on the door to see if they needed anything.

Nothing, Marina told her.

Nothing, for they had all they needed in each other, Eric added.

Peg's footsteps discreetly faded away.

In time, Marina fell asleep. She was deliciously tired, and there was no way better, or sweeter, to sleep than on his chest, her fingers curled into the crisp red-gold hairs on his chest.

But even as she slept, certain that any dreams that could plague her must certainly be good, she felt as if the darkness of a raven's wing was moving over her.

She felt as if she were on the beach again, walking along the sand.

And the raven came toward her. It made its unearthly cawing sound, sweeping down from above.

Then, suddenly, it landed. The wings adjusted, the head rose. It was a bird no longer. It was the old woman she had met on the beach.

"Now, Illora, now!"

"I am not Illora!"

"He will die!" the old crone warned, her arm snaking out to point toward the heavens, the black draping all around it. "With the morning's light, he will die!"

"Nay, he will not die. I will not let him die. I read the tombstone. I do love him. I love him with all my heart."

"Then hurry. Challenge him no more. Stop the blade that would pierce his heart. He has so little time... Look! Look at your hands! Already the blood flows."

She stared down at her hands. The old woman was right. Blood was beginning to stain her palms.

"Nay!" She shrieked the word, then screamed it out again and again, bolting up.

She no longer slept. The dream was done.

She was awake, and in her own room. Dreams were gone—

But shadows were not.

There in the darkness before her, she saw the shadow of a man. A man with his hand raised. Across the room, she could see his silhouette on the wall.

And she could see the dagger raised above her.

"Nay!" she shrieked again. And then she knew that Eric was up beside her, and that he was trying to cast himself over her, before the blade could fall against her flesh.

"Nay, not again, not again!" she cried. And she did not care if she died; oh, so much better that she should perish than him! In those awful seconds she heard him cry her name.

And she knew that it was her name.

Illora...

And twice she had lost him. Twice she had lived without him. She could not do so again.

"Nay!"

With all the force in her, she thrust him aside and leaped to her feet. The blade, already begun its motion, continued to fall.

There was an awful tearing sound in the darkness. She screamed.

"Marina, my love!" Then he was up, leaping to his feet, seeking out their assailant. "Bastard, henchman! Coward in the darkness!"

Eric! Eric was crying out the words. He was all right.

And she was all right...

The door was pounded on and thrust open. Light flooded the room as Angus was followed in by Peg and a number of the chieftains, wearing their nightdresses but armed for battle with dirks and guns and swords and daggers.

And in the sudden flood of light, Marina saw where the blade had fallen.

And she knew what had ripped.

Not flesh this time. She looked at her hands. There was no blood on them.

She looked across the room to where Eric now had dragged their assailant to his feet, his arms wrenched behind him.

"Kevin!" She gasped, astounded. And she stared at the cousin she had loved all her life.

Eric thrust Kevin toward Angus. He was one of their own. Angus and the chieftains would be left to deal with him. Marina ran to Eric, quickly finding shelter in his arms. She stared at Kevin again.

"Why?" she asked in amazement.

"Ah, Marina, why?" he replied bitterly. "I fought for the fortress, I bear the family name! I am a man, and I deserved to be laird of this isle. I did not seek to see ye suffer, lass. 'Twas not personal, fer I have cared fer ye, and deep. But I would be laird, ye see. And he,"—he inclined his head toward Eric—"well, he is laird by virtue that he is yer husband. If ye were dead with no issue, then the isle would fall to me."

"Get him out of here!" Angus cried with fury. "We dinna turn on our own! Betray our name!" he said with disgust. "Bah, blood of my blood!" he thundered. "My laird," he said to Eric, "what will ye have with him?"

Eric was watching Marina, staring down into her eyes. "We will have it as my lady wishes," he said.

"Banishment!" Marina cried. "I will have him banished. We'll not have the blood of a kinsman on our hands."

"He meant to murder you," Eric reminded her.

"Banishment, please!" she implored.

Angus nodded to Eric. Kevin, his head lowered, was taken from the room.

And then, suddenly, there was silence.

"You shiver. You are cold," Eric said to her.

Aye, she was shivering. She was shaking. She wanted to tell him about the dream.

"I saw the danger coming, Eric," she said swiftly. "I was dreaming. The old woman was in the dream."

"Was she now, lass?" he said softly. Blue eyes caressed her with the greatest tenderness. He picked her up gently into his arms and brought her before the fire.

"Eric—"

"Hush now, the danger is over."

"But, Eric—"

"Hush, love. I am with you."

She wanted to talk; she needed to talk. But the words wouldn't come. And in his arms, she felt the greatest peace, and the greatest exhaustion.

She should have been wide awake. She shouldn't have been able to sleep for all of the night.

But she did sleep. She closed her eyes, and she slept. Deeply.

With no dreams to plague her.

* * *

When she awoke in the morning, Eric was gone. She leaped up, feeling faint twinges of fear. She wasn't sure why she was so afraid—she remembered the night, but she knew that Kevin had been stopped. She still felt ill—she had loved Kevin, loved him deeply, and his betrayal was painful. It was incredible to think that he could have found the coldness in his own heart to murder her.

But though she had loved Kevin, she did not love him as she

loved her new husband. With the morning, she remembered that she had been dreaming of some danger when he had come, and that the dream had made her awaken; the dream had warned her of the danger. But try as she might, she could not remember the dream. It had something to do with a raven, and something to do with the warning, and something to do with the words, the legend, on Illora's tomb. But now it all escaped her.

She was desperate only to assure herself that Eric was all right, and that he was near.

She dressed quickly and started to run from the room, so very anxious to find him. She raced down the stairs, but he wasn't in the great hall, and Peg hadn't seen him. She ran back upstairs and searched the gallery, but he wasn't there, either.

At last she hurried to the stables, and found out from the groom that he had taken his great black war-horse and ridden out early that morning, and the groom had not seen him since.

Growing more desperate by the moment, she asked for her bay to be brought out. She didn't even wait for the mare to be saddled but leaped on her, urging her into a canter the moment she was mounted.

She knew where she was going. To the cliffs before the Irish Sea, and to the beach there. She closed her eyes, terrified that she would come to the beach...

...And would see him leaving. A Viking warrior again, laid out on a bier, riding the waves into eternity.

It could not be...

He was flesh and blood. She had touched him, loved him, lain with him. She had been tortured by dreams, nothing more. Even last night, the dreams had tormented her. Somehow saved her, but tormented her, too. And now the dreams were lost, and she could not remember them, but no matter how foolish she told herself she was being, she was afraid still.

She came to the cliffs at last. She gave the bay free rein, and rode haphazardly over the steep and treacherous footing.

But then she came to the other side. And a burst of gladness seemed to fill her heart like the startling gold of the rise of the sun.

She blinked against the fierce light. Aye, he was there, a man. For the briefest moment, she was certain that he stood tall in leather leggings and the short tunic of an ancient Viking warrior.

He stood tall, a ghostly figure of mist and legend.

A Viking, looking to the sea...

Nay!

It was a trick of the sunlight, nothing more. A trick within her own mind.

He was there.

Not a ghost disappearing on an ancient Viking ship, veiled in the mist of the isles. He was there, in the flesh. By agreement with the English, he had forsworn his colors, and so he stood in hose and breeches and shirt and frock coat, his tam cockaded but unadorned. His hands clasped behind his back, he looked out to the sea.

Aye, he was there.

Returned to her from the mists of legend? Or a man, nothing more, nothing less, come upon the isle just at the time of her distress.

Could she be a princess, risen for a chance once again to taste the sweetness of life, and of love?

Nay...

She did not know.

And it did not matter.

All that mattered was that they did have each other, and that they did have love, and now, life. Sweet, sweet life. Together.

"Eric!"

She shouted his name, leading the bay over the last of the rocks. He turned to her and smiled slowly.

In seconds she had the bay racing across the sands. The mare pounded the surf until she arrived before him. There, she leaped down and into his arms.

Strong and sure, they folded around her.

"I was afraid! So afraid!" she whispered.

"Why, love?" he asked, holding her from him. "The danger was gone with the night."

His eyes searched hers, puzzled, so very blue.

"I-I don't know," she whispered. "You weren't there. I was afraid."

"I'll never leave you now, you know. Never," he told her.

She smiled slowly. "You were willing to die for me," she said.

"And you were willing to die for me." He stretched out a hand, staring at it against the golden sunlight. "Flesh and blood," he murmured softly. He gazed down at her. "Are you going to ask me again where I came from, Marina?"

She smiled and shook her head slowly. "I don't care where you came from. Only that you are here to stay."

He wrapped her in his arms once again, and then they started down the beach together, arm in arm. His great black war-horse and her bay followed slowly behind.

Soon they neared the cliffs. Eric turned and lifted Marina, setting her back atop the bay. He leaped up easily on the black, then paused, frowning, as he watched her stare at the caves within the cliff.

Toward Illora's gravesite.

She smiled slowly and looked at her husband. "I think that I shall let her rest in peace, my laird. What do you think?"

He smiled in turn. "Aye, lady, I think that that would be best. Let them both rest in peace. Let the Viking Ulhric and his Illora go down in legend." He brought his mount closer to hers. "And as for us, my lady, I say, let us live this life, and savor each moment, for life is precious, and love even more so."

She cast back her head, feeling the sun on her face. "Indeed, my laird, aye!" She nudged her horse's flanks, and the mare pranced gracefully forward, ready to climb the cliffs again. Marina turned back, a light, a fire of mischief in her eyes. "Come then, Laird Eric, ride with me, live with me, savor the sunlight with me. For I—"

"I will love you forever!" he interrupted with a gallant cry.

And she laughed, and his laughter mingled with hers, and echoed throughout the cliffs, even as they rode off hard together.

Lovers, in love, forever.

The mist rolled out to sea, and the sun rose high above the Isle of the Angels.

ABOUT THE AUTHOR

New York Times and USA Today bestselling author of more than 125 novels, HEATHER GRAHAM has been featured in the Double Day Book Club and the Literary Guild. She has won numerous awards as both a romance writer and an author of thrillers, including: The Romance Writers of America Lifetime Achievement Award and the Thriller Writers Silver Bullet Award.

Heather hosts the Writers for New Orleans Conference each year in the city that she loves NOLA.

Find more information and links on Heather Graham and 13Thirty Books, be sure to sign up for the 13Thrity Newsletter at 13Thirtybooks.com

Books from
13Thirty Books,
That you may enjoy

Heather Graham's Christmas Treasures
Ripper – A Love Story
On Two Fronts

~~Never~~ Fear Series – Horror Anthology
~~Never~~ Fear
~~Never~~ Fear – Phobias
~~Never~~ Fear – Christmas Terrors

Zodiac Lovers Series
Zodiac Lovers Book One: Aquarius, Pieces, Aries
Zodiac Lovers Book Two: Taurus, Gemini, Cancer
Zodiac Lovers Book Three: Leo, Virgo, Libra
Zodiac Lovers Book Four: Scorpio, Sagittarius, Capricorn

More Than Magick
The Third Hour

Printed in the USA
CPSIA information can be obtained
at www.ICGtesting.com
LVHW091549010224
770661LV00005B/59